Cover Design – Jaycee DeLorenzo
Publishing Coordinator – Sharon Kizziah-Holmes

Paperback-Press
an imprint of A & S Publishing
Paperback Press, LLC

ISBN -13: 978-1-956806-67-0

DEDICATION

*To Dad, who started me down the prophetic path.
You are loved and missed.*

ACKNOWLEDGMENTS

This path that God put me on so many years ago has been a journey of paths crossed with those He so richly blessed me with on my way to this point. And for that, I am truly grateful and overly blessed.

My thanks and love to Shelly, my wife, and Hunter, my son, for their unconditional love and enduring patience as I worked on this book. To Mom, one of my biggest cheerleaders, thanks for the encouraging words in my times of self-doubt. To Grandpa and Vera for believing in me and for setting Dad on the path that led me to digging deeper in God's word. I love you all.

In making this book a reality, I want to thank Sharon Kizziah-Holmes of Paperback Press for all the work, advice, and introductions. You've been a blessing. Thanks to Kathy Garnsey for her copyediting, Shirley McCann for her eagle eye as a proofreader, and to Kay Lang for her help as a proofreader, as well. And a big thanks to Jaycee DeLorenzo, of Sweet 'N Spicy Designs, for creating a book cover that went beyond my expectations.

This book would never have happened if it weren't for all of you.

PROLOGUE

Jane Mason didn't feel like President of the United States of America. John Doe had dismissed her from the Oval Office like she was an annoying child. His arrogance surprised her in that she was expecting someone lauded for his patience and tact. After all, he was the one who brokered the Mid-East Accord, effectively bringing peace between Jew and Muslim.

But this man had the nerve to sit behind her desk and bark orders as if she didn't exist. On top of that, every single member of her staff listened, including the vice president. When she tried to take control of the situation, everyone laughed at her like she was a first-time staffer. A wave of his hand sent her out of her office, the symbol of American power.

Now, President Mason had retreated to her vacation home in the mountains of Virginia to reevaluate and prepare a new plan of attack to regain control of the dignity of the office she swore an oath to protect from despots like him. Her resolve was unwavering while she typed away at her speech on the presidential laptop. However, her nerve was shaken like the planet after the great earthquake that had happened just two and a half months prior and the subsequent aftershock. At least, that's what the new leader of Europe called it.

Nervous fingers typed the truth she would reveal to her constituents. A plate of untouched grilled chicken and waffle fries sat on the coffee table along with a half empty glass of sweet tea sweating beside the computer. Her notes strategically placed within reach on the coffee table in front of the soft leather couch. A Bible lay in front of the computer, opened to John's Revelation. Now her revelation. Many things were revealed to her in the previous six months. Some timely, and some not so much, which she regretted.

She had the upper hand when it came to the accord, being the only one who could sign off on it to complete its ratification. He would have to wait until she was ready, not the other way around.

While she typed away on her State of the Union speech, the infamous press conference played in the background. The one where John Doe entered the global spotlight. No one knew his real name. He called himself John Doe at the beginning of the Tribulation, claiming that his identity was not in his name, but his works. So, everyone gave him different monikers until Sovereign was adopted.

The world began picking up the pieces, desperately looking for answers to all the death and disappearances that took place before the earthquakes. John Doe started with a speech given at the European Union Parliament in Brussels. His presence was undeniable, and his energy was indefatigable. He spoke of a new society without the interference of Christians, who had held the world back from its potential glory with their antiquated beliefs.

After a whirlwind tour of Europe, John held a press conference to tell the world his plans for the conflict in the Middle East where war was about to break out on a scale that made the planet tremble in fear of nuclear response. During the Q&A, he was asked what he thought had happened to those who disappeared. His arrogance showed through as he scoffed at the reporter.

"They didn't disappear. They were murdered."

On the television monitor, his stare dared anyone to disagree. President Mason's anger rose as the echo of the keystrokes bounced off the mahogany paneled walls.

"Murdered?"

The reporter seemed awestruck by the statement.

"Of course. With their declining numbers, Christians were frustrated that their savior (he used air quotes) hadn't raptured (he used air quotes again) them yet."

"Sir, if they weren't raptured, then what happened?"

Like President Mason, the reporter couldn't write fast enough. But it wasn't to praise the Sovereign as the reporter had done in her article the next day. It was to expose him.

"Like I said. They were murdered. As the people of the world began understanding that their ridiculous preaching was a sham, Christians became desperate. So, they decided to make this rapture happen. Christians decided to kill certain ones, mainly the old and sick. Then the murderers made phony videos and photoshopped images making it look like their loved ones had disappeared before their very eyes. They faked this rapture."

His expression was of absolute surety. President Mason stopped typing thinking about how even she was fooled. His confidence wasn't just mesmerizing, it was addictive.

"But they killed millions. That would be impossible," a reporter in the back of the room said.

"Those were fake numbers. I'm guessing a hundred thousand at the most. They just reported the millions."

"So where are the murderers now?" the first reporter asked.

"Mostly dead. Either by suicide or when we killed them in battles all over the world," he said in a matter-of-fact tone.

It was the same tone he used when dismissing President

Mason. Her fingers ached from hitting the keyboard so hard.

"Why not bring them to the courts for justice?" an American journalist asked.

"That was justice. For the atrocities they committed against man, woman, and child, "he shouted as he slammed his hand on the podium.

The room went silent.

"They killed all the children?" A British reporter gasped.

"How else to complete the narrative? That is why so many Christians did not die. They were needed to kill all children under the age of fourteen."

Everyone breathlessly watched while his face reddened in mock anger.

"Then there would be millions of deaths you moron!" the president shouted at the television.

She knew the ridiculous explanation should've made him the laughingstock of the planet. But Second Thessalonians 2:10 said it best. *God shall send them strong delusion, that they should believe a lie.*

And they did.

Rage flew through her fingers at the thought of anyone killing that many children being believed by any rational person.

"And what happened to the bodies? There were graves that had been torn open, from the inside out," another reporter had asked. "And the parents of those children who are loyalists claimed their children disappeared?"

"They were drugged into believing the lie." He sighed. "And the bodies were cremated. The ashes were strewn to the wind. The graves were disturbed to make it look like the corpses had come through the soil."

Sovereign John Doe became stoic, and his voice cracked as if holding back emotion. "These deluded fanatics sacrificed their own and the children of the world for a lie."

After a long pause for effect, he raised his hands over his head and shouted, "And now they will miss the greatest leap in human evolution that history has ever witnessed."

President Mason needed a break to control her emotions that were spilling on the pages. After printing the speech, she went into the bedroom and changed into her bathing suit. Grabbing the wine bottle and glass on the kitchen island, she went to the sliding glass door. The night was uncomfortably still, no breeze or animal sounds of any kind. It was as if the world was muted.

The jets of the hot tub came to life at the touch of a button. Before stepping in, she dismissed her Secret Service detail and retrieved papers from the coffee table she wanted to look at while the jets worked the stress from her muscles.

She slowly stepped into the hot tub, allowing her skin to get used to the heat. Once settled, she stared at the page and took a long draught of freshly poured red wine.

"A nation divided," she mumbled.

The speech resonated from the screen fastened to the wall near the jetted tub as she sunk up to her shoulders in the hot, frothy waters. Fear and pain worked against the heat, making her muscles ache while she studied the pages and listened to the end of John Doe's press conference.

After a long ovation, his facial features calmed to a restrained fury.

"For their treachery to humanity, I have submitted legislation that not only makes this odious religion illegal but punishes the murderers and those who dare to share their abominable beliefs. Until it is passed, the new Head of Religion has already put into effect a religious law that punishes anyone found guilty of worshipping this child-killing God in which the governments of this planet will not interfere."

"What punishment are you suggesting?" a reporter asked.

"Death by guillotine."

5

CHAPTER 1

The suffocating air shrouded me like a heavy burden as I walked to the dead woman's head. But that's how it feels when God turns off the winds. Since the seventh seal judgment, the earth's airflow stopped, and the weather was unsettling in its quietness. It was hard to work and breathe in the stifling atmosphere. And we deserved it.

But I had a feeling that the woman didn't deserve what happened to her.

At least, I believed it to be a woman. I'd confirm the gender later with the medical examiner.

A grayness settled over the city that seemed to accentuate the depression of the world since the quakes, including me. The clouds overhanging the city made the purpose for my visit to St. Louis more disheartening.

The walk to the crime scene from my truck was uninspiring. The buildings surrounding the former home of the St. Louis Cardinals were either in a state of ruin or pushed into demolished heaps for public safety. But I wasn't there for the dystopic scenery. My old police academy instructor, the new captain of the Peace Forces in St. Louis, called me in from Kansas City to investigate the head.

Clark Avenue was cracked and filled with holes that

reminded me of tiny versions of the canyons I'd seen in Arizona. The earthquakes did a number on the planet. Seal judgment six sent the world into a torrent of motion that changed everything. Then there was the second quake. It wasn't as intense as its predecessor, but it still had its consequences. Even the sidewalks by the wrecked stadium were an obstacle course of concrete and protruding rebar in most places. But the woman's head lay silently by a tree near Gate 5, maybe the only spot on the sidewalk that was untouched.

"Will Thomas?"

I turned. "Who's askin'?" The captain of the St. Louis Peace Forces stepped out of the SUV police cruiser parked near the scene and walked to me.

"An old friend." He smiled as we shook hands.

Grinning, I looked downward at the captain. "A very old friend."

"Glad to see you, Will."

He punched me in the shoulder with a fist that had seen too many fights. Captain Frank Malone was my instructor at the academy before the Rapture, and an old family friend who attended the church Dad preached. If it wasn't for his thick chest, he would've looked fat. If it wasn't for the white flattop, he would've looked ridiculous.

"Thanks for the invite, but why did you call me, Frank? I'm still wet behind the ears."

This was my first case as a detective of the Peace Forces, a pretty name given to us by the Sovereign. To most, he was the magnanimous leader of the world. But to the Christian Resistance, in which I was a member, he was the Antichrist that was foretold in John's Revelation.

"I only have three detectives. The rest joined the military to fight the murderers. I heard you were in the neighborhood."

I watched him put his giant hands in his pockets and stared at the head with cobalt blue eyes that could pierce the soul. "That's a mighty big neighborhood. KC and STL are still two hundred and fifty miles apart. Even after the quake and aftershock."

"Close enough." His morose tone worried me.

"Why this one, Frank? What makes her so special? Why not hand her over to the Corpse Patrols and let her burn?"

Corpse Patrol crews were still wandering the U.S. trying to find all the dead to be properly identified and cremated. And I knew their jobs were secure for another five and a half years.

"I got a call this morning. Said it was an important case."

"How does the caller know it's important? How do they know she's even here?"

"Not sure. But he knows."

"Did he say who she is?"

"When I asked, he said people were listening and hung up. I tried to scan for a Loyalty chip, but either there isn't one or it got damaged somehow."

"Keep the drama going I guess," I said, shifting my weight from one foot to the other.

"Appears so," Frank said.

"Who is this he you're talking to?"

Frank looked at the crowd then leaned close to me.

"Senator Jon Staeger."

Frank's whisper was lined with apprehension. It was as if he wanted to be as far away from the head as possible.

"Oh." I felt like Frank sounded.

"He called my private phone. Said to make it top priority. And to keep it quiet." He shrugged. "That's when I thought of you."

I saw Frank look at the river like it was foreign to him, although he had spent the better part of twenty years patrolling its shores. "Again, Frank. Why me?" I looked up at the stationary gray sky. No winds meant no weather pattern. The St. Louis region hadn't seen the sun since the winds were hushed.

"One, this is your first case, and I want to see my best student in action. Two, there's no one I trust more than you. And three, my boss would spread this like wildfire to every politician she knows. The senator made it abundantly clear that I am to report to him, and him only, with the details of this case." He turned to me. "I need you, Will."

"No partner?" My gut twisted with the thought of working alone on my first case. No guidance in the tricky situations. It felt as if Frank was feeding me to the wolves. Otherwise known as politicians.

"Sorry, kid. Like I said, no one else I trust to cover it."

"I suppose I only report to you."

"That's right. Everyone knows already."

"Did you do the initial observation?"

"Nope. That's for you. I called in the CSU. Should be here in thirty, so you better get working." He slapped my shoulder, walked back to his electric cruiser, and leaned on the fender with his hands in his gray pants pockets.

The woman's shaved head was lying on its right ear facing Ballpark Village across Clark Avenue from the stadium. It was an obvious dump by the way the head was placed by the tree. It looked like someone set her head on her right ear so it wouldn't roll.

Leaning on the balls of my feet, I noticed a bullet hole no bigger than a pea above the right eye. It looked like a small caliber bullet hole. But no blood on the sidewalk drove home my idea that it was placed there. The murder happened elsewhere. But I'd have to confirm that in my final recheck. I wondered why she was shot in the head after being decapitated. Seemed senseless. Maybe target practice, but I doubted it. Maybe she was shot before, and the blood drained from the decapitation. Something for the medical examiner to determine.

Although I had seen plenty of fallen crowns over the last year and a half since the advent of the guillotine, I have never gotten used to it. Feeling a bit queasy, I turned my attention to the Mississippi River. Most of it was obscured by the mounds of rubble that used to be buildings. In between each mound, a slice of the Mississippi River flowed north to south. I took in a deep breath and experienced a similar smell to the one when I visited the Pacific for a week of sun and surf before I started my first day as a newly sworn in police officer in Kansas City, two years before the rapture.

"Salty air." I looked at Frank. "Just like the Missouri River, only the scent is stronger.

He sniffed and smiled. "Reminds me of the Caribbean. Clair and I went on a cruise there for our honeymoon. Geologists said that the sediments at the mouth of the Mississippi and her tributaries were shaken after the quake and aftershock. Could take a couple of years for the salt to clear up."

After the first earthquake, the Antichrist used his best tricks to keep people from either rioting or getting them out of their hiding places. But the way the sky turned into a free-for-all of darkened sun, blood-soaked moon, and a meteor shower that lit up the sky like a giant fireworks display shook everyone to their core. Then it immediately stopped. I always believed John the Revelator was trying to describe everything he saw through his limited perspective, but this time he had the right words. The sky parted like two pieces of paper being rolled apart. As if the Rapture wasn't enough, these amazing sights brought me to an awestruck, yet fearful, state seeing the Bible come to life. It reminded me that I chose the right side.

The Antichrist claimed that these events, including the first earthquake, were easy to explain. Everything was investigated by his scientists, and they agreed that what happened to the sun and moon was nothing more than dust from the quaking earth being sent high into the air and mixing with the burning debris from the meteor shower that was predicted by astronomers. He described the folding of the sky as an intricate optical illusion from everything happening so quickly. Then he referred to the second quake as a severe aftershock.

And the people swallowed it hook, line, and sinker.

I remember watching replays of several reporters during live feeds banging on bomb shelter doors begging the inhabitants for protection from the wrath of God. However, after the Antichrist's explanations, they retracted their statements and praised him for remaining a beacon of strength and composure during the crises.

But I knew these events were the sixth and seventh seal judgments based on Dad's prophecy journal he made from his studies of the Bible's prophetic texts and current events taking place prior to the Rapture. His descriptions of what was taking place in front of me was uncanny. I was glad I kept it, so I could put it to practical use. Kind of a survival guide to remind me of what's coming next.

"There's nothing I see that connects the head to its surroundings. And the way it's laying, I would suggest that she was placed here. The murder happened elsewhere. But that's a working theory. Once the drone has given the place a good going over, and the M.E. looks at her, it might change." I stood by Frank with my pad and pen out to take notes.

"Not bad, kid. Is there anything else?"

His smug grin made me paranoid.

The stadium and Ballpark Village were the only standing structures in the immediate vicinity. I scanned the area. The stadium looked like a skeleton with too many bones, and the brick was missing, probably removed in a pathetic attempt to rebuild. There was nothing that seemed to stick out.

Putting my hands in my Cardinals jacket, I felt the flash drive loosely moving about. My mind went numb with panic. I'd already forgotten my duty to the Christian

Resistance. Once I'd put my faith in Christ after the Rapture, I met some people at an underground church meeting in Kansas City. They introduced me to the higherups in the Resistance, who asked if I'd spy on the new police force, a.k.a. Peace Forces, to get the locations of any raids that were starting in the city. Although they weren't technically government sanctioned, the raids were sanctioned by the Global Church, and the government didn't meddle in those affairs by choice. After securing the drive in the hidden pocket within the pocket, I returned focus to the crime scene.

The sidewalk in front of Ballpark Village was lined with observers. No doubt media and internet reporters trying to get the scoop, even though the government would tell them what to report.

I pointed to the crowd. "Why are they so close?"

"They were closer, but our European Peace Forces friends over there thought it was far enough. And I concur." Frank folded his arms and glared at the uniformed officers.

They glared back in defiance. Frank was their superior, but the Europeans challenged all American leadership, right up to the Sovereign who challenged our new president on a daily basis.

"Then I got nothing for now." I shrugged.

"Good. That's what I'm thinking too."

He gave a fatherly smile, turned and rested his elbows on the hood of the cruiser.

I joined him as we looked at the river.

"Is it me or is the river closer?" I narrowed my eyes.

"The new shore is all the way up to Memorial Drive, a little over three hundred yards from Busch, about half the previous distance. After the first earthquake, the Mississippi River widened from its source to its mouth. In St. Louis, it went from about 1800 feet wide to over a mile. Then there was the aftershock, which widened it another quarter mile. And now, the river is experiencing mild tides."

Frank rubbed the scruff on his chin and looked at the river as if it was foreign to him.

"Why does she merit special attention?" I stared at the river, afraid to see the answer in Frank's look. "After all, the dead still float downriver after the quake and aftershock."

Every major faultline, including the New Madrid Faultline, fired off in cataclysmic concurrence. The fissure that formed from the dividing of the land dropped flood plains considerably. New Orleans, Memphis, and Minneapolis/St. Paul were underwater. Even after three months, the Mississippi River still carried the dead from these former port cities that were overwhelmed by the river surge to the Gulf of Mexico, the new tides, and the lazy Corpse Patrol agents who didn't want to mess with the rotting carcasses, human or otherwise. The Pale Horseman was hard at work. But for some reason, God spared St. Louis. The shore's flood plain only dropped a couple of feet. The rest of the city was less.

"All Senator Staeger would say is that she's no ordinary victim." He stood and stretched. "And I trust him."

It was best to leave it at that. Frank's stubbornness was something to avoid.

"I need wheels." I pointed to my pickup truck. "It's good for the open country, but it gets bad mileage in the city."

"You might need it. The rubble and road damage make the streets an obstacle course. Only the rich and business districts have smooth streets."

"I'm not putting my truck through this." I pointed to the ruins of downtown St. Louis. "It's worse than KC. That and from what I hear, my truck will be stolen by days end."

"All right, I'll request one for you, but don't get your hopes up on anything fancy. We're low on vehicles."

"Four wheels and a motor." I grinned.

"Check and check. If you need anything else, let me know." He patted my shoulder, walked back to his SUV, and left.

CHAPTER 2

There was a little time before the CSU team got to the scene, so I decided to do the sketching. It was an out-of-date thing to do, but Frank taught me to do it in case the drone didn't work. The new cameras on the high-tech fliers were second to none. The forensics pilots and computer analysts were able to get pinpoint accuracy that made sketching a thing of the past. However, sketching gave me a sense of awareness of my surroundings and an unequalled intimacy to the victim that gave purpose to my investigation. She needed justice.

While I drew what I saw from different angles and took the proper measurements, a sense of familiarity came over me as I stared at the head. Although all hair was removed, her face still looked familiar. Try as I might, I couldn't place a name with the face. DNA would give me an identity.

Movement from the crowd of reporters entered my peripheral view. A large black man in a red Cardinals jersey and wearing a navy-blue hat with broad shoulders stood out amongst the nosey onlookers across the street where Peace Forces officers cordoned off the crime scene. He seemed to be the typical don't-mess-with-me type. He turned his hat around and lifted a digital camera. I took note of him as I scratched behind my right ear.

Just then a high-pitched sound of three propellers introduced the coming of the drone. The triangular shaped machine rounded the tattered corner of Ballpark Village and slowed until it was stationary twenty feet above the head so not to compromise the crime scene. It was basic white with the Peace Forces falcon plastered on the underbelly. There were eighteen cameras mounted in various positions to get the best angles possible for accuracy in the distant pics and videos I would look at to see the crime scene. Another member of the CSU team still took the close ups.

The CSU van pulled up and parked on Clark and 8th near the scene. Two people emerged and started pulling out tackle boxes with a camera dangling from around one of the females' necks.

"Detective Will Thomas, I assume?"

The young woman wore a blue CSU jacket, with a matching baseball cap, black slacks, and bright yellow running shoes that matched the lettering on the jacket and hat.

"Yep."

"Jenny Lewis. Wow, you're a big 'un." Her green eyes gave me the once over. "Six four?"

"Yeah. Good guess." I put my hands in my Cardinals jacket pockets.

"Not really. Skill from experience. I see more dead people than live ones."

"You're on Corpse Patrol?" We watched the other CSU open her tackle box near the head.

"Was for a while, but the department couldn't do without me. I'm the best CSU tech out there."

Her grin had confidence, not arrogance. I liked her.

"Good. I need the best."

Jenny nodded to her counterpart. "That's Dr. Washington, the best M.E. there is."

The doctor waved without looking at me while she went to a knee and took a closer look at the head. She was a tall black woman who didn't seem to be the talkative type. Straight to business. I appreciated that.

"I have a question. If you don't mind." Jenny walked around the head to face me.

"Fire away."

"Why is this one so important? The head probably rolled off the C.P. truck heading to the crematorium." She raised her camera and fired off a couple of shots.

"There are those higher on the food chain who disagree with your astute assessment." I took a step back to see if the man in the crowd was still there. "Although I fully agree with you."

He was.

She smiled as she watched the drone take a different path. I was impressed. The pilot was thorough.

"This scene is staged."

Dr. Washington spoke to me, but still didn't look my direction. She leaned closer to the head.

"I was about to say that, Dr. Washington." Jenny frowned. "Yeah, I still think it fell off the truck."

"That's a long way to roll." The doctor deadpanned. "No Corpse Patrol trucks allowed through this part of the city. They take Chestnut to Broadway to go north of the river." She pointed away from the crime scene.

"Since the victim has been decapitated." I pointed to the bullet hole. "Why the head shot?"

"Didn't see that." Jenny took a pic of the face. "Guess that's why they pay you the big money."

"I saw it. There's just enough of a shadow from the nose to hide it. And you're right, it is interesting. Why do it both ways? Seems like overkill," Dr. Washington said as she leaned in for a closer look at the bullet hole.

"Psychotic?" Jenny got on her belly and zoomed the camera in on the gunshot wound.

"Aren't they all?" I grunted, watching the two women do their jobs.

"Not all, detective. But you already knew that." Dr. Washington still didn't look at me.

She was right—Cop 101. Then I remembered the question I wanted to ask her.

"Was the victim shot first or decapitated?"

"Since it was planted, it's hard to tell at this time. When I get her on the slab, I'll be able to tell."

"It doesn't make sense that a decapitated head fell off the Corpse Patrol truck. If it's bladed, how did it get to St. Louis?" I moved away from the head to see the street better. I needed to get a sense of where the killer came from to deposit the victim.

"You have a point detective. Capital punishment is completed at the penitentiary in Jefferson City." Dr. Washington stood. "Maybe got separated from the body during transport. Possibly a serial killer."

"Killers are known to dissect the victim. Maybe we'll find the rest elsewhere." Jenny said, with a tone that reminded me of some of the girls I grew up with in southwest Missouri. Just enough of a Southern twang to notice.

"Can you tell if the victim was bladed?" I asked.

"Maybe. But Jenny is right. Even if the cut is clean, it could have been from someone with medical training." Dr. Washington took off her gloves.

"So, we're back to the same question." I noticed the man in the crowd was gone. "Let's get some answers."

"We'll get answers when we get it to the slab." Jenny retrieved a plastic bag from her tackle box.

I walked around the crime scene once more. "Let me know your findings ASAP."

"Sure thing." Jenny smiled while Dr. Washington carefully placed the head in the bag as she held it open.

"You're five nine," I said, smiling as I walked away.

"You're pretty good yourself my friend."

CHAPTER 3

My hotel was between the crime scene and Peace Forces HQ. It was one of the few downtown buildings that survived the quakes and river surge. It used to be an apartment building, but the quakes, water, and the Rapture rendered it all but empty. Now, it was a hotel that rented by the hour. It's funny how a place like that can go from quiet cozy to roach ready in such a short time.

The bedroom was adequate with white walls and a queen-size bed that seemed clean. The taupe bathroom was somewhat clean, with only one roll of toilet paper and two towels. The mint green kitchen was useless. No appliances, and the water was shut off to the stainless-steel sink that didn't live up to its name.

Unfortunately, the odor was horrific. It was a combination of B.O., rotten pizza, and diarrhea. After unloading my suitcase and pointing a hotel-provided fan going full blast out the open window that did little to remove the smell, I decided to lie down for a fifteen-minute power nap.

My badge stuck me in my bicep. I removed it and looked at my identification. Although I didn't have the Beastmark, and never would, I still had a numbered I.D. chip inside the badge associated with the Peace Forces of the world government. It was placed in a way that when I decided to accept the Mark, the loyalty center simply removed the chip, disinfected it, and injected it under the skin of either my forehead or the metacarpal bone of my right thumb.

It scared me to think I had a number in the Antichrist's regime, but Tommy assured me that everyone was assigned a number whether they were American or not, according to his sources. It was the Beastmark chip I couldn't have implanted. One of the Jewish preachers told him that. It was a choice.

However, the chip in the badge was a constant reminder that Big Brother was always watching. It had a digitized key that opened up my file in any official's terminal, where my life would appear on the screen. Except the fact that I was a member of the Resistance, of course. There was also a GPS tracker in everyone's chip so they could be found if they got lost or committed a crime. I had to be judicious when dealing with being a Peace Forces detective and a spy for the Resistance. The badge never went with me to my meetings with my handler, or the government would pick us up immediately.

That wouldn't always be the case. At the halfway point of the Trib, no one would have a choice. Take it or face the blade. I knew the odds were against me to make it to Armageddon, but there were no guarantees in the Trib except the judgments.

After putting my badge on the nightstand and situating my pillow to an almost comfortable position, I tried to clear my mind and let the case unfold. The stress of driving the five hours filled with small crews of highway repair workers, mixed with the slow drivers sightseeing the damaged areas of Missouri, made me irritable and tired. The orange and white striped barrels made for one lane driving for more miles than I cared to travel. But that wasn't the hardest part of the trip. The missing Arch in the skyline made the city look no different than those of similar population. St. Louis became ordinary.

Closing my eyes brought the woman's head into view. Questions of her identity, importance, death, and being placed by the stadium ran through my mind with nothing pointing to any answers.

Answer.

Something inside told me it would be a single answer that would unravel her murder. With the senator's involvement, Frank playing the yes man, and my inexperienced detective's skills being called upon, I couldn't help but believe this was a setup to withhold something far bigger.

The conspiracy theories abound in my mind as I tried to remove the focus of the case while I turned to my side. The scent on the pillow was commercial laundry detergent that made the stench of the apartment go away. The cleaning person knew what they were doing. After deciding to sleep on either one of my sides or planted face down into the pillow for the rest of my stay in St. Louis, I drifted into a short sleep with nothing but chemicals and faux pine scent in my mind.

With a refreshed outlook and no desire to check the man in the mirror, I sat at the end of the bed and shook the nap webs from my mind and considered what I needed to tell my Christian Resistance handler. He was a demanding taskmaster who knew his business and the consequences of a job not well done. Deaths of fellow Christians at the cruel hands of a government who believed them to be killers troubled my tired mind.

Before my meeting with Frank, I had to meet Tommy, my Christian Resistance handler. The man I saw at Busch Stadium. Tommy turning his hat around told me he had scouted our meeting place he told me about before I got to the city, and it was safe. Scratching behind my right ear told him I'd be there.

As I spritzed a cologne/wrinkle remover on my person, I thought about Tommy, a founding member of the local Christian Resistance. The Peace Forces made it almost impossible to collaborate with the other groups, so we did the best we could with the resources at hand. Although it was difficult, we managed to keep some of our brothers and sisters safe while being a thorn in the side of the Antichrist.

Tommy's post-rapture story was similar to mine, only it was his sister who got the free pass through the Rapture. He was disowned by his family when he started telling them everything that was actually going on. I had to hold him as he sobbed after they took the Beastmark, the mark of the beast described in the Bible. It was voluntary, and he begged them not to make a rash decision. Unfortunately, the chip was advertised as the safest way to keep people from getting their identity stolen with the guarantee that if it was, they would get double the money they had lost.

The people flocked to the loyalty centers.

My truck roared to life, and I started for the meeting place. The police radio I had mounted on the dash was filled with Peace Forces overwhelmed by the daily occurrences of strife and struggle to maintain a city on the brink of collapse. The voices were a mishmash of dialects and accents that were local and European. Frustration between the two made for confusion leading to angry retorts and sinister mumblings that spilled to the victims and guilty alike. The Peace Forces were not subject to complete respecting of the formers laws that protected the rights of individuals. Many citizens were beaten or shot for the misunderstanding of a European Peace Forces officer drunk on their own power. But that's what happens when destruction takes control of a government filled with politicians looking for their next rise on the world stage. The U.S. citizens were complaining to a government whose hands were tied by the Antichrist.

After the quakes, all levels of law enforcement and

military throughout the U.S. were decimated, and criminal activity skyrocketed. Many cops and soldiers, overwhelmed with grief and long hours, committed suicide, making a bad situation worse. Because of this, the U.S. government had to take matters into their own hands. President Mason reached out to the Sovereign when our allies refused to help. The ones we continuously sent money to for decades, to help with their problems, told us to take care of our own. But the Sovereign chastised them for being unfeeling, and he sent money in the form of Earth dollars, the new global currency that coincided with the digital monetary system in place of the cryptocurrencies.

The Sovereign sent the Peace Forces to help regain social control. Although technically disconnected with the newly formed world government, America was slowly being absorbed. The Peace Forces took over and all local, state, and federal law enforcement agencies were put under the same umbrella as the military. Sovereign believed it best to have all organizations used to maintain peace in the world combined for communal information gathering, sharing, and acting as a single unit rather than quibbling departments more interested in one upmanship to gain notoriety and government funding.

The radio brought a white noise of confusion and anger inside of me that I knew was dangerous. Thoughts of finding the killer by any means controlled my thoughts. It was a rage that I couldn't afford. It made for a messy investigation that would lead nowhere, except a one-way ticket to the Internal Affairs office, and I knew it. Frank told me about cops, who lost sight of what's important, being fired and losing promising careers and pensions, all to emotions that were worthless to the investigation.

I took a deep breath and asked God to calm me for the investigation.

CHAPTER 4

After talking to a Resistance member in St. Louis, Tommy decided the safest place to meet was under a section of I-64 that had collapsed near the stadium, making a small alcove. It faced the railroad tracks and was close to nothing. There were no cameras in that area due to the lack of interest by the Peace Forces.

I parked my truck near a burned-out church in an area that was washed out. The only people around were a few drug addicts passed out for the day. The railroad yards were clean with just a hint of salt from the river surge. The only negative to the scene were the rusting tracks that looked like furry caterpillars before cocooning up for the change.

The cheeriness of the scene was overtaken by the clouds. There was a hopelessness that overwhelmed everything. The planet was feeling the ravages of the previous judgments and dreadfully looking forward to the rest. A melancholy fell over me as I walked to the alcove. The idea that I could've avoided the Trib made me angry with myself. The lost years. The bad choices. Family now in Heaven, like Mom and Dad. But my sister was somewhere on the planet. She didn't want to be found, and she was good at it. Off grid or name change. Either way, I hadn't found her yet. I felt lower still.

To avoid despair, I focused on the case while I finished the last hundred yards. Since the senator called Frank in on it, the thoughts of his involvement crossed my mind and made me wonder if the senator killed the victim. He wouldn't be the first politician to clean up after himself using cops in a murder investigation and definitely not the last. Concern for Frank started me thinking he might be a pawn. Thinking him part of the conspiracy was out of the question. Frank Malone was the straightest shooter in the business. And I needed my mentor to be innocent.

When I was twenty yards from the alcove, a large figure stepped out of its shadows. The frame of a very large individual would've made even a brave man give pause. I kept walking because Tommy's shadow was familiar.

"Hey, man. How're you doing?" he asked, smiling and holstering his SIG .45. He acted as if depression didn't exist. Just another day in the life of a spy, he always said.

"Peachy." I stepped inside the alcove and fist bumped my handler and my friend.

"Why did you get to the scene before the CSU?" He shrugged, lifting his giant paws. "Not that I'm trying to tell you your business."

"Standard procedure. I'm the investigating officer, so I need to be there first to maintain the integrity of the scene," I said, while following Tommy into the alcove. It was dark and smelled like asphalt and stale drugs. No doubt, we weren't the first to meet here.

"Interesting."

Tommy frowned as he searched his hoodie pockets, then sat on a chunk of concrete.

The only things I could see in the dark alcove was differing sizes of concrete and asphalt, making the area look like the meeting place of modern cavemen.

"Why was there a crowd? This seems like a simple enough case." I sat on a piece of rubble and rummaged through my jacket pockets. "A couple of reporters is usually all that needs to be at a crime scene. With all that's going on, why the interest?" My right hand gripped the flash drive.

"The crowd was journalists and internet paparazzi trying to get the scoop. I heard some say they were called in by an anonymous source." He paused and pulled out a miniature tablet and set it by him. "Probably because the woman was our former president."

My stomach did a swan dive down to my toes. "Seriously?" I nearly threw up.

President Jane Mason was the first ever female American president, elected a year before the Rapture. A couple weeks back she had disappeared right out of the Oval Office, or so the government media reported, but everyone took that with half a grain of salt. After two days of exhaustive searching, the Peace Forces announced that she was murdered by the northeast Christian Resistance who had been causing trouble in the capital area.

"Are you sure?" All I could do was shake my head.

If anyone would know, he would. Tommy was in the CIA before the Rapture. Afterwards, he deleted his identity–he'd never say how–and disappeared into oblivion. He took a few of his friends, former CIA, FBI, and military personnel and started organizing the western Resistance into something more effective. Although there were other Christian groups detached from ours, we all coordinated together the best we could to be a cohesive unit against the forces of the Antichrist.

I noticed a slight grin cross his mouth.

"You turd." I backhanded his elbow. Tommy always knew when I needed a laugh. "You really had me going. I thought the woman could've been the president." I thought for a second. "Timeline's all wrong. She was reported missing about two weeks ago. The head is in too good a shape for being dead that long."

"No one recognized the head. It was shaved, like the

killer knew what they were doing. I'd even wager the eyes were gone. If that's the case, it was done by a pro. And besides, who knows where the former president really is? If you ask me, she drowned in the tsunami after the first quake."

The first quake sent tidal waves to coasts all over the earth. Washington D.C. was far enough inland not to get the initial hit, but the Potomac River surged and ruined the already quake-damaged Capital Building, White House, and Supreme Court. Although there was enough time to escape for the politicians, the rest of the local populace suffered great losses. Philadelphia became the new capital. But there was one problem with Tommy's theory.

"She didn't disappear until long after the second quake."

"True, but I still think she's dead anyway. By the way, how do you know the head's a woman?"

"Just guessing." I shrugged. It was better than calling her an it. It didn't feel right. I felt as if I needed to give the victim respect for reasons I didn't understand.

"Looks like a head that fell off the C.P. truck." He looked me in the eye with eyes that were always searching for truth even from a friend.

"No C.P. truck routes go by the stadium." His stare bothered me. Even though I considered him a friend, our relationship was still tenuous considering our profession as spies.

"Was she bladed?"

"Maybe, but not necessarily by the Global Church. Not unless there's a new rule of shooting a prisoner before sending them to the guillotine." I stared back to see his reaction before he answered. Something he taught me in my spy crash course.

"I don't follow."

He shifted his weight as if he was expecting a long conversation.

"She was shot just above the right eye."

Tommy's eyes widened. "Wow. No one in the crowd mentioned that."

"How would they know?"

"Some started to get close to the head when a couple of cops pulled guns on them and shouted stuff about congregating groups being illegal. Threatened to start shooting if the crowd didn't disperse. When they scanned some journalist's Beastmarks, they moved us to where we were when you got there." Tommy looked down. "Cops sounded Eastern European."

"Peace Forces patrol fresh from Europe. No ability, but plenty of attitude."

Not long after Sovereign sent the personnel aid, all law enforcement in America wore the Peace Forces patches. Now, we're all one big happy storm trooping family.

His dark eyes narrowed. "Will, you need to make sure to stay on point. It's one thing to solve a murder, but your responsibilities to the Resistance are priority one."

"I know my job. Both with the Forces and the Resistance. But I need to be careful. Frank called me in because Senator Jon Staeger wanted this case investigated. Frank is supposed to report to him directly." Just saying it made me feel dirty.

"Why would he want this investigation to happen? He barely comes to Missouri anymore," Tommy whispered as if talking to himself.

"Is he a member of the Resistance?" I thought it would help a little knowing that one of us was a powerful senator helping in the background.

"Not ours. But I don't know about the others. I'll have to ask around."

Although he looked outside, his eyes were glazed with deep thought. Probably thinking of the people to contact and how to do it. Tommy always looked ahead of every situation.

"It seems there are more people interested in this Jane

Doe than I care to have. I don't want the spotlight treatment if she's famous." The idea of my image plastered all over the planet made the red flags in my mind fly at full staff. Nothing good could come out of it.

"Sounds like you're scared."

I knew Tommy was trying to get to me, and I didn't want to disappoint. "I'm not scared. Just looking at the facts the way a good detective should. And interested parties are part of it," I said shaking my head. Even I didn't believe me.

"So, what's the problem my friend?" Tommy's voice was filled with concern. He sat up and looked at me as a show of friendship. And motivation. He was a crack interrogator in the CIA.

I stood and looked at the gray sky, ran my hand through my hair, and sighed. "I didn't sign up for this. I'm just a rookie detective and a newbie spy. I feel like I'm in over my head in so many ways."

"What do you mean?"

"It's just that Frank didn't give me a partner. I'm doing everything alone on both sides."

I wanted to tell him how inadequate I felt. Being a newbie detective alone on his first assignment was one thing. Find the bad guy and arrest him. But to have so many people's lives depending on my spying ability was something else. One wrong move and good people died.

"God made you to be a cop. You graduated with a 4.0 in criminal justice. I mean really, you were the top of your class in the academy. The FBI was recruiting you."

His conviction in my abilities was always kind, which paled in comparison to his convictions for his savior.

"You're the youngest detective in the Forces."

"By default, through attrition. But I didn't sign up for this case. If this person is famous, and I find the killer, I will shoot up the ladder faster than I should. The Peace Forces are filled with sharks. Cops are always investigating each other so they can climb the ladder faster. It's like Philly. The politicians are in line to kiss up to the Antichrist to get the scraps from his table. If the spotlight shines too bright, somebody will figure out I'm in the Resistance. Christians count on me for survival." I paused. "The blade isn't something to play with."

"That's what you signed up for, Will."

He stood and placed his giant hand on my shoulder and gripped me tightly. I almost dropped to one knee from the pain, but I endured it to avoid embarrassment.

"You know things are only going to get worse from here. We need all the intel we can get. Brothers and sisters in Christ are going to be murdered faster than we can convert them. The higher up you get into the Peace Forces, the more information you'll have access to. The faster, the better. Lives will be saved."

Considering the limited time we had left on the earth, he was right. All it did was add more pressure to the cooker.

"That's the problem. That is a lot to put on my narrow shoulders. What if I get caught?" I walked out of the alcove and sighed. "Or worse, what if I fail?"

"You knew it would get tight. You read the scriptures, same as me. The guillotine is waiting for us all." He stepped up beside me, took a deep breath, and smiled. "If it's His will, Will." Tommy handed me a flash drive. "Just got it from Tech."

I pocketed it and handed him mine.

"According to ICON, the military is on the move in Cheyenne. And the raids in Nebraska are about to escalate." I patted his shoulder and stared at the sky. "Thanks. It's hard sometimes to see things clearly."

Tommy hesitated and rubbed the back of his neck as he looked in the direction I was. "Clouds are getting darker. Will the next judgment ever start?"

One of the most difficult parts of the Trib was that the judgments didn't come on a schedule we could see. God did it when He thought best. The first set of judgments kept us guessing for over a year and a half. With a little under two years until the halfway point when the next set of judgments began, we still didn't know when they would start and finish. We just knew they were coming.

"Yeah." I looked at the concern on his face. "What's the matter?" I didn't really want to know. He had a bad habit of saving bad news for last.

"It would be in your best interest to solve this case as fast as you can."

"Why's that?" Something inside me said to hold on. The ride was about to get bumpy.

"Some of our Bible experts talked to one of the Jewish preachers. You only have five days before the next one." He wouldn't look at me. "Counting today."

"Great." My stomach started protesting the new stress.

"You know the seventh seal is when the seven trumpets are passed out."

"Yeah, with thunder, earthquake, and voices."

That creeped me out the most. As the disembodied voices spoke, my wits had taken a vacation. I never heard what they said, but their tone wasn't happy, happy, joy, joy. Ominous wasn't even a strong enough word.

"And the 144,000 Jewish preachers have started spreading the Word." He kept his eyes on the sky.

"The two witnesses in Jerusalem put them on the road last year. I ran into three of them in K.C. Good kids. Lots of energy."

Tommy moved into the fading light outside. His emotions were always hard to read. But this time, his entire body was transfixed on the skies. "The first trumpet is about to be blown."

"And?" When I couldn't keep a Bible or Dad's prophecy journal on me in the field, I depended on Tommy.

He closed his eyes and bowed his head. "The first angel sounded, and there followed hail and fire mingled with blood, and they were cast upon the earth; and the third part of the trees were burnt up, and all green grass was burnt up."

"Great. Nothing like a bloody forest fire to cheer us up." My smile had no steam.

"This is no time to joke. The dangers will elevate with each judgment. We have to be careful." Tommy's tear landed on a blade of grass that wouldn't be there in five days.

"Sorry, brother. I'm just trying not to lose it out here." I patted him on his shoulder. "The judgments are for the unbelievers. We are immune."

He looked at me with surprise. "And what about the people who aren't?"

"Maybe just the Marks (what the Resistance nicknamed those who took the Beastmark) will get it." I shrugged. "God knows what He's doing."

"Always." He looked back at the sky. "These things I have spoken to you, that in Me you may have peace. In the world you will have tribulation; but be of good cheer, I have overcome the world. John 16:33."

Tommy knew I had limited access to God's Word, so he always told me a Bible verse of encouragement to keep me going. It was the first one he told me when I entered the spy game. He used it when he believed I was under a lot of stress, and this case was shaping up to be one that needed overcoming. And it helped. It reminded me that not only was I not alone, but that Jesus had experience doing it.

"We need to go." My fear subsided, but I still dreaded the next five days. It always seemed to get intense just before a judgment. And this one was going to be rough.

We bowed our heads.

He prayed for us.

CHAPTER 5

With limited time, I decided to talk to Frank, then see if the CSU crew had any preliminary reports.

The Peace Forces had their St. Louis Command Center at the pre-Trib metro police headquarters. It was just far enough away from the river to not be overwhelmed by the surge. However, there was enough water damage that required renovation of the basement and first floor that was about fifty percent complete according to a sign at the front entrance.

Frank waved me into his second-floor office.

"Did you get settled in, Will?"

Frank sat back in his office chair and pointed a crooked finger from his wrestling days in college to the chair across from his desk.

His office was filled with his past. The gray walls had pictures from his career mixed with pictures of his wife. The ceiling was off white from years of neglect with an old-fashioned tube lighting system that barely kept the room illuminated. They were never able to have kids. His desk was dark stained, yet simple.

"Yeah. The hotel cockroaches sat out a delightful mint on my pillow."

He laughed. "Sorry about the accommodations. But

that's the best I could do on short notice."

"Thanks. I'll remember your generosity in my memoirs." Frank laughed again. It was nice to have a boss I could rib. My K.C. captain was uptight and humorless.

"All right, all right. Let's get down to business. I know you just got one look at the scene, but what are you thinking?"

He interlocked his hands on top of his head as the chair grunted when he leaned back, waiting for my answer.

"It was obviously staged. I highly doubt that anything will show up on the drone cam footage. It feels like she was murdered across the river, the killer brought her here at night, and staged the head by the stadium." I crossed my outstretched legs at the ankles and sat back in my chair for a long conversation.

"Sounds like too much supposition to me. Stay with the facts. Focus on the evidence." Frank's gravelly voice grumbled.

"The lack of a body suggests that the murderer had a reason to decapitate. It might be a couple of possibilities. Either there was too much evidence pointing to the killer, or it was easier to travel with just the head since it was the only thing the killer needed to get the point across." I felt my brow furrow under the strain of thought. "I know there may be other reasons, but I think these are the most practical. Only more evidence will help eliminate them down to one."

"Anything else?" Frank had a way of dragging things out of students at the academy that they didn't realize they had to begin with. His legendary patience with students brought out the best in them.

"I believe that once we establish identity, the case will be easier to close. My gut feeling is that she was someone of importance due to the interest the media displayed at the scene. Someone told me they were given an anonymous tip that was strong enough to send them scurrying to scoop each other. I think we should only tell them what is absolutely necessary, otherwise the killer will be almost impossible to find." The heaviness of my words matched the inactive air.

"Good thinking, kid. You're sticking to your training."

He smiled at me like a proud papa. It reminded me of church before the Rapture. Frank was a deacon who always had a pocketful of candy for the kids. He gave the same smile to them while he passed out the cinnamon hard candies.

"What have you told our good Samaritan?" I asked.

"Nothing yet. Not enough to give any kind of report," he whispered, pointing to his ear.

His office was bugged.

"You're taking orders from a politician? Frank, I'm surprised. Does he even live here anymore?" I whispered back.

The red flags in my head were waving hard. I tried to ignore them out of respect for my captain. But I also needed to know he was on the level.

Frank sat up in his chair. "I'm not sure. But I do know he's still got plenty of pull in our state."

Frank's willingness to help the senator troubled me. He should know better. Staeger was obviously using Frank for his own personal agenda.

"Seems to me that the orders are coming from the wrong man."

"That may seem so, but things in Philly are crazy. Including the top man." He leaned back in his chair and used his loud voice. "You didn't hear this from me, but word from the higher ups is that America is about to sign a deal similar to the one Israel signed last year." He smiled.

The Resistance already knew that. The Bible predicted that all the world would comply at the beginning. Dad thought America would be the last holdout, and he was right. The thing he got wrong was that President Mason would be in favor of the treaty based on the way she spoke of keeping America more involved in the world's activity and focused less on our own problems. But she did an about face when the Mid-East Accord ratification was placed on her desk to sign.

"Sounds too good to be true." The speed at which prophecy was being fulfilled was staggering. At times, it felt like I was on a carousel that was moving too fast to see the surroundings, since God wasn't sticking to a schedule we recognized.

"Would you be optimistic for once in your miserable life? I mean really. Think about it. With all this death and mayhem going on in the country, wouldn't you like to see America back on top?"

Remembering the way Frank was then, and realizing he didn't make the faithful cut to Heaven, my paranoia revved up. I chastised myself for not checking the first time we met at the crime scene. Checking someone's right wrist and forehead for the Beastmark was something Tommy taught me to do when dealing with people. Tattoos were suggested for people to be proud of their loyalty. That made checking easy. The other way was to find bumps the chips made, which was difficult at best. Frank was clean for now. The Beastmark was still voluntary. Frank still had a chance. If he had it, that was the end. His afterlife was set in stone. Brimstone.

I shrugged.

I didn't have the heart to tell him that America had no important part in the times we were living in. He needed to hitch his wagon to a better horse. Jesus. However, that wasn't for me to say. When I was being prepped for undercover work, Tommy and the others made it crystal clear that my part was not spreading the Gospel to the world. That was for the two witnesses, their Jewish entourage, and other Christians.

"Yes, I do. But I can only do my part. One case at a

time." My job was to infiltrate the Peace Forces and provide information about such things as raids, safe areas for the Resistance to operate, and anything else I felt was important for believers to stay off the radar and keep up their diligent preaching of Christ and Him crucified, like Paul the Apostle.

Frank returned to business. "I'm having the medical examiner put a rush on the autopsy. The senator wants results."

"That sounds good to me. This being my first case and all." I stood. "I'll start with the CSU people. They should have a few ideas by now."

"Still sticking to your training. Just remember to keep me in the loop."

"Will do."

CHAPTER 6

On my way to the CSU lab, I began thinking about how the scene was in front of one of the most recognizable buildings in the city. Second only to the Gateway Arch, Frank told me that the only thing left was the peak that somehow stayed upright just above the waterline at the end of the other six hundred feet that had toppled into the river during the first quake, resting just below water level.

Placing the head there meant the killer was either brazen or working on orders that required him to stage her there. Only someone who believed the cops couldn't close in on them would do this whether the killer did it of their own volition or not. Especially if they knew the case would be given to a snot-nosed rookie. The only two things I hoped for was the CSU team figuring out the identity of the victim and where the murder took place. Otherwise, this case was already cold.

Jenny and a man I'd never met were the only people in the antiseptic-looking lab full of forensic testing equipment and shelves of scientific supplies. There was Trib jazz, a mix of blues and new age that sounded like humpback whales caterwauling in pain, playing on a wireless speaker. They were hard at work separating the evidence on a table. There wasn't much, and I wasn't optimistic that anything would be found to aid my investigation.

"Hello everyone. How's it going?" I strolled to the table and began perusing without touching.

"Detective." Jenny was bookworm pretty. Freckled, thin, with red hair. Although her bangs covered most of her forehead, she was devoid of a Beastmark there or on her open right wrist. "This is Bobby O'Neill, the second best in the forensics business. But he is the best drone pilot in the forensics business."

Bobby waved without looking at me. He was a short, thin man, almost sickly, with even thinner hair. His Beastmark tattoo was prevalent on his wrist, a falcon carrying an olive branch. His soul might've been Hell bound, but his physical movements were of a professional manner which left little doubt of his abilities. I could tell he loved what he did and did what he loved by the way he meticulously placed the crime scene paraphernalia in an order that he and Jenny knew. It made me feel like the rookie I was.

"We were just getting started with the physical evidence. The pics are in the computer. Take a peek while we finish this. Bobby is about finished with the drone cams. He sent the feed to a friend in the old FBI to confirm his findings. But don't get too hopeful, it's standard procedure."

The computer was one of the best I had seen. The Peace Forces pockets were deep because the Antichrist owned the global piggy bank. Any, and all, financial institutions bowed to his will since he was considered the one who stopped the global depression after the Rapture. And one of his ideas was to weaponize his law enforcement with as much money as possible. The pics came up on the screen. Nothing stood out.

Bobby came up beside me.

"Shaved head and eyebrows. Looks like a pro did this."

I echoed Tommy's assessment by carefully nodding, trying to look smart.

"Interesting," Bobby said, squinting as he enlarged the picture. "But why stage it there?"

"Good question. Maybe a Cubs fan?" I grinned when I looked at him.

"A what?" Bobby asked, looking at me with an inquisitively raised eyebrow that matched the vacant look of a man who had never heard of sports.

"Baseball team in Chicago. Cardinals' rival," I said as I quickly turned to the screen, hoping he didn't see my unintentional condescending grin. Even he should've known about the Cards. Unless he lived in a cave.

"Bobby, we talked about this already. The stadium where the body was at. That was where the Cardinals played professional baseball," Jenny said, raising her eyebrows at her cohort like a lawyer leading a witness.

"Oh, yeah. Sports. Tedious thing, sports. Keeps the mind numb and the butt number for the spectators." He mocked in haughty derision as he went back to work.

Instead of arguing, I let him have his fun. After all, we were playing for the same team.

"Anything else?" I returned to the monitor. Everything seemed the same on the surface, but I'd let the experts have a go on a deeper level. Then I saw a couple of street cameras in the pics.

"We should have a preliminary report in a couple of hours," Jenny said.

Her lawyer voice seemed to be leading me right out the door.

"But don't get your hopes up. The majority of this stuff is basically useless. But I never leave a stone unturned."

She grinned as she raised a stone from the crime scene.

I rolled my eyes. "Anything on the street cams in and around the crime scene?"

"Captain Malone is getting the warrants for them as we speak," Bobby said as he returned to the table and methodically separated the last of the evidence. "He just called it in."

Frank must've thought of it as I walked to the lab.

"Did you notice anything interesting on the drone cams?" I removed the pics from the screen and turned to face Bobby, who didn't flinch.

"Nothing I deem necessary to talk about at this time, detective. But I'm reticent to make any speculation until the footage is officially confirmed." The corners of his mouth curled into a knowing sneer. "Unless you believe in bucking protocols."

"Easy there, stud." Jenny frowned. "He just asked your opinion, and that is permissible."

Bobby slightly rolled his eyes as he said, "Then no, detective. It doesn't seem like there is anything important on the footage. But I would like to wait to have it confirmed by my colleague."

"Thanks. Please let me know when you receive word." I wanted to be snarky, but I doubted Bobby would retaliate by holding the results out of spite. So, I decided to keep my tone cordial, even if he didn't seem likable.

"Where's the coroner's office?"

"Turn left, last door on the right." Bobby pointed with his thumb and deadpanned. "Ask for Doctor Death."

Jenny shook her head and furrowed her brow.

"Thanks."

CHAPTER 7

It's interesting how death seems to smell the same in all morgues. Chemicals mixed with human remains are the kind of pairing that had to be invented by the devil.

"Who is it?" a voice from the examination room called.

"Will Thomas. I'm the detective in charge of the severed head investigation." I walked into the room. "Are you Dr. Death?"

She was pulling out the last of the woman's brains and carefully placing them into a metal evidence tray on the slab. My lunch plans were immediately canceled.

She turned around and glared. "The next time you see that lab rat, Bobby O'Neill, tell him his sense of humor belongs in here with the rest of the dead." She pointed a latex gloved finger at my Jane Doe.

"I guess this is part of my hazing. My apologies." I smiled as I stood across the slab from the coroner. It felt good to be sent through the wringer. It meant they were trying me on for size. Giving me a chance.

"Ruth Washington." Her mask moved up her nose as she smiled. "I'd offer a handshake, but as you can see, they are not in the best shape for niceties."

The last time I saw her she was slumped over the victim. She was a tall black woman, a little under six feet, who wore flats. She didn't need to lord over the shorties of the world. It showed a confidence I appreciated.

"Thanks. How are things with Jane? She didn't seem to be in good shape when I last saw her."

"A little worse for wear, but she's in good hands now." Ruth returned to her work. Her skill was as impressive as her gentleness. The head wasn't rudely handled or ignorantly tossed about. I could tell she respected the dead and loved her job.

"This is a woman? I'm just guessing."

"Yes, but I will confirm through DNA. She has the facial characteristics of a female. Good guessing for a new detective. And by the way, congrats on the promotion. I hope you solve every case that comes your way." Her voice was filled with conviction. Maybe her way of starting on the right foot. And I wasn't about to let that fall to the wayside. I needed all the friends I could get for this case. Especially if the victim was famous.

"Thanks. From what I hear, your help in cases will make my job easy." I knew there was a little-brown nosing in that, but I wanted her to know that I appreciated everything she could do.

She looked up at me with beautiful dark eyes, the kind a man would need a map and a compass to get out of. The mask covered her obvious grin. Something made me clear my throat. It was time to get back to work.

"Any idea about the cause of death yet?" Hoping she didn't see my cheeks flush, I peered into the brain pan that once housed Jane's thoughts and dreams. Yep, lunch was a definite no go.

"Easy so far. The gunshot wound makes it pretty obvious." She pointed inside the skull. "The bullet ricocheted a couple of times then embedded here. Her brain was turned into hamburger. Died instantly."

"Small caliber?" I was surprised.

"Yes, a .22 of some sort. Bobby, the comedian, will give

you the details later."

"Nothing suggesting anything else?"

"Just a trace amount of water in the ear. Not enough to suggest she drowned. But it could be from where she was murdered."

"So, she was shot before being decapitated?"

Ruth pointed at the bullet hole in the head. "The headshot was first. Then the decapitation followed by the head shaving, teeth removal, and eye removal." She opened the lids, then the mouth.

I cringed at the empty sockets. The mouth looked like my grandfather after taking out his old-fashioned dentures. "A pro, I'm guessing."

"I'd agree. Especially considering the head was wiped down."

"What else did you check for?" I leaned on the empty table behind me and started a mental file of the findings so far. It was a very small list.

"River flotsam, dirt, grass, and a partridge in a pear tree. Nothing suggesting where she was killed, except maybe the water."

"And then she was staged at Gate 5. Right across Clark Avenue from Ballpark Village." I had enough of the sight, so I focused on Dr. Washington.

"That was my favorite place." She pulled off her mask, walked to the sink, and washed up. Great margaritas."

Gorgeous wasn't a good enough description for her.

"I preferred Big Mac Land," I said, trying not to stare.

"Oh, a purist. My kinda fella." Her smile could have stopped traffic if her curves didn't. Then she pointed at the head as if she remembered something.

"And she was guillotined. The smoothness of the slice suggests either that or a very sharp blade. But that would suggest a very strong killer. Most decapitations require more than one swing, and the neck wouldn't be smooth, like this one." She walked back to the slab and pointed at the neckline. "See? No edges. This was a single swipe cut."

"Interesting," I said to myself.

"If you want to look at the hard copy, I just printed it."

She led me into the front office, pulled out an empty folder, and filled it with a short stack from the printer.

"Time of death is interesting."

"How so?" I tried to read the pages upside down, but she moved them too fast. She was efficient in everything she did at work.

"From the state of the head, I would have guessed a couple or three days. But she was actually killed two weeks ago."

She handed the file to me. Her wrist Beastmark was surrounded by an ornate tattoo of Earth with a lion on one side and a lamb on the other. The Antichrist pretending to be God.

My stomach churned, but not from the stench of the corpse. "Why did it fool you?"

"The skin is in good condition. But all the other factors, muscle deterioration, lack of entomological presence, etc., point to a two-week TOD." She frowned at the paper. "Now it's up to the jokers in the lab to determine why this is."

"Okay. Now comes the million-dollar question."

"Who is she?" Ruth's dark eyes penetrated mine. "No idea."

"Great."

"Sorry, but any ID markers were either scrubbed or too general. Seems the killer knew how to get rid of just enough evidence, like he's toying with me. Her dentals won't help either since the teeth were removed." She sighed. "There is no loyalty chip either or Captain Malone would've had that answer at the stadium."

"What about the DNA? How long will it take?" Even I could hear the beginnings of my frustration.

"The blood has been sent to the lab. Our DNA expert is

already on it. Should take less than twelve hours."

"That's fast."

"When you have ICON at your disposal, it can be quick."

She was talking about the International Cloud of Networks. It was nicknamed ICON, but the Christian Resistance called it the Beast. The Antichrist's people used it to keep tabs on everyone. It was linked to every camera and microphone, government or private, in the world. It also contained files on everyone in the world when it took over the internet, although the Antichrist denied it. America was plugged into it the day the Peace Forces put boots on the ground. But American citizens didn't know it. Just us cops, and we were sworn to secrecy. Now the entire planet was being watched by the Beast.

I got up and thanked her.

"I'll text you to let you know the rest of my findings before I submit them to the case file on the police, I mean ICON. Sorry, I'm still trying to get used to that. But it is nice to have everything in one place. Makes me wonder why America didn't do it ages ago."

"By the way." I turned just before I left the office. "Could she have been decapitated for transport?"

"Of course." She thought for a moment. "Makes sense. But let's let Jenny and Bobby, the comedian, help with that."

I winked at her. "Thanks, Dr. Washington."

"Call me Ruth. We're colleagues now." Her professional tone had a hint of flirtation. But it was probably my ego. I always liked curvy women.

I nodded and went to ask Frank for my office.

CHAPTER 8

Frank gave me an office away from the distractions of the daily precinct activities but within earshot of his office. It had four tan walls, one office chair, and two Hercules chairs. They were all gray, but not the same shade, hand-me-downs from a generation before the Rapture. The wooden desk with a light varnish was older. There were two windows. One in the door, and the other in the wall opposite my desk where I could see a former interrogation room loaded with files and other junk.

I turned on the fan I stole from an empty office to help forget the still air outside. Unfortunately, fans struggled to move the air like they used to. It was as if the air fought against the blades. Everyone sat closer to their fans just to feel the wind on the highest setting.

One of the difficulties I had when performing my Copley duties was that I sometimes forgot I had another job. The Resistance was counting on me to find out what the government knew about us and the Global Church's plans to capture and kill us.

The flash drive Tommy gave me was invisible to the anti-hacking search programs that the Beast used. Resistance hackers were barely able to keep up since the Beast had advanced A.I. programming that allowed it to vigilantly search for hackers twenty-four/seven. To start, Resistance Techs did this by keeping their own search programs in a place that was easily removable if the Beast was close to finding it—flash drives. The techs said it was also the safest way to transport the information. The Beast ruled the internet like Sovereign ruled the planet, with full reign and without remorse. Any spy program found was not only extinguished, but the user would be found quickly, then bladed for global treason.

Since I wasn't tech savvy, I put my faith in the nerds Jesus gave us.

Before he left my office, Frank wiped dust off the monitor and told me that the desktop computer in my office was a dinosaur that barely kept up with the constant barrage of new hacker proof software being downloaded at a daily rate. The various Christian Resistance groups weren't the only ones not pleased with the Sovereign's reign over the internet. Jesus had told his followers that wars, and rumors of wars, would sweep the planet during the Trib, and that apparently included the internet.

Waiting for the computer to update was maddening. I sat back in my chair, drummed my fingers on the worn armrest, and considered my situation. A barrage of emotion filled my mind as the case was slow in presenting itself to me. Anger at the lack of evidence to form a preliminary investigation list. Grief for the murdered. Like I thought earlier, my gut told me she didn't deserve this. Plus, there was the excitement to prove myself to my mentor. It was hard to reign these feelings in, but I tried.

After an hour of waiting for the computer to update, I plugged in the flash drive, entered the password, and let the software hide my presence on the Peace Forces network. My password was assigned to me by Tommy. It was 074 101 115 117 115, in the obsolete ASCII computer coding it meant JESUS. It was his way of reminding me of who I really worked for.

ICON was fairly simple if you had a degree in rocket science. Trying to find the plans for every raid was the proverbial hay stacked needle. The plans were never in the same spot twice. It was a good thing I had a couple hours, because it felt longer than that to find the folder. The file for the Midwest and Great Plains showed there weren't any raids planned near our safe site locations, which I downloaded.

The western Resistance leadership was trying to keep the Peace Forces out of the Great Plains region of the U.S. That was so they could send groups of new believers safely through to the encampments near the Canadian border. Montana and the Dakotas were filled with new converts trying to avoid the guillotine while the Resistance used Wyoming and Nebraska to train new soldiers to protect the region. Although the government seemed ignorant of these camps, I had a hunch there was little they could do about it until the northeastern and southern Resistance armies were defeated.

My biggest concern was the new West Coast. It took a beating from the quakes. Most of the Pacific Ocean overran California, Oregon, and Washington. In fact, the death toll from California and Nevada alone was by far the largest in the world for any one area. Corpses still floated to the shores of Utah and Arizona more than a month after the second quake. Still, there were enough military Peace Forces in those two states to do plenty of damage to the Resistance encampments until the new army was armed and trained.

Once enough troops were ready, the Resistance army led the Peace Forces army on enough wild goose chases up and down the Rocky Mountains to keep them busy. But that could only last so long.

I heard some voices coming my way, so I shut off the monitor and picked up an empty folder and pretended to study its contents. It felt like the days my buddy, Dwight, would do the same thing when I thought I heard his parents near his room while he looked at porn on the internet. Since porn wasn't my thing, I kept lookout. I'd lie about his parents' presence sometimes just to hear him panic.

When the voices trailed off into the bullpen, I turned the monitor back on.

I entered ICON's financial section that I didn't have clearance for, but the program on the flash drive cleared the way. I noticed an inconsistency with the disbursement of funds to the U.S. government in the amount of ten million Earth dollars, the global currency. It was under the heading of "Services Rendered." I had seen this account before. Tommy had his CIA friends trace the money to soldiers of fortune groups that loved getting paid to kill Christians without repercussions. But this was a small amount compared to the billions in the previous deposits.

It felt like assassination money. I wondered if Senator Staeger was in on it. Maybe he had a political rival killed. There was no clear answer until I knew her identity, so I shook the conspiracy theory out of my head, then downloaded a couple more files with his name on them. Maybe Tommy could get the information about our senator from them.

Every time I entered ICON as a spy, I always looked up my parents and sister. Although I knew my parents were raptured, the computer always showed them as murderers who were killed in the Missouri Uprising. At least that's what the government media named it. The narrative was that the Christians, after killing everyone they deemed necessary for the Rapture story, invaded the Missouri state capital to take it over and start a new Civil War. They were going to take over the country, then the world. Sovereign applauded the U.S. military for its swift justice filled protection of the state, the nation, and the planet.

Although President Mason denied that this event happened, the vice president was reported to investigate the place of the uprising and corroborated the Sovereign's version. The fact of the matter was there was no uprising. Tommy went to Jefferson City himself and inspected the grounds where the supposed uprising occurred. The grass was undisturbed. The trees in full bloom. There was no battle.

After the president begrudgingly accepted the vice president's statement, the Beast took control and put in the names of Christians that were confirmed to have disappeared, and their names were added to the uprising. I sat back in the chair and stared at their names. Jacob and Trudy Thomas—Springfield, MO—Combatants.

According to Dad, being a new believer made it difficult to sin without immediate regret. However, being a convert during the Tribulation, with no experienced Christians to help you through the struggles of early belief, made it hard to let out a good curse word or two without a sideways glance or an out-and-out admonishment to make sure I knew I had just sinned. So, I let it fly under my breath and let the Holy Spirit do its work. I'd ask for forgiveness later when I felt good and guilty.

However, Katrina, my sister, was still alive. I called her Kat because she was so unpredictable. She prided herself in this and did outrageous things to prove her independence. She broke Mom's heart the day she turned eighteen. Momma had a big party planned with Kat's friends and all our relatives. Kat never showed. She sent Mom a scathing email from her phone. Kat complained of never getting her way, that I was the favorite, and God didn't exist. She said she was tired of living a lie, and it was time for her to cut ties with us because she could never be under the same roof as ignorant people who clung to a deity that didn't exist.

Although I wanted to be done with her after what she did to Mom and Dad, I still loved her and wanted her to go to Heaven. So, I always looked for her when I was spying on the Beast. But her file hadn't changed in over a year.

She was in London working as a prostitute in a high-priced brothel frequented by Peace Forces and aristocrats. It hurt, but what could I do but pray?

So, I prayed, placed the unloaded flash drive in my jacket pocket, and went back to Busch.

CHAPTER 9

Frank requisitioned me a junker that was old even before the Trib. But it was exactly what I asked for. The gasoline motor ran smooth and strong, and the tires had new tread. The rest of the car was straight from the junkyard. The only other thing it had going for it was that it was a single color, white with no cherries on top, but there was no doubt it was a cop car. Even the computer terminal mounted to the dashboard looked like a dinosaur trying to escape its vinyl covered cage. The whole vehicle looked beat up, so I nicknamed it the beater after my uncle's old farm truck that never saw the open road when I was a kid. I left my truck in the safety of the Peace Forces fleet services' secure parking garage, then went to Busch.

After the quakes, the city tried to clear the rubble and rebuild in a pitiful attempt to bring baseball back. Unfortunately, the other stadiums in the league were worse off. And the west coast teams had no state to play in. No, baseball would never come back.

The stale twilight air was filled with growing judgment. I stood where the head was found and tried to piece together the reasoning for dumping her there. If the killer had put her by the river, I'd never consider this anything more than a drug deal gone wrong.

Although motive wasn't the most direct route for catching a criminal, I couldn't help but wonder why the victim was killed in this way then dumped at Busch Stadium.

Starting at the site where the body was found, I worked in a concentric pattern. I had learned to search in the inverted V, a common method used by military dogs who detected low, then high, then low again. Something I learned from Mom's dogs. Although I didn't have their sense of smell, I did have some success finding evidence using their method. My mother's dogs were some of the best searchers. Police departments from around the state, including the Missouri State Highway Patrol, called her frequently to use her dogs to search for missing people. Although they weren't certified cadaver dogs, they were the most successful pack in the state at finding the missing and dead.

The more I circled, the more I knew that this was a dead end. The street was empty of evidence. Any physical evidence the CSU had was, at best, confirming there was no evidence. No footprints or dropped flotsam from the deliverer, nothing. Hopefully, the street and drone cams saw something.

Memories of sitting in Cardinals Nation, the rooftop bleachers on top of Ballpark Village, enjoying a stormy summer night game, took over when I stood trying to figure out my next investigative move. I was eighteen, looking forward to college where I would study Criminal Justice. The atmosphere of the rooftop deck was incredible. The most diehard fans sat there that day. There were three rain delays, and the game took four hours to complete. But no fan in that section went home. The Cubs were in town and the Cardinals whipped them ten to nothing. Three Cardinal pitchers had a combined no hitter.

The sound of falling debris woke me from my nostalgia, and I turned in time to see a man darting out of the stadium rubble thirty yards from me. He made a beeline to Ballpark Village across Clark Avenue. By the time I hit my full stride, he had entered through the main entrance and disappeared into the darkness. I was able to keep up while pulling my Maglite from my jacket. Clicking the light with one hand while pulling my SIG .45 wasn't easy while I let my eyes adjust to the darkness of the giant room.

Navigating the broken tables, chairs, a fallen large screen that had been attached to the wall above the bar, and the debris from the ceiling and upper floors was difficult in the best of circumstances. Keeping my breathing steady from the short sprint and excitement made it difficult to focus on any one spot. The darkness of the area overwhelmed my senses. I became fully aware that this guy could have a gun trained on me to pick the right time to end me. Shaking the fear meant that I accepted that part of the chase as I focused on what the small light beam exposed.

On the other side of the former Cardinals watch/party hall were doors that led to the parking lot across Cardinal Way. This was the only way he could've gone, so I quickened my pace to the opposite side. The obstacle course was difficult for me to navigate, especially the shin busting sharp edged chunks of rubble. Ignoring the urge to rub my damaged shin, I kept my gun trained on what the light pointed at, ready to take action if necessary.

The entry door was devoid of glass, so I stepped through to see if he had stumbled or stopped. No luck. He was completely gone. Probably took a hard turn somewhere out of sight. I caught my breath and started back the way I came.

The moment I stepped through the door, a loud whisper came from under the overturned screen.

"Over here."

Paranoia and fear coursed through my mind, and I trained my gun barrel where the voice came from. "Peace Forces. Don't try anything."

"No prob, Bob." The man was trying to talk me down as if I needed it. And he was right. My heart raced adrenaline from my kidneys to my entire body.

"Why did you run?" I knelt to one knee and directed the light beam under the screen.

He squinted and covered his eyes. "We can't be caught talking."

His beard and hair were a disheveled sandy blonde, and his clothes were tattered and stunk of perspiration, urine, and drug use. That was all I could see. Where he slumped under the screen, sitting crisscross, was as dark as a cave.

"Who's listening?"

"Too many to count. And they're watching too."

He wiped his nose with the palm of his hand. No Beastmark anywhere. Made sense. Druggies didn't want to be noticed or tracked.

"How do you know that?"

"The first thing the government did after the two earthquakes was fix or replace the cameras. And they put plenty more up all over the city."

He looked around like he was searching for one that was unaccounted for.

I wasn't sure about this guy, but he was right. That happened all over the country. The politicians claimed the crime wave pandemic necessitated a more watchful eye for protection. He also called them earthquakes. I wondered if he was Resistance since we were the only ones to refer to them that way.

"Why are you talking to me? I'm a detective for Big Brother." I pulled out my badge.

"You're not one of them. You want to find the killer. You're a real cop. Could you put the light down? I can't escape," he said, giving a meth mouth smile.

I checked to make sure he wasn't lying. My flashlight showed that his hole had no back door.

Sitting on a smooth chunk of ceiling, I put my gun in its

holster near my armpit and pointed the light to where I could still keep an eye on him.

"You're right. I want to find the killer." I leaned over and gave a conspiratorial grin. "Can you help?"

He relaxed his shoulders, looked up, and tapped his bottom lip with a filthy finger, appearing to be in deep thought.

"I'm not sure." Then he smiled. "There was a man who dumped the noggin where you found it. But it was early this morning. Like three a.m. or thereabouts. I couldn't see his face because of his hoodie, but he was a big 'un. Bigger than me, but not bigger than you."

I'm six-four, two thirty. He looked about five-eight one thirty, almost emaciated.

"Did you see where he came from?"

"No, just heard the boots hitting the sidewalk."

He started rocking slowly like a nervous man not used to cop company. I'd seen his kind when I was a uniformed patrolman.

"Where did he go after he dumped the noggin?"

"To the river. I followed but kept a good distance." He pointed to his ear. "His boots never stopped. Then they did, near the Arch by the Old Cathedral. That's when I heard the boat."

He started chewing his thumbnail and rocked faster. He was either agitated, or he was in dire need of a fix.

"What kind of boat?"

"Not sure. It was fast but not very loud."

I could tell he wanted to run. Probably wasn't used to staying in one place this long, especially in the presence of a cop.

"Did he go upriver or down?"

He tightly closed his eyes as if saying a prayer.

"The sound went up. If he went down, he could've floated without the motors."

He opened his eyes, smiling at his own logic.

"I wonder who it was?"

"Mafia."

I could barely hear him. He stared at the ground hoping I was the only one who heard him. He was taking a big chance talking to me anyway. But something like this was a death sentence if the wrong people heard.

"You think it was the mob?" I whispered in an attempt to keep him calm.

"No doubt. They're dumpin' bodies all over the city. They like to make people think before buying more than they can afford. And they got the kinda boats that cops and military can't find or catch."

His beady eyes started looking behind me.

"I've heard about those boats."

Inheriting his paranoia, I gave the place a once over with my flashlight, then turned back to him. "Listen. Are you familiar with the local mob?"

"Mobs. More than one. Buy my drugs from the big one. They're the only people a soul can get a good score from, now that the Cardinals left town." His giggle was hidden by two hands trying to keep the noise to a minimum.

"Got a name for them—or their dons?"

"The Free Agents are the biggest and toughest. Dealers say they call themselves that because they're tired of having other people decide their fate for them. Top man is Hector. And he's a bad 'un. Never seen him, but they say he's a monster."

He started scratching his arm as he rocked hard enough to lift his backside off the floor.

"Can I go, officer?"

"Sure, but first tell me your name." I stood.

"Clay." He shivered as if he dreaded giving his name.

"Clay, nice to meet you. My name is Detective Thomas." I pulled a fifty from inside my jacket. "You can call me Will. I was wondering if you'd be my C.I. It means confidential informant. Could you do that for me?" It was barely enough to score the drugs needed for one short-lived high. But my instincts said he'd take it, or at least ask for more.

America was among the first to turn to the global currency. Insurance companies bankrupted the U.S. economy covering the wrecks and deaths from the Rapture. The devaluated dollar sent the country into an unrecoverable depression until the Sovereign bailed the country out with his remarks concerning the murders, aiding the insurance companies to deny claims from those considered part of the Christian conspiracy. Then he required the government to comply with new global economic policies. That included turning to the new Earth dollar in order to receive forgiveness of the loans the country incurred over the entirety of its existence. Without knowing it, America was on her way to the loss of freedom.

Clay stopped rocking and looked at the Earth bill as if pondering a deep philosophical thought. Then snatched it, smiled, and said, "Sure. What else you wanna know? There are two brothels on the other side of the river." He wiggled his eyebrows. "But it's a long swim." His giggle had mirth.

"That's all right. I'm not looking for a one-night girlfriend. What I really want is any information you can get me on the Free Agents and Hector."

He frowned and handed back the fifty. "I'm not sure I can do that. They find out, I'll be deep-river swimmin' for sure." He started rocking again.

I raised my hands to show that the fifty was his no matter what. "It'll be easy. Just hang around where they do business and listen. Don't ask any questions. Just listen when his people talk. Especially when they are selling to a junkie." I could see he needed me to sweeten the pot. "I'll give you one of those every time you give me good information."

"Deal!" He jumped out of the hiding place and pocketed the cash. "We'll meet right here every time."

"Right. I'll meet you here every day around this time. But you better wait and leave later. We don't want the cameras catching us leaving at the same time. They'll be on us for sure. It'll look like I couldn't find your hiding place." I raised my fist. "Go Cards."

"Go Cards!"

He bumped knuckles with me like fans did in the old days, then crawled back in his hole and laid down. No doubt thinking about his drugs, and hopefully a way to get more information.

As I went back to the beater, I decided to leave this C.I. off the books. If what he said was true, this informant's help would need to be as confidential as possible. If the mob had any ties in the Peace Forces, I'd never see him again.

CHAPTER 10

There was little else I could see, even with the flashlight. It wasn't just the coming evening. The clouds were getting darker. There was even a red hue in places.

It was past suppertime, according to my stomach. It was already angry from a small breakfast and no lunch. The downtown restaurant choices were few, and I wasn't in the mood to sit for a meal.

Frank told me about a food truck patio on the banks of the river near the stadium. The patio was settled on the corner of Walnut and Memorial Drive, where a business consultation company had a building that fell during the first quake. In fact, that building and the two next to it, a hotel and luxury apartment building, were all taken out by the two earthquakes. The city had already finished demolition but hadn't moved the debris from the site yet. In their places, a barren wasteland of twisted steel, concrete, and memories lay in heaps reminding passersby the new world had literally landed at the city's feet.

The food truck court participants took the chance to serve their fare along the new banks of the river. The city allowed it to give downtown employees a place to eat their lunches now that the restaurants were all but vacant or completely destroyed. Brown chat was laid for the trucks to park with a white gravel parking lot beside it. Picnic tables in two places offered amazing views of the river, and makeshift light poles helped illuminate the evening dining.

It was late, and a crude mom and pop hot dog truck was the only one there. The sign said they served the best chili dogs around. Fresh food was rare during the early years of the Trib. Even the moderately rich were losing money putting nutritious food on the table. The only thing going for people who couldn't afford the good stuff was government program canned garbage from European manufacturers that barely passed for food. The smell that radiated out of the truck made me believe these would not be the best chilidogs I'd ever eaten.

The mom of the truck was wiping down the serving counter when I approached. She stuck her head halfway out the window to greet me. "What'll ya have, sweetie?" Her deep southern drawl took me by surprise. She was a plump lady with greasy brown hair tied in a sad ponytail covered by a hairnet that had seen too many lunch rushes.

"I'll try two chilidogs with the works and a large, sweet tea." I grabbed my badge. The tea cost a lot, but as a member of the Peace Forces I could afford to splurge now and then.

She pulled out the scanner, flashed my badge's chip, and waited for the machine to chirp its approval. An internal cringe shot through my body thinking that the Beastmark I held in my hand was mine. Just a couple of inches away from Hell.

"I'll call ya over when it's ready, hun." Her toothy grin hadn't seen a toothbrush in a while.

The salty air from the river was not present the last time I came to St. Louis. It felt like I was looking into the ocean since the eastern shore was out of sight. Taking a full breath of the air helped as I cleared my mind to let the case simmer on the backburner. Something my dad did before a sermon. Although the stress of the day was still present, a calmness began overtaking it while I remembered the verse Tommy gave me earlier. For a moment the case didn't exist. For a moment the world wasn't Hell bound.

When my order was up, I leaned on the beater and ate. My thoughts kept going to the timeclock in my head. Although the Bible scholars were smart, accuracy was difficult. We were on God's clock, not vice versa. It could be five days, or it could be five hours, but there was one thing I could count on—it was coming. I read enough of Dad's journal to understand that even though we didn't know the exact moment things would happen, everything would be completed within seven years. Although my faith was strong, it was hard not to feel depressed for the lost time and the anxiety of the coming events. It also didn't help my digestion that my investigation was barely progressing. Not only that, but the chilidogs were nasty. A mixed flavor of cheap mystery meat and metallic beans covered in too much mustard, not enough ketchup, and onions that didn't have enough water to fully reconstitute them.

Giving up on the second chilidog, I sipped my tea and prayed for strength to solve the case before the judgment and for the protection of my stomach lining from what I believed to be a potential mortal sin. Then I went to the hotel.

When I walked in, my apartment's smell had not improved. In fact, it seemed to have gained an odor or two in my absence, though I couldn't tell exactly what they were. Deviled eggs maybe? With a side of feet, but not mine. The last chilidog went in the trash.

After a quick shower and a couple of antacid pills, I swore off chilidogs for the rest of the investigation. The living room wasn't in prime shape for me to start working, so I moved a few things around and turned on the almost useless fan. The table and two chairs were smaller than most hotels, but I figured I was lucky to have them at all. I sat my messenger bag on the table and started unloading. The laptop assigned me by K.C. was top of the line. I couldn't spy on laptops because they had special software embedded in the Wi-Fi that made it difficult to have it on for long periods of time without raising suspicions. Desktops at HQ, however, ran twenty-four hours, making it difficult to notice any hacking. After entering ICON as a cop and not a spy, I opened the file Frank had designated for my case. The first thing that jumped out was that Jenny and Bobby had only entered the pics I looked at earlier. Frustration set in my gut, but it may have been supper.

Switching to the autopsy report was no better. Ruth made it official that the woman was killed by the gunshot wound, but that was it. I remembered from my detective training that lack of evidence is evidence. We knew she was cleaned before she was dumped. It was one thing to shoot and blade the victim, but why would the killer scrub it, then pull all the teeth and both eyes before dumping it when DNA was still present?

It was also frustrating that no one could identify the woman. Ruth simply put "Unknown" in the identity section of her paperwork. Leaning back in my chair and giving an unsatisfied sigh, I worked through some possibilities based on what little evidence there was to see if anything made sense. They didn't.

The only thing that came up was a drug deal gone wrong, and the victim was a junkie. The problem with that theory was the clean, shaved, toothless, and eyeless head. No hitman would take the time to do that to a junkie. She was somebody.

Since I had nothing to add to the file, I hit the sack after deciding to talk to Frank about the local crime families. Plus, I needed to talk to the CSU team to find out why they hadn't posted anything yet.

CHAPTER 11

Frank was finishing off a homemade breakfast sandwich when I entered his office. I looked at his spreading midriff, smiled, and shook my head while I sat in the chair across from him.

"Watch it. I'm sensitive about my figure." He scowled.

"I can see your concern." I smiled.

"What do you want? Or you just want to discuss my dress size?"

"Jenny and Bobby haven't posted anything yet. Is that normal?"

"I had them working through the night. They'll post everything when they're finished."

"That's a lot of work with little rest. Won't their findings be off?"

"We know what we're doing."

He whisked toast crumbs off his tie with one hand while grabbing his plain white coffee mug with the other. "That and lots of caffeine."

"How many mobs you got in this city?"

He nearly choked on his coffee. "Where did that come from?"

"You mentioned this could be a drug killing. Right?"

"I might've mentioned it in passing." He wiped coffee

drops off his shirt and desk with a greasy paper towel. I almost laughed.

"So?" I did my best rookie stare down.

He grinned at me when he tossed the dirty paper towel in the waste basket.

"Needs work. But you're young. Keep practicing."

He sat back in his office chair, giving the "old man grunt" all the way back. "I can confirm that there are three mobs inside the city, and two more outside the city limits, but they're small time. One is an offshoot of one inside the city. Won't last long. They don't have the resources to keep it up much longer. The other is brand new, and they will be taken care of soon enough."

"How's that?"

"The biggest mob got the go ahead from the top to take them out."

"They that powerful?"

"Not sure, but rumor has it that the big mob made a few calls." Frank shrugged. "Now they're out."

"This happen a lot?" Red flags were spinning in the front and back of my mind.

"More, now that the…" Frank sat forward and looked out the window facing the hallway. "Let's take a walk. I need to get some of this breakfast worked off, since your wise crack about my figure." He laughed.

We left the building, then strolled down 20th Street a couple of blocks towards Busch Stadium without saying a word, like old friends avoiding an uncomfortable subject. Unfortunately, the clock was ticking, and I wasn't in the mood for this nonchalant attitude Frank was taking. I had to remind myself that he probably wasn't aware of what was coming down the spiritual pike. For all he knew, everything was better since the second quake had happened a couple months ago. The Antichrist had ensured the world that the best was yet to come, and the worst was behind us. He was right in one way, but very wrong in another. Things would get better in a little less than six years. Unfortunately, the coming judgments and other events were going to ramp up beyond imagination. My heart rate rose just thinking of what was ahead and wishing I had missed it like my parents.

When we reached Union Station, Frank led me to where the St. Louis Wheel was lying on the ground in a twisted heap of metal. It had partially landed on the building next to it where Frank was heading. We entered a small area beside the wreckage that was a miniature golf course. There were only a few holes unaffected by the quakes and fallen Ferris wheel. The rest were damaged beyond repair or completely covered.

Frank went to the pay window and retrieved two putters and two different colored golf balls. He motioned for me to join him at a tee box and handed me a putter and a pink ball, his silent hazing.

"I found this place not long after I was stationed here. The precinct was a madhouse after the quake and aftershock, and I needed a break. I passed here a couple of times escaping the madness." He putted his red ball straight into the cup for a hole-in-one. "This is one of the few places I can get some peace and quiet." He waved his putter at the surrounding walls. "No cameras or mics."

My pink ball rolled past the hole and bounced back to within a few inches of it. "It's nice to have some sort of privacy these days."

He grunted when he bent over to retrieve his ball. "Will, I knew you a long time before all this. And I remember your parents before they died. Your dad was a great preacher. And there wasn't another woman as good as your mom, except my Clara." He smiled. "That is why I requested for you to investigate. That and the fact you were one of my best students. You have a patience that only my most seasoned detectives have. You allow the investigation to come to you." He chuckled. "The patience of Job."

Taking it all in, I was trying to decipher why he was telling me all this. I'd known Frank since I was in middle school. He was the one who made being a police officer look like a noble profession. My admiration and respect for him and his wife ran deep. Then I remembered the question I'd been meaning to ask, putting off why we were really there.

"What happened to Clara, Frank?"

He dropped his head. "Murdered." He said it as if he were afraid to say the word.

"The same time my parents were killed?" I tried to see if he knew what I knew.

Frank went pale and stuttered. "Where do we start?"

My emotions got the best of me. I could barely manage the response. "In the beginning."

Only members of the Christian Resistance would know this password sequence. It was the only way two members could discover each other without raising suspicion from anyone who was not a member.

Frank's tears landed on the Astroturf. I patted his shoulder, holding back my own excitement. When we both regained control of our emotions, we shook hands.

"I was prayin' for ya, boy." He let go of my hand and crushed me in a bear hug he was notorious for giving when emotionally overcome.

"Me, too. Brother." I grunted as the air left my lungs.

We went to the next hole to calm ourselves. After he aced it, and I got another birdie, we took a break and sat at a nearby table.

He wiped his eyes with a handkerchief and blew his nose. "Clara was Raptured out of my arms. I was about to leave for work, and she gave me a hug. She looked up quickly and was gone." His hand shook while putting his handkerchief back in his shirt pocket. "I felt her leave me."

Considering what other people had witnessed and experienced during the Rapture was nothing compared to

Frank's experience. There were no stories about loved ones leaving an embrace. Watching your wife was one thing, feeling it happen was another.

Knowing it was my turn, I started. "I was stationed in Springfield here in Missouri. I'd met a cop friend before our shift, and while eating breakfast downtown it happened. My friend was eating right beside me, then he wasn't. I heard his fork hit the plate. I knew what happened immediately." I fiddled with a chunk of wood from the table. "Then I went home. Knowing what happened, I wasn't surprised the smoke alarm was going off. Mama had just started cooking breakfast when she disappeared. The sausages in the skillet were smoldering."

Talking about how my parents left was difficult. It reminded me of my lack of faith. How I played church and ignored Dad's sermons and my Sunday School lessons. I spent more time on the back pew of the sanctuary flirting with the girls. Never thinking about my spiritual future.

"When did you pray the prayer?"

"Right after I took the skillet off the stove and opened the windows. I saw the blue sky. They went beyond it." I hesitated. "You can fool some of the people some of the time, but you can never fool Him." I pointed up.

"Amen, brother." His grin lacked joy. "For me, it was after I saw the Mid-East Accord signed. I never believed Israel would ever sign a treaty with the Muslims. But I remembered your dad's sermons about the Tribulation when they did, and I hit the ground praying."

The moment spread out over a few minutes while we became lost in our memories of missed family and Rapture.

My dad, the preacher, and my mom, the prayer warrior, tried to protect me and my sister for the coming apocalypse by getting us to believe in Jesus, who would take us to heaven to avoid it. But there I was, a year and a half into the Tribulation trying to act like a nonbeliever in order to get all the information to keep the other believers safe from the Antichrist and his guillotines. On the bright side, I now had someone else to confide in.

CHAPTER 12

Something we are never to ask another Resistance member is, "Who do they know that are members?" That way if we are caught and questioned, A.K.A. tortured, everyone is safe. So, I changed the conversational focus to the case. "Frank, we need to get back to business. Who are the mobs?"

He wiped his tears from his cheek and righted himself in his seat. "The two outliers are on borrowed time. The three inside the city are fighting for every inch, on land and river." He ticked off the mobs on his fingers. "The smallest bunch is from New Orleans. They call themselves the Spirits. They were big there until the first quake. Unfortunately, the tidal wave that sank the city killed over half of them. Then they came upriver. Now, they're scraping by trying to get new members. They dabble in a little of everything. But they're known for their moonshine, thus the name. Since the second quake, the big distilleries are trying to rebuild, while the small stills are making a killing. And those Southerners can make it fast and in larger quantities than people think."

"Sounds like they won't last long after the big distilleries get back online."

"They'll last longer than you think. Rumor has it they're

about to be soaked into the big mob. But that remains to be seen. Now the second is from Chicago. The Survivors Crew. Although rebuilding in Chicago would've been their first choice, the city is still underwater. So, they came here. They have almost cornered the market on prostitution. Brought all their pros who survived when Chicago was taken by Lake Michigan after the first quake. More prostitutes than any other mob had at the time, and they're getting more from up north every day. Snatching girls right off the farms. However, they're struggling with growth because they have no ability to get drugs to keep the girls hooked, and customers are hard to find since the economy tanked after the first quake. Even sex addicts are playing it safe until everything turns around."

"But it won't turn around according to the Bible. It'll get worse."

"True, but it seems everyone is drinking the Sovereign's Kool-Aid. The way I see it, the more money that gets passed out by Europe, the Johns will come back with a vengeance."

They both shook their heads at the thought of getting that industry restarted. "But remember, that won't last much longer. The Earth dollar won't be around in a couple of years."

The loyalty chips, what the Resistance called the Beastmark, would become mandatory at the halfway point of the Trib when Satan possesses the Antichrist's body. Then all hell will break loose. You either accept the Beastmark—or get bladed. Satan's way of separating the Loyalists from everyone else.

"And that's when the Antichrist will get his grubby paws on both sides of the law. Control the addiction by calling it the cure. He'll legalize everything and control it through government regulation."

"So that's why the mobs haven't started taking the Beastmark."

"With the streets and internet under Big Brother's protective eye, the mobs haven't taken it yet. They know the chips have GPS in them. But like I said, it's only a matter of time before everything becomes legal."

I saw Frank's left eye twitch a couple of times, and he acted as if he didn't want to say it. We were talking about things neither one of us wanted to discuss, but it was part of the current reality.

"Senator Staeger told me that. He said the federal politicians are already meeting behind closed doors to plan how they will implement the planned takeover of all the vices."

At least Frank was getting some information from the senator in return for his allegiance.

"Okay, what about the Free Agents?"

Frank gave me a grin of disbelief.

"How do you know about them?"

"I got a C.I. earlier today. But I'm not putting him on record."

"Smart. I like the way you think, boy. Unfortunately, the Free Agents got people already on the force. Tell me what you know about them, and I'll fill in the rest." He got up, led me to the next tee, and aced the hole.

"Only that they are called the Free Agents because they're trying to take control of their own destiny. Also, they have high speed narco boats that will amaze you, especially since they have very low sound."

"And narco subs. The Survivors Crew and Spirits have the boats, too. All are used to move their products. But it's the Free Agents who have the government's ear. They deal in everything, including secrets. The way I figure it, the leader of the mob, a guy named..."

"Hector. Sorry, I forgot I knew that." My pink ball sailed past the hole but snuggled up close after rebounding off the brick border.

"He either has plants inside governmental departments

all over the country, or the Free Agents are way bigger than anyone realizes."

"My money is on the latter. I think his boats and subs carry more than just illicit products. I believe that's how he moves his information." I tapped the pink ball in for another birdie. "Because the Antichrist's people rule the internet."

He smiled. "Now you're thinking like a detective."

"Or a criminal." I smiled when I reached down and grabbed my pink ball from the cup.

"We're criminals now, boy." He putted his ball straight into the next hole. "It just hasn't been officially announced."

"You have good informants." It was a matter of time before it would happen, but Tommy had told me before I left Kansas City that the Unholy Prophet, known to the world as the Head of Global Religion, had already announced a new spiritual law banning any religions that didn't follow his new religion. He believed all roads led to the Possible Divine, as he called it, so believing there is only one way to God is blasphemous and narrow minded. I knew he believed the Sovereign to be the Divine One. He was just waiting until he would confirm it to the world at the halfway point of the Trib.

"Same as yours." He moved to the next hole of the seven-hole course.

"How long have you been in the Resistance?" I asked as I walked with him.

"I'm not technically in any Resistance." He wouldn't look me in the eye. "I wasn't made for the cloak and dagger life. I'm a cop. Creeping around, stealing secrets, and letting law breakers go isn't in me. I'm from another breed, Will. I just can't do it. So, the ones I know tell me what I need to know to stay out of their way and know when the next judgment will happen."

"You won't help them if they break a law that is against

God?" My tone was sharper than intended, but I couldn't fathom Frank sending a fellow Christian to the guillotine for breaking a law that is wrong.

"I took an oath to protect the law. Whether I agree with it or not doesn't matter." He blew out a sigh of frustration and screamed. "It's part of the job."

"I get it, Frank. I just don't agree with it." I knew Frank was upset, but so was I. "We are at war with the devil. And he will use our rules and oaths to his benefit. The way I see it, when America signs the treaty, it will cease being America. Then my oath is fulfilled. But I will remain undercover to help as many as I can before I get bladed."

He leaned on his putter in deep thought. "Okay. I'll go along with that. When it happens, I'll join the Resistance and do my part. But not until that happens."

I let him calm down before restarting the mob conversation.

As if on cue, Frank started talking again.

"You have to be careful with Hector. That man is devious. He'll take over the city soon. And without repercussions from the Peace Forces."

"So, what you're saying is that the Free Agents use their pull with the government to maintain power in St. Louis."

"For the most part." He placed his red ball on the AstroTurf tee. "They also have the biggest drug trade in the city, maybe the state. Rumor has it that they have a former pharmaceutical lab west of the city where they make cheap designer drugs. Even the DEA is having a hard time tracking the drugs down. People are buying them at breakneck speed. Plus, the DEA and FBI cannot get anyone to flip on any of the mobs." He shot another ace.

"The DEA and FBI are dead, Frank. It's time to get used to it. The Peace Forces are here to stay." I shrugged. "The mobs use fear. Like any other time in history." I teed up my pink ball.

"There's that, then there's the fact that people are seeing

resources dwindling. They hoard everything now, including drugs. From what we hear, all the mobs are struggling to keep up with the demand."

"They should like that. It drives the prices up." My ball sailed past the hole, bounced off a barrier and hid behind an obstacle.

"True, but they have to keep the druggies happy, or they'll find another source."

"The other mobs?" I looked at the impossible line for my next putt.

"That's why the Survivors Crew split. One of the capos decided to take matters into his own hands and started making his own drugs."

"So why do you think they won't last that long?"

"Because the Free Agents have already announced they are going to handle them. I'd say the new guys have about as long to live as we do to find this woman's killer."

"Why don't they cut bait and run?"

"They believe they have the manpower to endure an all-out war."

"Do they?" I tapped the ball away from the obstacle, but it was still a ten-foot putt.

"Not even close. The Free Agents have already contracted the Spirits to help." Frank leaned in on me. "That's how they'll take the Spirits out. Lure them into being overconfident and safe, then soak them in. And the Spirits' leadership?"

I watched Frank make a slashing motion across his throat.

It sounded like the Free Agents were taking a page from the Antichrist. He was doing the same to America. I wondered if that was what happened to President Mason. She got in the way and was killed and planted who-knows-where.

"Interesting, so how does the victim play into all this?"

"Not sure."

"And why does the senator have any interest in this?"

"Not sure of that either."

"What does the superintendent have to say?"

"She is adamant that this is just a drug deal gone wrong. But she is interested in it enough to tell me to keep her in the loop."

"It's not important enough to be important." My putt snuggled up to the hole without dropping in. I withheld a curse.

"Yeah. She has the feel of someone being told what to do."

"As much as I'd like to go further into that conversation, we need to focus on the task at hand. This woman is dead, and no one seems to care. Except the senator."

Frank looked at me and frowned.

"I have been talking to his chief of staff and she told me to be thorough and take our time."

I grimaced. "That reminds me. We may only have four days to solve this case, counting today."

Frank gave me a surprised look. "Why is that?"

"My handler told me that a Jewish preacher told them." I paused for effect. "Hail and fire mixed with blood. A third of the earth's trees and all the grasses will be destroyed."

"God protect us," Frank whispered. "My contacts haven't told me because they haven't been told yet. They were waiting for word themselves. Why is that important to the case?"

"Think about it. Any uncollected evidence will be destroyed." I ticked each item on my fingers. "The fire will burn it up. The hail will melt and wash it away. The blood will corrupt everything else that survives."

"Great. It sounds like we're putting this into high gear." Frank perked up. "Let's get back on it. I'll have Jenny and Bobby give the scene another good once over. You get started looking into the Free Agent mafia. They could have done this for themselves, or they did it on orders from the

Antichrist."

"First, we need to identify this woman."

CHAPTER 13

The clouds were changing from gray to black, and the redness was becoming bloody. Frank walked beside me down the sidewalk on our way back to HQ as if they didn't exist. We kept our voices low to avoid detection from the street cams that had mics.

"So, what did you mean about the superintendent being part of a group? Mob? Government?" I still stared at the ominous clouds.

"When I was reassigned to be the captain here, I was told that things weren't the same as they used to be. The superintendent of this city is scalp deep in the new world government. She wants to climb the political ladder so fast she's willing to throw anybody, and everybody, to the European wolves."

"So, we can't trust her," I said matter of factly.

"You can trust no one." He shook his head and grumbled like a bear waking from hibernation. "I shouldn't have brought up our faith. If one of us is found out, it'll be more than the guillotine we need to worry about. It'll be torture to get all the information they can out of us." Frank's face cringed, and he shook his head. "I'm sorry, boy. This one's on me."

"We'll just have to make it to the end of the seven

years." I patted his forearm, and he went pale.

"Will, we are in deep. Deeper than anyone in the Resistance. They were recruiting me hard. Using any tactic to get me to turn on my oath. The new government will be far worse if we get caught. We must tread lightly. If anyone, including the superintendent, has an inkling of an idea we are Christians, death won't come fast enough to suit them."

"We'll just have to play everything as close to the vest as possible. We can use the mini golf course to talk about stuff off the books, not just our faith."

He smiled. "I'd like that. But the chances that both of us make it to the end is slim at best. We need to be careful. The new cameras they put in after the quakes have mics that catch everything, even a cat purring. Top of the line. And the Free Agents are connected to the government by way of information. They sell secrets about anyone in power to trade for the government's leniency and to cover their illegal trades."

"Which are about to become legal."

After the Rapture, I studied Dad's Trib journal. He seemed to see what was coming down the pike and connected it to the prophetic texts throughout the scriptures. One set of his notes covered the new world government and how the Antichrist would handle policy concerning everyday living. Most of the prophecy experts seemed more interested in the global government's relationship to Israel and how it set off each of God's judgments. Dad, however, was interested in why America wasn't in prophecy. Based on what he found, he put together the journal as an outline of the possibilities.

I kept it in a prepper's bunker near Kansas City that I took over after I transferred to the KCPD. Tommy showed it to me and said the owners were Raptured out.

Frank's assistant was waiting for us.

"She's here." The mousy brown-haired assistant with

wide hips and a narrow waist looked nervous beyond measure.

"Thanks, Claire. In my office?"

"Yes. She's sitting in your chair." Claire seemed more offended than Frank.

"Thanks again." Frank smiled at her.

"Who's she? And why is she sitting in your chair?" I had an idea but wasn't sure.

"St. Louis Peace Forces Superintendent Joy Everhart, and trust me, she does not live up to either name." Frank growled. "She sits in everyone's chair. Makes her feel empowered."

He'd put an emphasis on the last word.

Sure enough, when we entered the office, Superintendent Everhart was leaning back in Frank's office chair and staring at us with a scowl that would've been cute on anyone else. Yep, despite my Christian faith I already hated her.

"Captain Malone. Where have you been? My time is valuable, and I don't have time to waste waiting for a subordinate." She tried to stare him down, but she was more of a rookie at it than me.

"We were on our way to the crime scene."

"On your way? You didn't make it?" Her eyes moved to Frank's computer monitor. She was looking for us on the cameras.

"Had to make a pitstop. Nature called and with my prostate I couldn't ignore her." Frank's lie almost had me going.

She stood and stared at me. She was five six on a good day, small but well built. Probably spent more time in the gym toning up for the cameras than getting in shape for a chase or fight.

"Detective William Thomas, I presume?"

She made her way around the desk. Strike that, she was five three. Her extremely high heels, saunter, and sneer gave the impression of the Napoleon Complex at its peak.

"Yes, ma'am. But you can call me Will." I accepted her overly aggressive handshake. She needed to work on that if she meant to intimidate.

"I go by proper first names, William."

She didn't have a Beastmark on either location, which was one thing she had going for her.

"But that is my proper first name."

"Well, aren't your parents informal?"

I sat in the guest chair and put my feet up on Frank's desk, crossing them at the ankles. I decided her manners could use some improving.

She gave me the stink eye before the eye roll and returned to Frank's chair.

"Why you're here is beyond me. I thought Detective Evans would be the obvious choice."

"I've known Will almost all his life. He is more than capable of finding the murderer. And Detective Evans is investigating three crimes in the Spirits' territory. I thought her time would be better spent in an area she's more familiar with." Frank maneuvered around the desk and stood beside his chair and stared her down. I almost laughed at the pissing contest playing out in front of me.

She frowned at the last part. "She is more than capable to handle the added caseload. But my sources tell me the murdered woman is connected to the Spirits. So, Detective Evans would be the obvious choice."

"So far, Will has found some things out that seem to point to the Free Agents and not the Spirits."

She turned abruptly. Fury emanated from her entire body. "So, are my sources not as good as a rookie detective on his first assignment? One who is not even from here?" She turned and gave a sarcastic grin. "Kansas City is not that close. Is it?"

Her deep blue eyes widened, surrounded by a terrible fake bake.

"No ma'am." I decided to play it stupid. "Two hundred and fifty miles."

Her grin turned into a full smile that ate at me. She was using me against my mentor.

"Joy, please let me do my job." Frank tried to keep an even tone. But failed. It was obvious how he felt about her. She didn't even try to maintain a semblance of professionalism. I wanted her gone.

"Superintendent Everhart. We will maintain full decorum Captain Malone." I almost laughed at how she could say such a thing after acting childish a second before.

"Sorry, I got emotional. I remember back when you were good people." Frank's eyes widened as if he wanted to catch the words midflight and return them to his brain.

"And what is that supposed to mean? Soon to be ex-Captain Malone."

Her voice echoed off the walls when she looked up at Frank. I wanted to de-escalated the situation, but I didn't know Joy well enough to know how to do it without getting me and Frank both fired.

"Sorry, ma'am. I meant to say when you were in the lower ranks. Remember when we said that to our higher ups behind their backs and laughed? I let it slip out to see if you remembered the good old days."

She softened. "They were good, weren't they? But they are in the past. We need to remember the hierarchy and follow it." She looked back at me. "That'll be all, Detective Thomas."

"Yes ma'am." I looked at Frank as I stood. "I'll go back to the crime scene and do another sweep. Maybe catch a break."

"I need you to update the file with what you know first." Frank used his stern voice for Joy's benefit. "And the videos of the street cams have been uploaded into the file. Bobby is already viewing them."

"Yes, sir." I used my best respectful voice for Frank's

benefit.

The door didn't fully shut when I heard Joy start dressing down Frank for being casual in the workplace. My guffaw wasn't used until my door was shut and out of earshot. Rumors in Kansas City about Joy usually included incompetency and advancements due to threats against the officers in charge of promotions and not her actual abilities, which I had yet to see.

CHAPTER 14

The computer file for the case was still lean and the little I had to include didn't help its growth much. However, I received an email from the CSU team to come see them later in the afternoon. Bobby wanted to talk to me about the street and drone cams. I checked the clock on my cell phone. There was enough time to grab a bite to eat then head to the crime scene. Maybe I'd catch another break, maybe get another C.I.

When I logged out, a knock on the door that wasn't meant for a response was followed by Joy marching into my office with a look of determination that made me uncomfortable. She stood by me as if I was in her office occupying her chair, raising her expectant eyebrows.

"Can I help you, ma'am?" I sank into my chair to challenge her to see how she'd respond.

She stared at me for a second and didn't answer.

I returned the raised eyebrow expectations and let the awkward moment stand.

She rolled her eyes and moved to the chair across from me.

"I'm not sure how it's done in Kansas City, but here people allow the one in charge the seat."

"We are more of the person whose office it is assigned

to has it." My unemotional response clearly irritated her.

"I'll let it slide this time. Just remember the rule here." She sat with perfect posture, probably rehearsed it all her life.

"Hopefully, I won't have to remember it. If I can finish this up, quick like." I smiled at my rookie mistake.

"From what I'm reading, this could take years. If it is ever closed at all."

She obviously didn't know that the Bible said in less than six years it won't matter.

"I'm a rookie, which makes me an optimist."

"Yes, you are." She smiled an unhinging smile. "And that's why I wanted to talk to you in private."

"What about, ma'am?" The red flags in my head immediately raised and were flying high and hard.

"I was wondering if you could do me a solid."

Her use of vernacular was as fake as her skin color. It's one thing to get a fake tan, but the unnatural orange that covered her face and hands made her look like a cute alien baby who overdosed on orange soda and carrots.

"And what might that be, ma'am?" The innocent schtick was getting harder to do by the minute.

"I need someone." She considered her words carefully with a glance at the ceiling. "An outsider, like you, who could keep an eye on things here at headquarters."

My pulse increased through rage. "And why would you need outside eyes, ma'am?"

"There have been complaints that Captain Malone isn't playing completely by the book." She stretched out the last four words like a person who was embarrassed to say them.

"I've known Frank for over twenty years. There's no straighter shooter than him. I'd stake my reputation on it. And besides being an outsider, why pick me? He was my academy trainer. I'm obviously biased when it comes to Frank's character and professionalism." I paused, then followed it up with, "ma'am."

She leaned forward, put her forearms on my desk, and smiled the same snarky smile she used earlier. "Captain Malone is on borrowed time. Remember, he'll retire out in a few years. And if I had my way, he would never see one Earth dollar of his pension. He's insubordinate, arrogant, doesn't follow protocol properly, and is a general pain in my keister. When I'm done with him, he'll be lucky I don't send him to the state penitentiary myself. And it would be in your best interest to take this assignment. If you know what's good for your career."

My first impulse was to put a slug between those big, beautiful blue eyes, where the Beastmark was supposed to be. But I didn't want to get up close and personal with a guillotine that way. If I see the blade, it will be for Christ, not this two-bit halfwit cop.

"Can I have a day or two to think it over? I mean, he is a family friend." Stalling for time was the only thing I could come up with. I'd tell Frank about her then hold her off until either the case was solved, or the next judgment made her forget about the offer.

She sat back in the chair and smiled. "One day ought to do it. I mean, there's really only one choice."

"Thank you, ma'am." I tried not to grit my teeth too hard as my words echoed off the walls.

"Now, how's it going with the investigation?" She returned to the same manner as she started with.

"Not much. CSU wants to see me this afternoon and Frank and I..."

"Captain Malone. Please keep up with decorum." Her jaw flexed. Then it hit me. She could have OCD along with the Napoleon Complex. I added that in my mental file.

"Sorry. Captain Malone and I have discussed the probability that this might be tied to either a drug deal gone wrong or something to do with the mafia, probably the Free Agents." I hesitated to decide how much more she deserved.

"Or both." She grinned. Her overly white teeth contrasted with her orange skin.

"Yes, or both. Thank you for the insight, ma'am." It hurt to say it when I'd already considered it, but Frank's career was on the line.

She gave a mock frown and turned her attention to the back of my flat screen monitor. "If this is the case, then why did Captain Malone bring you in on the investigation? I mean, we have perfectly competent drug enforcement personnel to finish a drug deal gone wrong, and we have a top-notch organized crime unit in Philadelphia that I can call in at any time." She sighed and smiled that snarky smile. "So why investigate this case when it seems so run of the mill?"

"I'm not sure. Frank...excuse me... Captain Malone said that someone had requested me. That's all I know." I shrugged.

Her eyes glazed in quick thought. She didn't know.

After a very long pause, the glaze melted and she asked, "Did Frank say who requested the investigation?"

It was the first time she ignored decorum. Using Frank's first name told me she wasn't in the loop.

"No, ma'am. He didn't," I lied.

The redness from her anger mixed with her skin tone that made a red orange unlike anything I'd ever seen. In fact, I thought she was about to have a stroke.

"Interesting."

It was all she could say. My mind scurried to understand the implications. She looked down at the desk. Her eyes darted from left to right as if she was reading something not in the physical realm, just her own mind.

"Why's that, ma'am?" I could barely hold my own snark.

She looked up, quietly composed herself, and stood. "You have one day."

Then she left. I took a long, satisfying breath, relieved

she was gone. If there was anyone more annoying than her, I didn't know. And she did it so naturally, like she was born this way. I wondered what her parents were like.

I immediately hurried to Frank's office, but he had already gone to lunch, according to his assistant. So, I decided to go for a drive to get the lay of the land and to clear my head of politics, antichrists, and blind ambition.

CHAPTER 15

The drive around the city was as depressing as the sky. God's judgment was becoming too real again. The clouds above had movement, but not from the wind. They were rolling in place. The red puffs mixed with the black ones, like a painter mixing colors. The river was reflecting the red sky, looking like a bloodstream flowing to an unknown destination away from the land of the living. The scene gave the impression of an age-old anger churning before being released.

On top of that, trying to focus on the case was difficult with what just happened at headquarters. After our meeting, Joy left the building in a hurry. One of the officers told me she went west on Olive Street as if she was going home. The officer said it seemed pointless since the superintendent had no one to go home to, being thrice divorced. She actually used *thrice* in a sentence. I was impressed.

However, I couldn't get one question out of my head. Why was this case so important that a senator was involved off book?

I figured when the body was identified, we might find an answer that would lead us to the killer. But that was probably only wishful thinking. Chances were that what we might discover would convolute the situation even more. Especially since a politician was involved. One that stayed in the background, which made the red flags in my head dance to the point of giving me a headache.

There was a map of the mob territories in the ICON computer terminal in the beater, but I wanted to get the feel of the boundaries for myself.

The territories of the three mobs were more clear-cut than I was used to. The invisible boundaries in K.C. remained because they were constantly shifting, but in St. Louis there was no problem figuring out who ran the show in the different parts of the city. Mobs marked their territories like local governments marked their city limits. Hand painted signs were strewn about the streets to let travelers know whose turf they were treading without saying the name of the mob.

The Survivors Crew had the area from the zoo to downtown and everything north where lower working-class citizens lived, but Frank said the Peace Forces didn't know where they kept their base of operations. The Free Agents started downtown, then moved west to the zoo where the big money was, then down to the slummy southwest where the cheap drugs were sold. Their base of operations was in the Missouri Botanical Gardens. The Spirits had the southeast side where they made booze and discreetly sold it on the streets in all territories without people knowing it. Their territory was from Route 66 to the river, with their headquarters on the riverbank in a beached riverboat casino. The Peace Forces and city government had downtown. And the mobs were fine with that since downtown was a mess from the recent quakes. Business was sparse. Few people worked there and fewer lived there.

Driving through the territories wasn't hard in an unmarked police cruiser. People stared but kept to themselves. The looks were a mixture of disdain and hopelessness. Frank said the Peace Forces were not respected because of the political corruption used by the Free Agents. I was guilty by association.

My trip was sidetracked while passing the new construction going on at the site of The Religious Center. The old domed football stadium had taken on enough quake damage and water that the city leveled it and began constructing the new edifice that was to be the centralized place of worship for the central U.S.

Although it creeped me out to no end, I had to see it.

It was about halfway finished but the exterior was nearly complete. The building was garish to say the least. Every religious symbol had been placed into the granite with marble trim using precious stones that were associated with each religion, except Christianity. Even though it was a Holy Site, as they were called throughout the world, it was not yet open for business. I still sensed the evil in and around it.

The pluralist religion set forth by the new Head of Religion required the local Decreed Holy Person to consecrate the ground before building could commence. Frank said the false priest had the main entrance facing east because it was the holy direction and the river was now a holy river when he consecrated it after the first quake, promising that it would not take another life. Frank laughed because a dead body floated by while the false prophet spoke. The crowd ignored it for fear of the holy man's wrath, meaning the Peace Forces would be visiting blasphemers' homes at night.

At the front entrance of the monstrosity, something from my past looked straight at me. The Eros Bendato Sculpture of the severed head of the Greek god was sitting on its neck facing east as if Eros was searching the river for a new mate. The City Garden Sculpture Park was missing a major attraction. I parked the beater in front of the metal sculpture and got out.

When I was younger, my family came to St. Louis on

vacation. The City Garden Sculpture Park was my favorite. The sculptures and interactive fountains made my overactive mind soar. But I'll never forget Eros. His bandaged, decapitated head lying on his right ear gave me the chills. Mom tried to explain the significance of it all, but I was too busy trying to climb the fountain and see Eros's brains through the empty neck.

Kat, however, paid attention to Mom and told me later that his long-lost love found him the day before a major battle. After a long night of kissing, (she was eight at the time, so kissing was the only sexual move she knew) he was too tired to fight properly and lost his head in battle. The enemy's king left his head on the battlefield to punish his daughter for kissing the enemy.

Maybe the woman's head in front of the stadium was Eros's long-lost lover?

Dad wasn't too happy that his family was looking at and talking about a false god. He did a twenty-minute sermon on the evils of worshiping false idols. Mom asked him to calm down and reminded him that we were on vacation. He needed to stay away from the pulpit and enjoy the city. Dad smiled, kissed Mom—in public no less—and said that the sculpture creeped him out.

Remembering that time was running out, I turned to walk away. A clicking sound coming from behind the head of Eros made me pause. A woman in high heels came around the bandaged head. My heart skipped around in my chest. She was medium height and build and wore a red sundress with white flowers and red pumps to match. She delicately rubbed her hand on the sculpture as if the artistic flow would enter her body. Her jet-black hair circled her right ear and covered the left. There was nothing pretentious about this lady. She saw me, moved her sunglasses down her nose, and looked over the frames. No Beastmark tattoos or bumps.

"Take a picture, why don't ya? It'll last longer."

I kept my hands in my Cardinals jacket, looked around to see if anyone heard, and turned back to her. "Nice line. Did your great-great grandma teach you that?"

Her laugh was like a summer breeze, just warm enough to feel, but slight enough to keep you guessing where it was coming from. While I slowly walked to her to insure she was alone, I gripped my SIG in my jacket pocket to make sure this wasn't a honey trap for a holdup.

"You're a funny guy. I like that. Most women want a tough guy who makes them feel safe. I like a man who can make me laugh. Forget safety." She put her hand on her hip and waited for my response, like she was goading me into some kind of debate over male-female preferences.

"You really know how to make a fella feel special," I said to avoid social debate.

I tried my best smile on her as I tried to case the place without her noticing my eye movements. Something Tommy taught me in my two-week crash course in spy craft training.

She sat on a bench near the art display. "Fella? Where did you time travel from? 1930's Chicago?"

Even her smirk was cute.

"I've always been at the wrong place at the wrong time, I guess." I sat near her so I could see where she came from. It was the only point I couldn't scope out.

"Maybe not big boy." Her wink made me forget what I was doing. That rarely happened. But she was gorgeous. She was medium build but not pudgy. She worked out.

"What brings you to the Religious Center?" I tried not to sound like a cop, but I knew I failed when her eyes narrowed.

"Looking to pick up a quick solicitation arrest?" She stood, daring me to keep her around.

"I'm not that kind of cop. Homicide detective." I almost whispered for reasons I didn't know. Probably because my mouth was drying out from nerves.

She whispered mockingly, "Is the murderer around here?"

"Maybe so, little lady." I grinned to de-escalate the situation. For obvious reasons, I wanted her to stay. She was easy on the eyes, which I needed right now. There was nothing like a beautiful distraction to reboot the brain. Or fog it up worse. I was willing to take the chance.

She laughed. "Touché, my new friend." She sat closer to me. Enough so that I caught her perfume, a spicy, zesty scent with green undertones. My throat constricted out of desire, not allergies.

Her eyes were a layered liquid gray, like a morning fog on a dewy meadow. Each level on top of the other. If I got a good side view of her pupil, I believed I could've witnessed each stacked layer. But she wouldn't let me have that intimate of a look. At least not now. Her skin was a soft alabaster, and I wanted to run fingers over her forearm. It was close enough to try if I wanted—and I really wanted. Yet something inside told me to keep her at arm's length until I knew her better. My Copley instincts had returned.

Taking a moment to not look desperate, I begrudgingly focused on the statue. Eros, the god of love, looked at me as if saying, "Don't make my mistakes."

I ignored the false god. "By the way, I'm Detective Will Thomas."

"Amelia Longstreet." She winked at me.

Grinning, I looked at the beautiful Brit. Her smile almost made me forget that in a few days the world would have to endure another judgment from God, and that I needed to solve this case.

"It's a beautiful day to sightsee." Using the moment to finish my perimeter search for a partner, I looked around some more. She was definitely alone.

She looked at the sky. "Yeah, the sky is blinding."

I blushed from my idiocy. "Are you from around here?" I asked, changing the subject.

She had an accent that felt European, but it was well hidden.

"Very good, flatfoot. I'm not from around here." She changed her focus to the reddening river.

I thought I'd test her to see if she was spying on me.

"I'm from Springfield, but I was transferred to Kansas City. The St. Louis Peace Forces called me in on the case."

"Interesting. I'm from England. West Sussex, to be exact. Near River Stor."

Her smile was hypnotic. And she knew it.

"We had river stores in Kansas City until the river claimed them." I knew what I was saying.

"No, you git. S-t-o-r. It's a river that flows near West Sussex."

I grinned.

She elbowed me in the shoulder. "You have heard of it. Haven't you."

"Yes. My dad was a preacher. He was asked to preach at a missionary church just outside London near Horsham. We went to West Sussex with the pastor to meet another pastor at Pulborough Brooks Baptist Church. Beautiful country."

"I went to that church a couple of times when I was young. Until I went off to college here in the United States." I expected the accent to come out more, but it didn't. She was either in America long enough for it to turn, or she must've learned to hide it until she knew if people liked England or not.

England was a difficult subject for Americans after the Rapture. The new king had made friends with the Antichrist. He made horrible comments about the U.S. when our president wouldn't sign off on the Mid East Peace Accord. And even applauded when he heard the American death toll after the quake. British-Americans felt the brunt of American anger.

The long pause made me go into cop mode and fear

entered my mind. I didn't know if it was the expediency of the case due to God's coming judgment, or that I would say something stupid to lose her. Something gave me the feeling that I needed to cut the conversation short.

"Sorry, but I got to go. This murder has a time limit. My captain told me to have it wrapped up in a few days." I stood. "But I'd like to see you again." I was never smooth.

She gave me the twice over. Smiled. Nodded. "Tonight. Seven o'clock." She stood and walked away. "I like chili dogs and a stroll along the river. Meet me there." She called over her shoulder.

I began questioning her taste, at least when it came to food. After she drove off, I gave the Religious Center a final look. It almost seemed like Eros smiled at me. But his empty-eyed stare returned before I made it to the beater.

CHAPTER 16

Remembering Clay said the person who staged the crime scene disappeared around the Old Cathedral, otherwise known as Basilica of Saint Louis, King of France, I took 4th to Walnut and parked at the shoreline of the river. The limestone, with a sandstone façade, structure was almost waist deep in water at high tide. It was still difficult to remember I was in St. Louis because the remnants of the Arch were behind the church, barely sticking out of the river. It used to tower over the basilica in a way that a person could miss it looking up.

Using my phone, I discovered the time Clay said it happened was low tide. Made sense. The killer rode the river current to the church, waded to Memorial Drive, and walked Walnut to Broadway to Clark. He used the same path to return and drove back upriver.

The walk near the Old Cathedral did nothing to inspire me, so I decided to walk the path the killer took. Believing there wouldn't be anything to find, I still hoped he'd made a mistake. I knew the drone footage would paint a clearer picture, but experiencing it myself seemed more natural. Like an old-time cop walking the beat. Sweeping the streets to and from the crime scene was a bust. Nothing to see here, officer.

The old man's head was visible in the passenger seat of the beater. He stared forward as if waiting on his family at the grocery store. My first impression was a homeless man wanting three hots and a cot for the day or two, but his bearing told a different story. He had life experience beyond the streets. His posture was upright and rigid, and his gaze was full of confidence, not helplessness. He felt like a politician.

With my SIG in both hands, I was about to use my cop voice to command him out of the beater when he looked straight at me and smiled and waved me over to the cruiser. The sight of my senator made me pause. Jon Staeger was in my car wanting me to join him. I holstered my SIG under my armpit and looked around to see if anyone was looking. My gait was hurried while I went around to the driver side, trying to figure out what was going on.

He returned to looking out the front window when I shut the door.

"Busch Stadium. And take the long way around, detective." He said it as if I was his chauffeur. Then he looked at me and blushed. "Sorry, Detective Thomas. I'm used to talking that way when I'm in the passenger seat. Please take me to the stadium. There's something I'd like to discuss with you, so please take the long way around. But not by the Gardens or your headquarters, if you will."

"What if my car is bugged?" I whispered, pointing to the computer mounted to the dashboard.

"I had this car specially made. There is nothing in here that will compromise your investigation. No dash cams or microphones planted in here." The senator smiled like a grandfather giving his grandson his first car. "The gas engine is important. It's turbo charged. It'll outrun any electric vehicle on the road. Including Peace Forces cruisers. Which may prove useful. But do be careful. Keep it as far away from the fleet services as you can. I had it planted there so Frank would be covered. It is in your name as if you owned it from before the disappearances."

"Thank you, senator. But..." I held up my chipped badge. "Superintendent Everhart is vigilant."

"Oh." He reached in his pocket, pulled out a small box with wires that ended with alligator clips. He connected them to the chip and pressed a button that turned a red light to a green light. "Now we can go anywhere."

I started the beater and went back to 4th. "I could use one of those."

"It's yours. My tech guy has several of them."

I needed to know. "Sir, to what do I owe the privilege of a visit from you?"

"Kennedy, my Chief of Staff, said it'd help talking to Frank and you face to face. It's hard to contact people via the internet and phones. The Sovereign sees everything in the air and on the computers." He sighed. "And she's right. To get anything done in this new world, a person must be willing to get out of the office and make it happen."

It made sense and it was nice to see someone willing to get out into the mud and slop with the rest of the working slobs. I was a little proud to have voted for him.

"Can we go by the crematorium? I need to ask a guy about a headless body."

"That'll be fine. But not until our talk when you drop me off at the stadium." He gave a conspiratorial grin. "I'm not here."

"Yes, sir." I went north. I-70 was drivable because the city fixed it first since the crematorium they built, which was erected across the highway from O'Fallon Park near Bellefontaine Cemetery.

"You're wondering why this clandestine meeting. I just wanted to get the lay of the land. Captain Malone is an old friend who thinks very highly of you. He didn't hesitate to say your name when I asked for a discrete investigator." He looked at me to see my reaction, but Tommy was a great teacher when it came to reading and being read.

"Not to be disrespectful senator, but why is this particular woman of interest to you?" I tried to keep an evenness to my voice to not give away my trepidation of the case and this meeting.

He smiled, looked forward, and said, "She was a dear friend, and I want her killer and the one who ordered it, brought to justice."

The red flags almost ripped from the flagpoles in my head. She had to be someone famous to be friends with a senator and have a hit put on her. The queasiness in my stomach turned to full on nausea. I could almost hear the blade singing down the montant towards my neck.

"I have to ask senator, or I wouldn't be doing my job. Did you have her killed, and are you just sending me on a feral goose-chasing expedition to look like a concerned friend?"

"I appreciate your candor, Will. But I assure you that if this leads to where I believe it will, the ramifications will be staggering." He looked at me. "On a global level."

My breakfast almost joined the conversation. If what he was implying included the Antichrist, then spotlight would not be a strong enough word for the illumination placed on me. The Sun might not either. My first instinct was to drop the senator off at the stadium then find Frank and tell him I quit. But my curiosity and the feeling deep inside told me to stick it out. Lives were at stake. My pettiness had to be tabled forever.

"Who is she, senator?" I wasn't the patient politician Staeger was, I had a schedule to keep.

"I'm not completely positive. You see, my friend died a couple of weeks back, but I'm not sure where the assassin took her remains. So, if this victim isn't her, I'd like to keep her identity anonymous. When you get the DNA results, you'll know why." The senator's deadpan delivery made the hairs on my arm stand.

We approached the turnoff to the crematorium, and my

mind became calm. It was as if my soul knew death was near. Cold chills ran through me when the oversized warehouse came into view. A dark smog hung above the building since there was no air flow to take it elsewhere. The parking lot was filled with workers' cars for the day shift. I had seen enough Corpse Patrol trucks humming through K.C., but I'd never been to the crematorium. My mind went blank with dread. I knew the ash trucks pulled out the opposite side from where the corpse trucks emptied the remains for identification. The bodies were then processed through the furnaces and sent to the mass grave in an undisclosed area in the middle of nowhere Missouri.

"It is sad that these places are still necessary."

The senator finally showed an emotion.

Although I knew these centers would not stop until Jesus took control of the planet, I couldn't help but agree. I turned the beater around and headed downtown.

"Is there anything you can tell me, or do, to help with the investigation?" My anger was increasing at the thought that he was wasting time.

"Until her identity is verified, I can only offer future support. This conversation is just what I said." He smiled and gave a sideways glance. "Seeing Frank's choice. And I must say, you are mature for a first timer. Most people your age would be yelling at me by now for wasting your time. But you must understand that when you reach my age time is relative. I want this case solved as soon as humanly possible, so I can expose the corruption in the new global government before that idiot in the White House signs our freedoms away."

His face reddened and his voice struggled to keep the calm that was obviously just on the surface. Inside was an irate senator trying to keep the country out of the hands of a megalomaniac.

I started liking him. But he was still a politician. Friend today, enemy tomorrow?

The rest of the ride to the stadium was me informing him about the case, which he already knew. Frank must've been constantly in the senator's ear. Which I didn't care for.

The senator had me drop him off in front of Gate 2 on the other side of the stadium from the crime scene. He said that a friend looped the cameras around it in order for the senator to move about freely.

"Please know that if she is who I'm afraid she is, that you will have all the support you need to complete your assignment. And maybe The Public Safety Officer Medal of Valor." He reached out to shake my hand, giving a political smile. "If I need you again, I'll send my Chief of Staff to bring you to me. Until then, detective."

With that, he walked around the stadium towards Gate 3.

The short drive to the crime scene was slow because I idled there. Instead of answers, he confused me with nothing, not even questions. He was just feeling me out. I almost believed him.

CHAPTER 17

I approached the stadium, and when I got closer, I saw movement at the doors of Ballpark Village. A scruffy sandy blonde bearded face stared at me from behind the glass door, his dull, drug-addled eyes willing me to come see him.

I obliged but walked around the crime scene a few minutes for the camera's sake. Then I went to the entrance and walked in like I was looking for a bathroom.

There was no life in the room, but I knew where Clay was hiding.

"It's a little early for our meeting." I sat in the same place as before.

"It's big, Will. Real big." Clay was rocking and chewing his thumbnail. He had used my fifty for drugs and was wanting another hit.

"Clay, you need to eat some real food. You keep snorting that junk you …"

"Shoot." He looked insulted. "This nose is clean." He stopped rocking, raised his head, and pointed at his nostrils.

"Sorry, I didn't mean to offend." I raised my hands.

"Snorters are the real addicts. Shooters, like me, can stop anytime we want." He raised a sleeve of his tattered hoodie. Some track marks were fresh, others formed scars that looked like a connect the dot game.

I knew if I hurt his feelings too much, he might shut down on me. If the fear didn't drive him to it first. I decided to let it go.

"What have you got?"

"Like I said, it's big. I was standing outside the Gardens mausoleum entrance, listening like you taught me. And there was these two guys who guarded it. They was talking about what was happening over at the stadium." Clay thumb pointed at Busch. "Me and these other guys were sitting near them. I was listenin' real good. And those two guys was talking about how that noggin was throwed on the ground and all. And that's when I heard it." He wiped his smiling mouth and looked at me.

"Well? What did they say, Clay?" I raised my eyebrows.

"The littler guy asked him if Hector did the killin'. And the big guy said that Hector didn't do it, but he knew who killed her. Then the little guy asked if she was from around these parts. But the big guy said no, she wasn't from around here. Neither one knew why she was killed. But if you ask me, she was probably the girlfriend of a cartel kingpin. Hector did it to make a statement to that guy." He giggled into his hands and started rocking again.

"What statement would that be, Clay?" My mind was sprinting with all the possibilities.

"Stay out of St. Louis." Clay stopped rocking and gave a knowing nod. "I wouldn't even be surprised if she was the girlfriend of the Spirits' Godfather. She was his type."

"And what type is that?"

"Breathing." He laughed and started rocking faster. "That's a joke everybody says about that good for nothing. Spirits' leader jacks up the prices on his booze and gives no mercy to anyone who owes him. Not even his own people. He'll be outta business soon. Mark my words. Hector's about to do something big."

"Is that so?" I remembered what Frank told me. "You know what it is?"

He shook his head. "No, but word is that he got an army comin' from the east. Enough guns to take over the city. Maybe eliminate the Peace Forces." He frowned. "I'd hate to lose you, Will. You're good people."

He looked at the cash in my hand expectantly, twiddling his fingers as if silently asking for the fifty.

"Thanks." I handed him a fifty. "Please get some food or you'll die of starvation. And I need you." I wondered if he meant that the military Peace Forces or the local police were going to be eliminated. I was still learning Clay's junkie way of thinking. A hard thing to read.

He took the money and stared at it with half glazed eyes. I knew he didn't hear a word I said.

"Thanks. See ya tomorrow." He laid down. "I'll take a nap, and you leave so the eyes won't see us together."

"Thanks, Clay. You do that." I stood, stretched, and went back to the stadium, pretending to zip up my fly.

My police training told me not to be too anxious to assume everything Clay said was gospel truth. Then there were his assumptions. I knew better than to trust a drug addict's gut. He was just trying to sweeten the pot to ensure his payoff. But I did know not to completely ignore him either. That's why I employed him as a C.I.

The rest of my time in front of the stadium was filled with the new information I had just received and thinking about the date I had that night. The thought of that beautiful woman wanting to spend time with me was distracting. But God blessed me with a pragmatic mind. When an emotionally charged thought threatened to take control, the realistic side of my brain interceded to bail me out of a potentially dangerous reaction.

The most important piece of information I got from Clay was that Hector knew who killed the woman. I pulled out my cell phone and used the map application. It said the Gardens were about five miles from the stadium. I got in the beater and made my way through Free Agent territory.

CHAPTER 18

The road to the Gardens was torn up. The local government was doing their best to get the necessary resources to repair the infrastructure. The problem was workers. With the death count crippling the workforce, the unused resources were subject to theft. The streets were the first to suffer. Only business streets and those of the rich were fixed. The poor neighborhoods were ignored. And during those days, that was a lot of miles of roads.

Instead of going to the mausoleum entrance where the drug addicts hung out, I decided to go to the main entrance and act like a cop. I figured that might get me a meeting with Hector. Or killed.

Parking wasn't that easy since most of the streets were either blocked by rubble that was obviously stacked as a barricade, looking like walls that stretched from house to house, or roadblocks crewed by Free Agent soldiers. After a couple of badge pulls and two phone calls, I parked near the entrance and was met by a woman and a man carrying automatic weapons. They let me keep my gun after verifying my police credentials. The woman took my badge, scanned the chip, and sent the information to their superiors. She complained that all cops should have the chip, Beastmark, implanted on their persons to make life easier for her. I knew that was soon coming.

They led me down a walkway, past the Climatron plexiglass dome. We then entered a building with a sign that said, Kemper Center for Home Gardening. While I walked with my entourage, I noticed mild damage to the structure. In fact, a little plaster and some paint, and it would look like it did before the quake. The woman walked me to another door that took us outside to the back.

There was plenty of movement going on in this part of the Gardens. In fact, it was a garden. Full of life and food. Construction vehicles were parked near what looked to be a large fence that protected the entire yard. I assumed that overnight thieves had their fill of the rich bounty of these gardens.

"The boss is over in the vegetable garden." She glared at me. "Remember, you're on his property. Be respectful." She pointed to the heavily armed guards surrounding the gardens.

"Just had a couple of questions. It won't take long." I nodded while walking out the door.

The garden was squared off into twelve raised beds that were about eight feet by twenty feet. Each plot supporting its own variety of vegetation from green beans to corn, tomatoes, and other sundry fruit and vegetable plants. There were no drug plants to be seen. I assumed those were being grown in the greenhouses on the other side of the Climatron and possibly inside it. Or maybe offsite. I couldn't be sure without a search warrant that I knew I'd never get, if the rumors of Hector's political strength were true.

Although there were five people tending the beds, it was obvious who the man in charge was by the armed security people who kept their watchful eyes on him.

He was an older man, about fifty to fifty-five, tall, broad shoulders and large hands. His strength wasn't hard to discern. This man had worked hard all his life. It was obvious he was formidable. I needed to be cautious.

Although he was physically strong, he had to be intelligent if he was running the largest mafia in the city. And cunning to have the government backing him.

"Hector?" I tried to be polite.

"Yes, Detective Thomas. I am Hector." He kept his eyes on the plant he was pruning. Although his gloves were well worn, he dressed well. A polo shirt, khaki pants, and brown work boots.

"I'm sorry I don't know your last name, or I would've been more formal."

"Hector will be fine." He finally switched his focus to me. His brown eyes were almost golden and a little unnerving.

"Hector it is. I was wondering if I could ask you a few questions concerning…"

"The head found near the baseball stadium," he interrupted. A grin came across his face. The type that said I was supposed to be amazed.

"Yes, by Gate 5." It was hard not to be unnerved by his knowledge of what went on in the city he believed he controlled. But I played it cool based on the way everyone talked about him. Don't poke the bear, or you will get the claw.

"Of course, detective. I have nothing to hide." He smiled and took off his gloves. "Let's talk over here."

He led me to a green park bench with wrought iron armrests near a small greenhouse that looked to have seeds germinating on enclosed tables.

"What can I do to help, Detective Thomas?" The bench gave a slight grunt when he sat.

"My captain told me you lead the largest private group in the city, and that you may have some insight into what happened to the deceased woman." I tried to choose my words wisely, but I felt like I missed the mark. This kind of questioning wasn't taught at the academy. Real world experience through fiery baptism.

"Private group? Detective Thomas, my group, as you call it, is a community of people trying to make their way through these troubling times. I mean, America isn't what she used to be. In fact, we are nearly a third world country compared to others across the Atlantic." A troubling grin crossed his face. "Or Israel."

The last country made me pause. Was this man aware of what was really going on from a Biblical standpoint? But since I had already made a mistake, I decided to table it for the time being.

"America is resilient. I think we can overcome our recent setbacks." I tried not to sound too resolute. His forehead was devoid of a tattoo or bump, and his wrist was covered by the sleeve of his shirt. I would've been surprised if he had the Beastmark.

"Yes, and it is communities like ours that will spearhead this triumph." There was a hint of Sovereign speech in his words. However, he didn't captivate like the Antichrist.

It was obvious I was out of my element. It was time to focus on the case at hand.

"I agree, and one way is to keep law and order. We would be barbarians if we weren't civil. Don't you agree?" I tried to sound like a cop. It was my only play as a rookie. A more seasoned cop, like Frank, would have fared better.

"I do. So, what questions do you have concerning this unfortunate event?"

The edges of his mouth turned up in a slight grin at his victory. It was to let me know my place.

"We believe she could be the victim of a drug deal gone wrong. We also have reason to think that it concerns another community, as you call them, who deal drugs on the streets of this fine city."

"Are you referring to the Survivors Crew or the Spirits? They are the only other communities inside the city limits." He crossed his legs and leisurely wiped some dirt from the sole of his boot. Having full control of the conversation made him arrogant.

The first mob he mentioned was probably the one he wanted me to suspect. If Frank was correct about the upcoming mob war, Hector might try to use the Peace Forces to do his dirty work. If Clay was right, either the military or the police Peace Forces would step in.

"I'm not sure as of yet. I was wondering if you knew who the woman was? We haven't had enough time to complete the autopsy or run her DNA, and I'd like to make progress to show my superiors that I'm the cop for the job. Anything you may know would be more than helpful." I knew I was treading on dangerous territory. If he gave me the name, I'd owe him. That slippery slope would lead to servitude.

"Why would I know her? If she was killed during a drug deal from one of those communities, I wouldn't have any idea who this random woman was."

I hoped he would take the bait and give me something in return for a favor down the road that I decided I'd never repay, even if it advanced my case.

"My captain said you are well connected and might already know things we don't." I was working off Clay's information, hoping to confirm it or not.

"Frank Malone knows this city well. I'm impressed." Hector shifted his legs. The mention of Frank made him uneasy. They butted heads before. I kept that in the mental notepad and would ask Frank about it later.

"So, have you heard anything?"

Hector paused. I didn't know what to make of it. He had the upper hand. Why not go in for the kill and blame one of his enemies to throw me off the trail?

"Detective Thomas, it might not be in my best interest, but I need to confess something." He shifted his weight. Was he nervous?

"Confession heals all wounds."

"Last month, I received word from outside the city that

someone was going to die. I must admit that I still don't know who she is, but this contact requested I stage the deceased in a place that will be easily found."

I almost lost my mind. "Who is this contact?"

"You wouldn't believe me if I told you." He grumbled. "Besides, they want to remain anonymous. And it's in my best interest to keep it that way."

The corner of his eye twitched when he stared me down. His first tell. But what was he telling?

"Why's that? You're already an accessory by your own admission." I knew I was out of my league, but this was a different sport entirely.

"Maybe, but my contact assured me that this matter would be quietly dispensed with, and life here would return to normal." He looked around and gave a modest shrug. "As normal as can be expected."

"Are you saying that corrupt cops are going to make this go away?" My anger rose. The thought of pulling my SIG .45 and arresting him came to mind, but Frank taught me to not allow emotion to get in the way. Plus, the armory that surrounded him guaranteed the Corpse Patrol would find my body somewhere around the Gulf of Mexico.

"There is some corruption in the Peace Forces all around the world. But my contact made it sound like this corruption is on the political side. I'm afraid you are the second domino to fall. The first being the unfortunate victim."

He grimaced as if he didn't want to talk about such things to avoid insulting me and my profession. It was the first time he acted out of character. He was blatantly rubbing it in my face.

"How so?" The fear I told Tommy was confirmed. This was bigger than I wanted it to be. And I didn't know anything yet. My stomach churned. Maybe the chili dog from the night before still wreaked havoc in my digestion processes. Maybe not.

"Why would a woman, who is seemingly insignificant, be required to die and left in our fair city? Then a rookie, such as yourself, be brought in from the other side of the state to investigate, alone?"

He sighed as if he was put off by spelling it out for me, making my inferiority complex, and my anger, grow.

Although he made the situation appear to be far above my pay grade, he was a liar by trade. He was also a seller of secrets. Political secrets. So why was he spilling the beans about this?

"You say you don't know who this woman is?"

"Correct."

"Like you asked. Why is she so important for all of this attention?"

"Now you're thinking like a detective." He slapped my thigh. "Now, if you please, I need to tend my gardens." He looked skyward. "The weather will turn on us soon."

I stood and shook his hand. "Thank you for the insights. I might have more questions later."

"Please, don't hesitate to ask." He nodded at his security woman looking out of the window beside the door I came out of.

Following her, I made it back to my beater safely, but angry. He was teaching me my job. Although he knew who she was, he was going to make me find out for myself. It felt like I left with nothing. But he did admit to being part of the crime. If only as a cog.

CHAPTER 19

The headquarters was abuzz with military and police Peace Forces personnel coming and going with great speed. A sergeant told me that the Survivors Crew had been attacked by the outsider mob that broke off from them near University City. The attack took place at Forest Park, near the zoo, and well within city limits. The police went in first to stop the shootout. Then the military came out of nowhere and joined in. It was a bloodbath. New laws dictated that the Peace Forces were allowed to use deadly force to end any violent confrontations between factions, including the military.

Frank was doing his best to maintain peaceful order with little success because Joy was giving orders to kill all combatants. She was given temporary control of the military since she was the superintendent. He had no choice but to relent to her authority, which she wielded like a child finding the key to the gun cabinet.

His head was in his hands while leaning his elbows on his desk when I walked into his office. The dejection of the moment pierced the air between us. It's hard to force peace when the Peace Forces are part of the killing.

"Hey, Frank. Heard your boys are getting trigger happy." I plopped in the chair in front of his desk. I didn't smile for fear that he'd think I agreed with what was going on.

"It's not funny. People are dying, and my commanding officer is pulling the trigger." His eyes bulged with anxiety. "They could've been saved. But now." He choked on the thought.

"Easy captain. Let's not say anything that could get you in hot water with the boss." I pointed to my ear.

He got the point and nodded at his desk. "How's the investigation going, Will? Anything new?" Nobody listening would've believed his intention with that tone.

"Not much." I snapped my fingers to get his attention and gave a simulated putting motion when he looked up.

He nodded. "Why don't you go to the lab and see if there's anything new. I haven't had the chance to yet. I'll see if there's anything new with the shootout."

"Yes, sir." My heart went out to the old guy. This was completely new, even to a young guy like me. Cops were to stop the violence, not join in, and the military was to fight foreign invaders, not kill its own citizens. The oath I took felt hollow, like a lie that politicians give to unsuspecting voters. The treaty that brought America into the global fold wasn't getting here fast enough.

The hallway was flooded with cops and military personnel trying to get in line for Jenny and Bobby. Instead of waiting my turn, I knocked on their door and barged in. The language thrown at me from the outside would've made a sailor blush. Europeans know some very colorful expletives. But I had the ability to do this since Frank and Joy put this case in the top priority classification.

"Detective Thomas, so glad to see you. Bobby's in his office updating your case file." Jenny smiled as she opened a machine that I'd never seen before. The canister had the biohazard label on it, but she didn't even wear gloves. So, I assumed it wasn't too dangerous.

"Do you have time to talk, or do I need to wait for the

116

upload?" I sat on a stool and eased to the table loaded with guns and ammo.

"Yes, we can, Detective Thomas." Bobby walked into the room and sat at the computer near the evidence table and loaded the drone cam feeds first.

"Oh, by the way. Ruth told me to tell you to keep your day job. Comedy isn't in your future." I hesitated to say it but took a chance that it might alienate him from me. "She called you a lab rat, too."

Although he never cracked the slightest grin. Bobby's eyes lit up enough for me to know this was probably an ongoing thing. It almost felt flirty. It was fun being the messenger boy for a potential office romance. Then I felt guilty for looking at Ruth the way I did at the morgue and shot a quick inner prayer for forgiveness.

"Find anything good?"

"Nothing out of the ordinary, detective." He clicked on a feed that seemed to cover the killer's path. "As you can see, the best way to the crime scene is from the south. The killer should have cut through the southern district, through the defunct railroad region, and right to Gate 5." He pointed to an adjoining monitor that had a digital map of the city with a red line showing the supposed trail.

"I came to tell you I have a lead that the killer came from the river. Probably tied off at the Old Cathedral." I pointed to the route Clay gave me on the monitor.

"That would be illogical. Given the time of night and the current of the river, the killer would be stupid doing it that way." Bobby shook his head and ran the cursor around the red line. "But your source is right. I'll show you in the street cams in a minute."

While he clicked to another feed, I thought about what Hector and the senator told me about the head changing hands for the staging. Why didn't the killer be the one staging the crime scene? No experience? Not familiar with the area?

"I did a thorough sweep of the possible routes yesterday, without knowing what the street cameras held for me. Fortunately, one of the paths I investigated was the correct, albeit illogical, path. Unfortunately, there was no evidence the killer dropped anything, and there were no footprints of any kind. I'm working on why that is." Bobby rubbed his chin. "You were not right about one thing. He wasn't a pro. He was caught on street cams."

"What if the person who staged the crime scene wasn't the killer? This may sound like a conspiracy theory but hear me out. Let's say the victim was murdered outside the city, maybe another state. The killer wanted to stage the head here but wasn't familiar with the city layout, especially since the quakes move things around a bit. So, he hires a local, maybe a junkie looking for a quick score. The killer arrives by way of the river, hands off the cargo to the planter, and waits for him to return for a quick payoff and escape."

"It's possible considering the street cams feed." Bobby adjusted his glasses with one hand while clicking on one of the feeds with his other on the mouse. "This is the planter. Notice the backpack he's carrying." Bobby minimized the video and clicked on another. "Here he is after planting the head. The backpack isn't slumping."

Bobby was right. The man's backpack had less of a load.

"Where's the stadium feed?"

"Too distorted to get anything. This was at a little after three-thirty a.m. yesterday, and most of the lights on Clark Avenue have been out of service since the aftershock. City's behind on fixing them. But the cameras were installed shortly after."

"What's his path exactly?" I looked a little closer. The man wore a ski mask, black shirt and pants. He wasn't very tall, but he was well built. Maybe a Free Agent enforcer looking for extra cash.

"He shows up near the Old Cathedral, then takes Walnut to 4th, then Clark." Bobby points to the different angles on the multi-monitor setup. "Then he takes the exact same route back."

Clay was right and slippery. As hard as I looked, I never saw him following the planter back to the church.

"Any way to clean this up for a better ID?"

"This is cleaned up. The tech and I worked all night on it." Bobby sat back in his chair, took off his glasses, and rubbed his eyes.

"Thanks Bobby. This helps with the timeline and where we can look next." I patted him on the shoulder.

"I'll go over the path with some uniformed officers after dinner." Bobby smiled and left the room.

CHAPTER 20

"**Y**ou got anything for me, Jenny?" I walked over to her side of the lab.

"Give me a sec. I just need to move this over to the mass spec. The military insists that everything associated with them be worked on first with full classified nondisclosure." She winked and giggled. "Eurotrash think they're our bosses. But they're not."

"And who is your boss? I've been curious about that." I shifted the seat height.

"Captain Malone is my direct supervisor in this case, but Superintendent Everhart has been on my phone every five minutes. She won't let us work without bothering us."

Jenny blew her bangs from her eyebrows as she pushed the button to start the mass spectrometer.

"The shootout?" I knew better but wanted confirmation.

"Oh, no. Her questions are only for your case." Jenny went to her table and retrieved a file folder.

It's funny how priorities change when you're in charge and don't have all the information. Joy was probably fit to be tied knowing she wasn't in on this. But I'd let Frank give her the information as he saw fit. Getting in the middle of that battle would just turn me into collateral damage, and I wasn't in the mood for that.

"What questions would those be?" Another one I knew the answer to.

"It's interesting. She doesn't seem to care about the woman's identity, which we still don't know, or who dumped the head. She seems more interested in any evidence of who the murderer is." Jenny sat across the table from me and opened the file while reaching for her coffee mug. "I keep telling her there's no way to find that out because she was washed clean."

This was the first piece of evidence of Joy's incompetence. To find the killer in this case, the best we could do was follow the trail backwards to the killer, not the other way around.

"Washed clean by the killer?"

"Yes. But there's something interesting about the scrub down." Jenny stared at the file in her hands, looking for the information. "She was scrubbed with water containing plenty of chemicals." She thumbed through a few pages before removing two pages.

Jenny's matter-of-fact tone startled me.

"She was cleaned in a pool?"

"Probably not. Tap water and bleach were used to clean her, but not submerged or this wouldn't have been found." Jenny handed me the top sheet. "Dr. Washington pulled a trace sample of water mixed with bromine from her ear. My guess is a hot tub, where it's more commonly used. And this had plenty. I took a closer look at the tap water, in both the ear and on the skin, and found that it was most likely from a treatment plant back east. I can't be sure of it exactly because treatment centers from that region tend to use similar formulae due to government regulation. But I am sure this came from the east. And that's not the interesting part. You see." She pushed the second sheet to me. "She was refrigerated."

"Why refrigerated?" I took the sheet and wracked my brain for the lessons on freezing and refrigerating corpses from college while I read the report.

"My guess is the killer knew about forensics. Freezing would be too obvious and easy to test. But refrigeration is harder to detect and makes it more difficult to find T.O.D. Especially when she was warmed up. That was genius." She stretched her arms above her head. "Once Dr. Death figured that out, it was easy."

"Probably did it for transportation from back east to here." It made sense.

"That's exactly what we thought. Extra credit for the detective." Her whimsical comment bothered me. After all, we were dealing with a murder. But she dealt with this all the time, especially now that the murderers were our own in her other case.

"How was she cleaned?" I studied the sheet.

"Most likely, the killer took the head, wiped it of any forensic evidence using the bleach solution, removed the other identity markers, and placed it in a refrigeration unit of some kind. Maybe even a beer cooler full of ice for easy traveling. The killer then moved her to St. Louis and warmed her up for a few hours before dumping her at the stadium. Probably set it out in the warm air."

"She was in the area for a few hours?"

"At least a day."

"This city is perfect for hiding a body but having the time you're talking about is another matter."

"Not really. All you need is a sound structure and no one watching. Maybe out in the country near here or across the street. It's easy to be invisible these days. Even with the cameras invading our privacy."

"Needle in a haystack?" I grinned.

"Not to that extent, but close. Almost all the major buildings downtown have been torn down. I'll be dead before the city gets it all cleaned and rebuilt."

The street cams reminded me. "Bobby showed the planter taking the head to the crime scene from the river."

Her face twisted in thought and concern. "That means the killer could've thawed the head out anywhere. According to the T.O.D., the murder could've taken place anywhere on the planet. But we know she was back east sometime around the killing. The killer would've had time to get close to St. Louis, thaw out the head, and stage it at the stadium." Her shoulders dropped in defeat. "Sorry, detective. I'm afraid the only thing I can give you as far as the scene of the murder is somewhere in the eastern United States."

"We have the timeline, an area where she was possibly killed, and that our crime scene is the secondary. This is a lot more than we had this morning." I looked around, and Bobby had left the lab. "And Bobby and I agree and believe that the person who staged the head wasn't the killer. Maybe a junkie paid off to do it."

She started a small smile while she perked up. "Cool. But Bobby told me the drone footage didn't show anything."

"I can confirm that. Following a lead, I walked the path and can confirm it's clean. It goes by the food truck court on 4th and Broadway by the piles of buildings."

Her eyes glazed in reminiscence. "I had an apartment at One Cardinal Way. Fifteenth floor. Just high enough to catch a game now and then with my binoculars. I was at my parents in Howell County in southern Missouri when the quake hit. I was almost to St. Louis during the aftershock."

"Howell County? West Plains?"

"No, just south of Peace Valley."

"I went hiking on Devil's Backbone."

"Cool. I never got into hiking. I was more into fishing. Norfork Lake was just a little over an hour from home. I almost became a Conservation Agent." She grinned. "But forensics was my calling."

"And you're the best. I was raised near Springfield here in Missouri. Fished and hunted around Stockton Lake. Dad was a preacher and Mom bred German shepherds, but I was made to be a cop. That's what Mom said. And I guess she was right."

"So far, you're doing great." She grinned as she passed the other page to me. "Your mother must be proud."

"She was. But she was murdered." It always hurt to say that, but it was part of the spy business. "Thanks for the compliment." I returned to reading the page. "A .22 mag?" My mind went into overdrive.

"A .22 magnum rifle from about one hundred yards." Jenny leaned on her forearms and let me process the info.

"Why did the killer choose that small of a caliber?"

"A good shooter can place a bullet anywhere." She shrugged. "Any shot that penetrates the skull is an almost guaranteed kill no matter the caliber. I read about a person getting killed by a .177 pellet gun at point blank range. Went through the eye and into the brain."

"The killer was that close. Wouldn't the victim see her killer? The bullet went in just above the right eye."

"Not likely because any terrain can make someone obscure. Unless she was looking for the shooter."

"Why a .22 mag? Why not a Barrett M82? It's still used by military snipers today."

"Maybe it was all the killer could get their hands on. Since guns are outlawed now, a person can't just go to the local gun or pawn shop and walk away with one. Most people scavenge nowadays."

She was right. Scavengers were everywhere looking for food, shelter, and protection after the quakes. In fact, the Resistance sent many people to find weapons from retail stores to homes to help arm the growing army when the Peace Forces entered the picture before the quakes.

"But to hit her from that distance, and in that place? That's quite a shot." I slid the page back to her.

"That's true. Probably military trained? Can use anything in the special forces. But that's supposition. These are the facts. I'm not sure there's anything else I can give you."

Beeping sounds came from the mass spec.

"Thanks, Jenny. You helped out a lot." I got up to leave. "And tell Bobby thanks for me, will ya."

"My pleasure." She stood and walked to the mass spec.

CHAPTER 21

Frank's assistant told me he went to investigate the scene of the shootout, so I left headquarters to get ready for my date. I only had one date since the Rapture, just before the Trib began. She was a 911 dispatch operator for K.C. working on her degree to become a pharmacy tech. It was only one date, but it was one to remember. She was childish and tried to pick a fight with the couple next to us at the movie theater to see me in action. Said it turned her on. I de-escalate the situation and took her home. She called me a coward and slammed the car door because I refused to walk her to the door.

My hotel room seemed to stink even more when I walked in. Like old onions had mixed into the fray. I could taste the smell. Then I saw the rest of my chili dog in the trash can. The housekeeper didn't clean my room. I hadn't set out the Do Not Disturb sign on the door. So, I tied the bag off and went to the front desk to complain.

After a long argument with the hotel manager, I went back to my room to take a shower. It seems that the new rules for the hotel industry are about self-service. The workforce shortages brought that about. There was only one housekeeper for all shifts, and she didn't like to work fast or efficiently. But she made sure the towels were clean and replaced on a timely schedule. For that I was thankful. The rest I'd live with.

At least the water was hot.

I rummaged through my luggage to find something appropriate for a casual first date. T-shirt and cargo shorts were my choice, but I left the Cards hat in my room, which was almost white tie for me.

The drive to the food truck area was stifling. The angels were doing their jobs of holding back the wind. The air hadn't so much as stirred since before the seventh seal was broken. The clouds were still rolling in place, maybe a little faster, and getting darker. It was getting difficult to tell day from night. The bleakness of the city's skyline was enough to instill depression. But not me. I had a date with a beautiful woman, whose smile, and curves, could turn a bleak day blindingly sunny.

Arriving ten minutes early gave me a chance to scout out another place to eat. The chili dog still barked in my bowels. I couldn't wait to get rid of it, but it seemed to be holding on for dear life for reasons unknown to me.

The menus were interesting because of the lack of fresh food. Most of the stuff was canned from before the beginning of the Tribulation. Taste and nutrition were for the rich. Or for people like Hector who could grow their own.

A long line to one of the trucks caught my attention. I walked to the end and talked to the tall, thin lady dressed in pale skin, high end clothing, and anger.

"This is my first time here. Why is this place so popular?"

"Fresh food. Not like that canned crap everywhere else. Not only that, but it's local organic. Grown right here in the city."

I thought for a second. "This wouldn't happen to come from the Gardens."

She pointed to the truck. "Can't read or something?"

The sign was clearly printed, *The Gardens*. Hector had his hands in just about everything in the city. That got me to thinking about his eye twitch. Most people can't control their entire body when talking. It was definitely a tell. He was lying, but to what extent still remained for me to decipher.

There were just two people in line when I got a tap on the shoulder.

I turned. The blonde hair would've been beautiful if it was moved by a breeze or light wind. Blonde? The eyes were the same layered gray, but the hair was no longer jet black.

"Surprise. A real blonde." Her smile put me in a full body pause. "This is my natural color. The black was a wig. I like to play around with colors."

She frowned.

"Sorry. I was just thinking about you. Wow, your hair is beautiful."

She smiled and punched my shoulder. "You about gave me a heart attack. I thought it turned you off."

"You could be bald and never do that."

"You're smooth." The flirty way she said it made her seem younger than I imagined. "I thought we agreed on chili dogs?"

"I had one last night that's still with me. I was wondering if I could talk you into fresh meat and vegetables. They say this is the only place to get it." I waved my hand at the menu.

The angry lady in front of me put in her order.

Amelia looked at the menu. The inquisitive frown on her face gave her an intelligent beauty. When she shifted her weight from one foot to the other as she crossed her arms made me think she had done some modeling or acting. At least in my mind's eye. High fashion, not that sleazy crap on the internet, television, and movie theaters.

"I'll have a Cobb salad and sweet tea." She smiled at

me. "I'll go find us a place to sit."

Once I got her salad and tea, and my BLT with fresh chips and bottled water, I found her sitting at a table that was close to the now blood-colored river in a secluded spot. We didn't talk while we ate. The food was marvelous. I hadn't had a fresh BLT since before God's judgments started falling on the earth. I had to hand it to Hector, he had great food. If he'd only get out of the rackets and focus on farming and restaurants, he'd make a fortune selling his foods.

Unfortunately, guilt came with every bite. The prices were through the roof. As a detective in the world government's police force, I made more than enough to sustain myself. However, there was a large part of the populace who didn't make enough to feed themselves, let alone their families. I said an inner prayer for God to take care of them, then tried my best to guiltlessly eat the sandwich He provided.

After we finished, we stared at the river that used to flow loud, even roaring at times. But now, it meandered almost silently. There was little beauty in this apocalyptic world. I never allowed myself to ignore it when it made its rare appearances. Before the quakes, a person had no problem seeing the Illinois side of the river. On our family vacation, I imagined swimming across it. Now I could barely see any land, and I had no intention of swimming away from this beautiful woman.

"It's been so long since I was on a date." She sighed, staring at the river. "Over a year."

"It's been longer for me." It's funny how the Rapture and God's judgment can put a damper on a man's social calendar.

"Wow, I thought cops got all the girls." She giggled.

Even the increasingly furious sky didn't obstruct my growing feelings for her. Even a small giggle took my full attention.

"Hardly. It's difficult to maintain a romance when you're on the beat."

"I thought you're a detective." She seemed disappointed.

"I am now. But this is my first case. In fact, I work in Kansas City. The captain here asked me to help with this case." I nearly slapped myself for divulging this much information to a veritable stranger. She had a way of making me want to talk. Maybe she should be a cop. Then a paranoia hit me. Maybe she was a cop from Internal Affairs. It'd be like Joy to do that. My Copley intuition set up walls faster than my conscious self could think.

She turned her attention to me and smiled. "You must've done something great to be called away from your city to work a case."

"Not really. Captain was my academy instructor and he's an old family friend from my childhood." I almost got lost in her eyes. "It's who you know, I guess."

"It helps to know people in this world." She turned her attention to the river again. On a clear day, the river would've reflected on that light, but deep gray, palette.

The winds needed to return their normal flow. Even as a believer, the punishments God was rightfully handing out still affected me. It's hard to believe that something like a breeze would carry so much weight for a guy like me, who never sat down and enjoyed it.

"I guess it does. It might've helped that woman."

"Who is she?"

"Sorry, I can't talk about an open case." I looked at her profile. The gray layers of her iris started showing themselves. I became entranced.

"Oh, it's not a case if you don't even know her identity, right?"

"It became a case when the bullet entered her brain pan."

"She was shot. Won't that get you into trouble?" She side-eyed me, breaking the spell.

"That's common knowledge. It's all over the internet. Superintendent Everhart put that in the press release." I almost shook my head to wake up the rest of the way.

"Oh." She seemed disappointed knowing something everyone else did.

"The killer must've been a Cubs fan." I tried to make the situation lighter.

"Because she was found at Gate 5?"

"Yeah."

"Was she gunned down right there?"

"We're not sure right now." I lied, knowing what was happening. She was pumping me for information. "By the way, what do you do for a living?"

She turned quickly. "You think I'm a journalist trying to get the scoop?"

Wow was she quick.

"All I know is that you're from England. After coming to America for school, I'm not sure who you are. That's why I'm asking." I shrugged. "Besides, it's something they train us at the academy. To avoid contact with the media."

"So, now you're giving me standardized questioning methods. Is that it?" Even her pouty face was beautiful.

"It's in the interest of global security that I know everyone that I encounter. Dead or alive." I recited the Peace Forces manual and smiled, hoping it would calm her.

She stifled a smile for a second before letting out a guffaw. I laughed with her.

"All right then. I studied to be an architect in New York. But the earthquakes took the city and my livelihood. A friend told me that St. Louis was starting to rebuild, and I took a chance. So, here I am." The way she talked and the lack of any noticeable tells made me think she was telling the truth.

"Are you working now?"

"Yes, with the city planning and zoning commission. We're working on clearing the destruction and refiguring

131

the new flood plain, so we don't experience what just happened again." Amelia looked at the devastation near the riverside. "The old riverside dropped over a foot after the earthquake and aftershock. That's why it's so far inland."

Now she sounded like she was reciting a manual. I still wasn't certain of her story. She could be a great liar.

"Maybe you can tell me something that's been bothering me since I saw the river a couple of days ago. If my Earth science is right, wouldn't a fissure develop when the river widened? And if so, why did the water increase, instead of decrease?" This time I didn't know the answer.

"I talked to a geologist and a seismologist about this topic not long after the aftershock. They said that the beginning of the river had widened and started spouting water at an alarming rate. If that hadn't happened, and the river widening didn't cause the fissure, the Mississippi River would have overflowed exponentially. Maybe even expanding the Gulf of Mexico to overrun Central America and splitting North and South America permanently."

"Wow," I muttered. "My mind never went that direction. I just thought that maybe the Great Lakes got connected somehow."

"Don't be ridiculous. It would take a catastrophe that would crack the planet like an egg for that to happen." She took another bite of her salad. "At least that's what the seismologist said when I asked the same question," she said, covering her mouth with her wrist to avoid showing her chewed up salad.

According to Dad's prophecy journal, there was going to be a quake that just might make that happen in the second half of the Trib.

It was then the heaviness of the Trib weighed on me, so I changed the subject. "Since the river hasn't made it to the ballpark, will the city rebuild Busch Stadium?"

"Not in the first few phases. This city needs its infrastructure rebuilt first. The problem is the almost nonexistent workforce." Her eyes glazed a little like she was still trying to solve the problem.

"No end in sight?" I knew the answer to that from Dad's journal.

"It'll turn around when people learn that it's over now." She took her last bite of the salad and sipped her tea. "That and the incentive program."

"Do you really think the population can be improved by paying people to have babies?"

After taking control of the European countries and many others around the world, he put into effect an incentive program to replace the lost generation of children who were raptured. Not only was there money given, but people who helped increase the population were given privileges to lowered prices on food and utilities. On top of that, marriage was nullified when he announced that a couple needn't be joined in any capacity. What happened was a massive increase in STDs across the world. But the government-run media made sure that was not reported. The Peace Forces were forced to take an online seminar on the dangers of unprotected sex. It was overly informative and humiliating to boot.

"The Sovereign seems to think so. Fertility clinics are pumping out repeat customers by the thousands now. The first wave of babies has been born, and the second round is on their way. My only concern is that there are more orphanages than ever before. There are four in the city with talks about two more being built. That paired with the workforce shortage will make it difficult for the children to be raised properly. But I think he'll get it figured out."

"How can you be so sure?" As a Christian, I was supposed to be looking at the sunny side of life. But it was difficult when you are bombarded by crime and death on an almost daily basis as a cop, and that's not even counting the death toll from the judgments. The thought of ill-raised children turning criminal made me want to quit the force and live in seclusion until Armageddon.

"Optimist, I guess. At least it can't get worse." Her smile was unsure.

The truth was that it was just the beginning. I'd never considered the effect it would have on a child. Even though they were protected, like the ones already raptured, it didn't seem fair that the innocents had to endure what was coming next. The next seven judgments were about to start, and they'd make people forget about the first seven. Then God would turn loose his full fury. A heaviness filled me. And from her response, I could tell she shared the same weight.

We closed our containers and put them in the trash receptacle. Then we started walking up the river shoreline sipping our drinks. The day was waning according to my phone, and I knew it was best to keep the walk short. You never know when a speedboat will come in and deposit another head.

She broke the silence by turning the conversation to typical date talk. Favorite colors, music, movies, etc. By the time we got back to the food truck patio, it was dark and empty. Just two cars in the gravel parking lot.

I walked her to her sports car.

"Can I see you again?" I stood close to smell her perfume.

"It depends." She sounded defensive but closed the distance.

"On what?" Her lipstick beckoned to be on my lips.

"If you solve the case, so you can tell me everything." She gave a kiss-me grin.

"I'll do my best. How about a year from next Christmas?"

"Trail gone that dry, huh?"

"Maybe." I still had enough of my senses to deflect the prying.

She leaned in and kissed me on the cheek. "You'll get the rest on delivery of a killer."

"I guess I'll have to put in overtime."

She smiled and got in her car. The electric motor mildly hummed as she drove away.

This case just became more interesting.

CHAPTER 22

The smell in my hotel room was added to by me from last night's date. Desperation. Amelia gave me a timetable that for some reason felt important. Everything about her made working hard worthwhile. Sleep evaded me. The case and the woman fought for my mental attention. The pressure of finding a killer and information for the Resistance took control of me in a way that made me feel ready to burst at the seams. Amelia made the pressure diminish enough to breathe. Maybe God sent her for that reason.

After leaving the hotel, I swung by the Peace Forces fleet services and filled up without so much as a glance from the supervisor. It occurred to me that Frank must have been in on making it happen, after I had remembered what Senator Staeger told me about the car not being in the fleet. I grabbed a dozen donuts from a local vendor next to fleet services for me and Frank. I had a feeling he needed Copley sustenance after dealing with the nonsense in the park.

While I was getting in the beater with a donut box in my hand, Tommy peeked around the corner of a building across the street with his hat already turned around. I scratched in the rearview mirror and left for headquarters.

The podium in front of the headquarters building was

surrounded by the media. They were camped all over the front of the building, either talking to their camera, or on their phones, probably to their producers. Camera operators of those not reporting were in circles with compatriots gossiping about the goings on in the industry, no doubt.

I parked close enough to hear the buzz when I rolled down my window. The ones already reporting talked about the shootout. I could tell the old school from new school talking heads. The old school still operated on the premise of freedom of the press, saying the streets need to be cleaned up in a more peaceful way. But they would be heavily censored by Antichrist's media inspectors who used the black marker heavily on anything that would paint the new society, and its leader, in a bad light. The new school reporters would just listen, then report whatever they were told to report.

The sky was churning faster than the night before. The clouds looked blacker and bloodier, like God was filling them with his fury. I needed to solve this case quick or take the chance of losing the killer. And the kiss.

Superintendent Everhart stepped out of the building, looking like a woman who relished the attention. She was using everything she had to take control of the crowd, but it was difficult. The questions started before she even gave her statement. Orange-redness filled her face when her assistant raised her finger to her mouth, and everyone silenced.

She began with a kiss up to the Antichrist about being patient with the city's efforts to clean up the streets. Then she lauded him for sending the necessary personnel and supplies to take the city back. It was hard to watch, so I decided not to indulge blind ambition. I entered through the side entrance and went straight to Frank's office where he was stewing.

"Got some sinkers, if you got the java." I held up the box.

He didn't smile. "Let's go." His gait out the door was that of a man at the end of his rope. Although he walked quickly, he trudged.

We exited where I entered. Joy's annoyingly squeaky public speaking voice echoed off the buildings across the street talking about the justice that took place the day before. I stopped long enough to hear that she blamed the Christian Rebels for inciting the shootout. That they were the ones in the park and not the Peace Forces.

It felt like she was reading straight from the Sovereign's playbook. A bad feeling came over me. I was too focused on the kiss and not enough on both my jobs. It was time to return to my serious nature as a cop and Resistance spy.

Frank went to my beater and got in the passenger seat.

"Mini Golf." He barked. It almost felt like a harsh version of the senator's commands the day before.

We entered the Union Station Mini Golf like last time. Frank went to the table, sat down hard, and waited for me to follow suit.

"What's up Frank?" I asked glumly, sitting the donut box between us. It was a serious moment, but I was hungry enough to take care of the dozen on my own.

"We got a bad problem." He shook his head like a teacher whose entire class failed the exam. "A real bad problem."

"What's that?" I was expecting to hear about the shootout.

"We got an ID on the woman." He paused, but not for effect, hanging his head in defeat. He seemed to dread telling me.

"And?" I prompted with raised eyebrows. "Who is she?"

He raised his head and focused to a spot on the wall next to us. His mouth started quavering. "I'm sorry, Will. I got you in deep. Too deep. I shoulda had Evans do it, but she's one of Joy's people, and I needed someone I could trust." He rubbed his face with his oversized hands like he was trying to shake a bad dream from his memory.

"Frank, it's okay. I'm good for this. Tell me what I need to know, so we can get this figured out." The red flags beat against my skull, and I became a little nauseated.

"Will, you got to be careful of the new government and their leader. They are going to bury this in the deepest pit they can find. And us with it if we don't play ball."

"What are you talking about, Frank?" His demeanor started worrying me more.

"The Antichrist." It barely escaped his lips,

"Yeah, Sovereign John Doe. Everybody in the Resistance knows his power. But Frank, who is the woman I'm investigating?"

He stared at his palm as if searching his next line. "Former President Jane Mason."

"Confirmed?" My mouth barely held the word.

"Confirmed. Jenny put the DNA through ICON and my fear was validated."

"What fear was that?"

"That the Antichrist had her assassinated."

I let it sink in. Dad's prophecy journal said that if any world leader resisted the Antichrist, he would have them assassinated.

"Why?"

"To make sure the U.S. signs the treaty. The new president is a fan of the Antichrist. He even said the world's a better place with the Sovereign in charge."

I remembered the speech he made after his inauguration, a week after the president was apparently assassinated. He looked like the typical placeholder. No authority in his demeanor or tone. The blame of the president's death was placed solely on the eastern Resistance, and he never discussed America without pointing out the Antichrist's amazing leadership skills. It was a subtle way to indoctrinate Americans into giving their freedoms up without a fuss, let alone a war. Dad called that one.

"But why now? Her term is up next year. They could've waited and put in their own person."

"Remember we're on a tight Biblical schedule. I think that even the Antichrist knows he has less than six years."

Then I remembered the case timeline. "She was reported missing two weeks ago, and the TOD is two weeks. And Jenny said the head was refrigerated, then warmed up before being planted at Gate 5."

"That sounds right for an assassination," Frank agreed.

"That's why nothing's been said about her disappearance, like she never existed. The vice president was sworn in without any moment of silence or any dedication to President Mason." My hat bounced as I scratched my scalp. I chastised myself for not seeing it sooner. America was set up right under our noses. The Antichrist used the assassination to his advantage. And we bought it completely.

"Sounds right. She was becoming a hindrance to the Antichrist's agenda. Jon said she told him that her speech was going to expose the Sovereign and keep America from joining the global government."

"This goes beyond a coverup. Frank, this was a President of the United States…"

"Which, for all intents and purposes, doesn't exist anymore." Frank raised his voice in frustration. "I tell ya kid, we'll be lucky to survive until the next judgment let alone the end of the Tribulation."

"It'll be fine. God has our backs." I reached across the table and patted him on the shoulder.

"Against the judgments, but not the blade. If He wants us, nothing will stop it." He was a man with experience burying loved ones, watching both parents die suddenly. His mother of a massive stroke and his father of the widow maker heart attack two months later. It was as if he was starting to give up.

"Then we'll be in Heaven." Frank was scaring me. If

this didn't help, nothing would.

He sniffed and wiped tears off the table. "Thanks, kid. I needed that."

I got back to the case. "When will the Secret Service come to protect what's left of her?"

"Not coming." He gave a disgusted look. "It's their job to stay with an assassinated president until they are interred."

"Not now. The Secret Service was soaked into the Peace Forces with the rest of us and are under strict orders to protect the current president from the Christian Resistance. I called them the second I found out her identity. But the director wouldn't budge. We are to send her remains to her family who will take care of the memorial and funeral."

It was hard to make the jump from one set of rules to the next. Every branch of service trained their incoming personnel at a level of patriotism that was second to none. We believed in America. But America was dying, and our leadership did nothing but bow to the wishes of a foreign dictator. I felt our forefathers crying for patriots to stand and fight. But they wouldn't.

Something hit the side of the building. A small thud that I almost didn't notice. Frank's eyes widened as paranoia got the best of him.

"We got to go. It may be best for us to meet somewhere else. Joy has people all over the city doing her bidding." He got up. "I'll walk back to headquarters. You take the car and keep going on the case." Before I could say anything, Frank was already out the door.

I looked outside. A bird had hit the side of the building. It was as if the lack of airflow threw off the birds' landing.

The beater groaned to life as I fired it up to see Tommy, then plan my next move.

CHAPTER 23

The darkening sky made the alcove harder to see, which was good for the meeting I was about to attend. Tommy stayed in the depths while I entered the cave of fallen concrete and asphalt. His demeanor was somber at best.

"You okay?" I went into the alcove and sat on a chunk of road.

Tommy didn't take his eyes off the skies. He just nodded, caught in his stupor. I'd never seen my friend like this. There was a fear in him I couldn't place. As if he could see the spiritual realm and it wasn't rainbows and sugarplums.

"Tommy, snap out of it." I clapped my hands.

As if he'd just woken up, Tommy gave a slight shake. "Hey, Will." He nodded to the sky. "I dread this part of the Tribulation."

The little that had already happened compared to the coming judgments still caught those of us who knew it was coming off guard. The next judgment would be like that of a nightmare. Hail and fire mixed with blood was something only the Egyptians, in Moses' time, had witnessed. And I had a feeling this one would be far worse.

"Tommy, you were right." I took off my Cards hat and rubbed my head, still trying to wrap it around the new information.

"About what?" He finally looked at me.

"The victim was President Mason." I paused to let that sink in.

He stood and looked at me, eyes widened. "I was only kidding."

"I don't think she was killed to make you feel bad," I said.

He sat down and put his hands in his hoodie pockets. "I know. But she was helping us."

"What are you talking about?"

I thought Tommy was losing it.

"She was a believer, Will. She put her faith in Jesus right after the Mid-East Summit. My boss said she knew he was the Antichrist when he sat behind the Presidential desk in the oval office. He was ordering everyone around like he was the president, not her. She tried to order him out of the chair. Everyone in the office laughed at her. Even the vice president. They started treating her like a spoiled child. Making her feel as if she didn't belong in their secret meeting. Then she was dismissed and forced to leave."

"But why have her killed? My guy says it's because the Antichrist knows he has a short time, but the more I think about it, I'm not so sure. Time might not be a luxury, but the election is next year. Or if time was a concern, why not trump up some charges and have her removed?"

"That's a good question."

His response was in an almost out of body tone while he sat and stared at the blood-soaked sky some more.

"Tommy!" I slapped his large shoulder. "Snap out of it."

"I'm afraid of fire."

He blinked and looked down, which told me he was coming around. But his words didn't make sense.

"What are you talking about?"

In the short time I knew Tommy, the one thing I never doubted was his nerve. He had a way to control his fear that made me believe he could stand in front of Satan and not turn and run.

"When I was a kid. My house caught fire. It burnt to the ground. A wire in the basement shorted and sparked near some dust, according to the arson investigator. We barely made it out. I can still feel the heat on my skin when we were trying to get out. Since then, I've been afraid of fire." He rubbed his forearm like a nervous parent waiting for their teenager late for curfew. He was feeling the flames when he returned his gaze to the sky.

"Tommy, you know we're protected. Right?" I patted him on the shoulder. "God's on our side. We won't burn."

"I know that. But my fear doesn't."

"Why don't you go back to K.C., get in your bunker, and hide out until it's over? That's what I plan to do."

He turned to me. It was hard to see him, as dark as the alcove was, but I saw enough to know his anger.

"I will never shirk my responsibilities." He towered to his full height over me. "Give me the flash drive." His hulking hand opened, holding the new flash drive.

"Okay." I did the exchange. "I didn't mean anything. Just trying to help."

"I'll have my people look into the cover up. Maybe there's something to slow down the Antichrist if we can connect him to President Mason's murder."

He left. No verse of encouragement. No pat on the shoulder. It was as if he turned me loose. It felt like I was moving closer to the Antichrist and farther away from God. I tried to remember my favorite verse. Even that felt far away. Maybe I was fooling myself. Maybe my faith was false. I just reached out of fear and not true belief.

A new fear entered my chest. What if I was doing all this for the wrong reasons? What if I was placating God without truly believing He could get me out of any situation? The thoughts of how the quakes and the voices didn't affect me gave a peace of mind and a calmness that helped. Maybe I should've never volunteered for the undercover work.

Maybe I should've ran and hid from Tommy.

I sat there regretting entering the Resistance, and my mind wandered to my other job. My fear that this case would be front and center had just come true, and that took root in my unsettled gut. This case was too big for me. Solving it would shoot me straight up the ladder. Something I didn't want this early. People like Joy wouldn't like losing the spotlight. They'd turn their sights on me and empty the clip until my head landed in a basket. But I didn't have a choice. Slow and steady might win the race, but we were in a sprint to the finish line—the world's demise.

The dark clouds looked thicker and churned more than when I entered the alcove. It was as if God was telling me to get this case closed soon. I knew I couldn't go after the Antichrist, except maybe slow down his agenda, like Tommy said, but I was able to go after the killer. I sat there in the comfort of the dark, stuffy alcove and thought about how I might go about doing that. But the more I thought, the more impossible it seemed. I didn't even know where the murder took place, just that it might have happened in a hot tub somewhere on the east coast. Not much to go on. No evidence is evidence. Maybe it didn't matter where she was killed. According to Dad's journal, the Antichrist will kill people who oppose him and spin it in a way that the masses will believe. But it was important where the head was planted.

Maybe he did this to implicate the Resistance like Joy was saying. That would enrage the citizens away from God and send them to hunt us down at a faster rate. Blades would be drenched in believer blood.

I mulled the situation over. The thought came to me that if the Antichrist wanted the body to be placed on display, he would probably use it to go after someone else.

Someone specific. I couldn't let my personal feelings cloud my judgment. Other scenarios creeped into my thoughts and made me consider other options of being the target. If not the Resistance, then who? Who in St. Louis was worth the attention of the Antichrist?

The mayor of the city was completely for the Peace Forces intervention because the mobs had taken over the city not long after the first quake. Plus, he had a Beastmark front and center on his forehead with a gaudy tattoo of the Arch around it. Unless the Antichrist had something on him that I wasn't aware of, killing him didn't make sense.

Something else that made sense was the clearing away of all the mobs. The Survivors Crew were just taken out along with one of the outliers. All that was left was the second outlier, the Free Agents, and the Spirits—which according to Frank was about to be soaked into the Free Agents. Was the Antichrist after Hector? Was the Don's reach in the political world too great? Is Hector stronger than I gave credit?

It was thin, but I needed to look into the possibility.

CHAPTER 24

It was dark enough that I had to turn on the beater's headlights, and it wasn't even noon. The sky was disturbing enough to bring fear to the stoutest hearts. But when adding the river reflecting the blood red hues, it was enough to cause an unholy panic within. I tried to ignore the scene with no success.

At the intersection where Broadway turned from south to north by Kiener Plaza Park, I noticed a tall woman standing on the sidewalk by the park entrance. She looked my way and started mildly waving at shoulder height, as if she didn't want anybody to know.

Although I figured she was a street pro, I stopped at the sign and waved her over, laying my gun in my lap and covering it with my jacket. Instead of coming to the driver's side, she crossed the car and got in the passenger seat.

"Detective Thomas, I am Kennedy Brown, Chief of Staff for Senator Jon Staeger. The senator requests your presence at Busch Stadium." She looked forward like I'd follow instructions without question.

She was wrong.

"Requests my presence? This isn't Philly, kid. And how do I know you're telling the truth?" The red flags weren't at full staff, just waving mildly.

She looked at me as if she didn't believe I'd question her. "Detective Thomas, why would I jump into your car and make up something like this?"

"Any number of reasons. You're homeless and need a ride to the closest shelter. Maybe a street pro looking for another John. How about a dumb kid playing a prank? Take your pick."

The conversation was already annoying, and I was about to drag and drop her out the beater.

She sighed like a spoiled princess. "How would I know your name and occupation?"

"The internet is an amazing place. Some I.D. would help."

She heaved a deep sigh and pointed at her forehead. The chip stuck out just enough to see, if you're looking for it.

"No loyalty tattoo?" I snarked while pulling the trigger of the chip scanner.

I never got over the feeling of using a scanner to see a person's life. All I could think of was her future. And it looked hellishly bright. Yet, something inside told me to trust her, but not too much. So, I decided to play her game but keep my cards, and gun, close.

"I haven't decided what to get. A falcon for the Sovereign or a shark for me being in politics," she said.

I couldn't tell if she was joking.

The dash computer confirmed her identity. I accelerated toward the stadium.

Parking near the crime scene, I put my gun in my holster before I slipped on my jacket and clipped the senator's machine on my badge and hit the button. As if knowing where the cameras were, she led me into the stadium through a slight maze of crumpled steel and broken seats.

The smell of hot dogs and popcorn floated around in my memory while we walked from the visiting bullpen, around the outfield warning track where would be homers died just before the wall, down first base line that signaled fair or foul, and into the Cardinals dugout full of championship trophies and losing seasons.

"Sit here and I'll get the senator."

The assistant walked into the hallway that led from the dugout to the clubhouse.

My hand cocked the hammer while still in the pocket. My heart rate increased, ready to go into a full adrenaline rush if anyone but the senator walked out. The novice in me said to blast the first person out of the door, but Frank's voice echoed the lessons that made me wait.

He walked out and looked at me. No expression, but it was same face that was in the beater the day before when he said a lot and told me nothing. At least I got to see him upright. A bald, lean man in the beginning of his elder years, about five feet ten. His dark eyes matched his wrinkling expression.

His picture was plastered all over the news recently. He opposed the vice president's sudden thrust into the Oval Office, even demanding that until President Mason was found, dead or alive, the vice president must stay in his role as acting president.

He sat close enough to hold a conversation but far enough to keep me comfortable.

"It is good to see you again Detective Thomas. Do you have any news from the investigation for me?" He folded his arms and looked expectantly at me.

"I figured Frank already filled you in." It was odd to see the senator and feel that he was out of the loop.

"Captain Malone is too busy with the unfortunate incident at the golf course to talk. I was hoping maybe you can pick up the slack." He still talked like a politician. Maybe he hadn't decided on me yet and was testing me to see if I liked to play ball.

"The victim is who you think she is." I kept it discrete because I saw Kennedy's right eye peering around the corner of the hallway. I decided not to trust her for that.

He stared at the visitor's dugout across the field.

It took a long minute before he responded.

"I was born and raised in Defiance. It's just across the Missouri River, due west from here. Some believe I'm too much like my hometown's moniker."

"In these times, a little goes a long way."

He gave a slow laugh then scanned the seats. "My family had season tickets." He pointed to the third base dugout. "Our seats were second row behind the visitor's dugout. Dad wanted to see the Cardinals players on and off the field. Said he could get the full feel of the game. It was that piece of information that made me a good politician. See all sides and you can better predict an outcome."

Silence entered the conversation. The type that shows one of the participants trying to figure out how much information is needed without saying too much. It was something he excelled at, and I lacked.

"Me and Jane both threw the first pitch on that mound. Separate dates of the same season. She won a bet we made when the schedule was announced. She got it to the catcher. My pitch sailed over the catcher's head. I had to send her a gooey butter cake."

His eyes glazed and a smile formed as if he was reliving the past.

"I'm sorry for your loss. But do you know that the Secret Service is not coming to get the remains?"

He gave a contemptable sigh.

"I'm not surprised. The illegal president wouldn't have it any other way."

"Sir, if you don't mind me asking, why are you here in St. Louis? I remember what you said about the phones and internet, but why is it so important to be over this case the way you are?"

"Jane Mason was my friend and champion. But most important, she was my president. That filthy despot, who hasn't even stepped foot on this country's soil, is trying to take us over. I aim to stop him even if I'm the last true American standing."

His patriotic speech was genuine. Although I didn't see a Beastmark anywhere on him, I still didn't know what that meant.

"Not to be rude, sir." I adjusted my crossed legs. "But I have a dead president's killer to find."

He grinned. "You're blunt Detective Thomas. I appreciate that." His grin disappeared. "The president was a Christian and fought to keep America out of the new global government. What she didn't know was that the Sovereign is about to sign a bill that officially outlaws Christianity. Anyone caught worshiping Jesus Christ, or even follows His teachings, will be immediately and publicly executed."

"I thought that was already happening."

"That's the Global Church's rules, which is illegal in this country."

"Hold on. We have guillotines all across the country in government places."

"It's not what it appears. The Missouri State Penitentiary is not an official federal or state government facility. It was opened as a temporary facility when the last prison was destroyed in the earthquake. If you look at the records, the Global Church owns it. If you do your research, it's the same all over the country. Think about the last beheadings. Only a Decreed Holy Person oversees it. No politicians on any level are present in official capacities. That will change once the treaty is signed."

He crossed his arms and took a long breath. "Christians will be arrested by law enforcement, immediately court martialed, taken to the public execution station, and be beheaded."

"No other ways of execution?" My gut churned at the thought of more fallen crowns in the basket.

"No. The Sovereign feels that beheading will be a strong device to deter people from worshiping a God who doesn't allow people to do as they please." He bowed his head and dug a finger into the wood of the bench.

Anger rose up from my depths. "Freedom of Religion…"

"Has been dead for over a year, my boy." His solemn words held in the air. "The United States of America died when all those people died. They were the spirit of the country."

He meant the Rapture, but I didn't know if he knew it.

Even though Dad's prophecy journal spelled it out to the letter, the thought of America's death was still hard to swallow.

"What about the new president?"

"A puppet." He shook his head. "Just a puppet of the Sovereign to appease the people until he signs the treaty." He turned and faced me. "President Mason refused to sign it because she knew she'd be giving away the country to a petty dictator. But no, the people of this country came out to protest her decision. They didn't want to be free anymore. They wanted to be saved."

His choice of words troubled me. Saved. That's what my dad, the preacher, called it when someone put their faith in Christ, because Jesus saved them from their sins. I didn't understand it till Dad was already gone, and I was facing a hostile world alone. My doubts earlier with Tommy left me. My faith was there, it was just weak in the wake of the argument I had with Tommy. I let my fear of losing my friend and confidant crossover into other parts of my life, including my spiritual side.

Now, I was more than just saved from my proclivity for giving in to temptation. I was also safe from God's wrath. Although the quakes shook me to my foundation, I had a calmness that I wouldn't get hurt. And I didn't. Because God's wrath wasn't for me anymore. Jesus took it fully on the cross. I wished I could tell the senator that. But I still had a job, and the senator wasn't a confirmed member of the Resistance.

We sat quietly for a while.

"Will, I need you to help me do something." He finally looked at me.

"What's that, sir?"

"I need you to help me hang the Sovereign." Fire entered his words and demeanor.

"It'd be awfully hard to pull that one off. But maybe we can discredit him."

The Antichrist's future was already spelled out for him. He still had about two years before being assassinated, then three and a half years after he resurrected with Satan possessing his body. But if we could discredit him to enough unmarked people, maybe the two witnesses and the Jewish evangelists could take that opportunity to reach them.

"He needs to be taken out of power immediately for this country to survive."

"By discrediting him, the people might take him out of power for us. It'd be easier to do that way." I knew taking the Antichrist head on was suicide, but I needed to keep the senator alive for as long as it took to get Tommy to send a witness to him.

He stared at me for a second longer than I wanted. "You may have a point. Let them do the dirty work." A smile crossed his face. "Maybe I can use you when I run for the Oval Office next year."

"I'm just a cop, sir. Let me help clean up the streets in law enforcement, and you fight the good fight on the executive side." I returned his smile. "You have my vote." But I preferred to know for sure his faith was in Jesus Christ.

We stood and shook hands. "Detective Thomas, I wish I could help you with your case, but my friends are growing fewer by the day. People are drinking the Kool-Aid by the gallon in all sectors of Washington." He paused and slightly shook his head. "Sorry, old habit. I mean Philadelphia. And the whole country for that matter. But I'll do everything I can to help. Just tell Frank what you need, and he'll contact Kennedy."

After he walked back into the hallway, I sat down. He'll never make it through the primaries, I thought. In fact, he may never see another election if he goes against the Antichrist. Then again, if the new president signed America over to the Antichrist, there will never be another election. I said a quick prayer for his safety and spiritual direction.

I walked out of the stadium with the red flags waving hard and fast in my head. If he didn't have anything to help with the case, why did he reach out to me?

But he did help with the case. Maybe the new president's lack of patience in getting into the oval office and using unconstitutional methods to do so meant he was in on the old president's assassination. It was plausible. Especially if his agenda was bowing America's knee to the Antichrist. Then I remembered Dad's journal. Maybe the new president wanted to secure his spot as one of the ten kings described in Revelation seventeen.

Or maybe the senator was still feeling me out. Staring at the place where Big Mac Land once stood, I considered what the senator said. He never used words that gave me the impression he was a believer or a nonbeliever. And no Beastmark. Politicians.

CHAPTER 25

Walking back to the beater, I tried to piece together the meaning of the meeting. If it wasn't for me looking in that direction, I would've missed Clay's face in the door of Ballpark Village looking like my uncle's old rock album covers where the band members heads were surrounded by a black background. He smiled when I diverted my path in his direction.

"It feels like our normal time is whenever I'm at the crime scene," I complained while sitting on my new normal chunk of ceiling.

"This is big, Will." He was already rocking. "Real big."

"I trust you, Clay. The last time you said it, you were right." For the most part.

"There's been a person in the cemetery meeting with someone else." His rotten teeth were visible in the bad lighting.

"Which cemetery?"

"Bellefontaine." He snuffed like it was common knowledge.

"Why were you there?"

"Having a private meeting with some friends."

His smile meant that either he was partying by the cemetery or coming down from a high.

"No food?"

"Maybe." He looked at the fallen screen above him for the answer as he picked at a rip in the fabric. "Maybe not."

"I told you I can't afford you starving to death. You need to eat." I raised my voice louder than I intended. There was a responsibility I had for him. Jesus said to feed the starving person food before feeding them the Holy Spirit. Since the latter was not possible, I could at least do the former.

"Yes, sir." He saluted with one hand while holding out the other.

"I'll need more than that for this." I held up the fifty.

He thought for a couple of minutes. "It's getting darker earlier. Hard to see who the people are. One is real tall, and one is short, a little shorter than me."

"Is the tall one taller than me?"

He closed his eyes. "Maybe a little taller. I'd hate to live off the difference." He opened them.

I figured closer to Tommy's height of six-seven.

"And the short one?"

"About my height."

"You're what five-eight?"

"Five-nine and a half." Clay sat up straight.

"Did you hear them talking? It might be a drug deal."

"Nope. No merchandise changed hands. That's why I got suspicious. Like you would've been." He tapped his finger on his temple.

"Why is this important?"

"The short one lives in there." He pointed at the stadium. "I followed him there. Maybe he's the one who planted the noggin."

"Interesting. Anything else you noticed about them or the meeting?" Senator Staeger entered my mind. Maybe he wasn't who he portrayed himself to be. As long as he'd been a politician, I bet he could out act an Oscar winner.

"The shorter one seemed to be in charge. He talked the

most. The other mostly listened."

It might have been the shorter one Hector was talking about. The one the Antichrist put in charge of the assassination.

"And this just happened today?"

"No, the last two days. If I'm right, they'll be meeting at about fifteen hundred hours."

Clay must've held this information back in case he had a slow day. It's what I would've done if I had multiple pieces of information, an addiction, and a sucker.

"So, they're keeping to a regular schedule, unlike us." It was hard not to raise my voice for his inability to stay at the Gardens doing his job. It was possible to scare him off and never see him again. He was too important as a C.I. I hoped he got the message.

"You report the information when you can."

He had a point.

I looked at my phone. Almost twelve-thirty. "I'll go see if they're there." I handed Clay his money.

"Anything from the Free Agents?" I asked.

"Nope. Business as usual." He eyed the fifty.

"If this doesn't pay out, you owe me fifty."

"All sales are final." He grinned again as he took the bill.

I went to the beater and returned with a couple of nutrition bars and a bottled water in my jacket pockets to avoid suspicion. "Here. It's not much, but I can't have my best spy going hungry or thirsty."

"Thanks, partner." He tore open the first bar and devoured it in two bites. He held up the second, leaned, and put it in his tattered jeans pocket. "Save this one for later."

It was comical to hear him mumble with a full mouth.

Before I walked out the doors, I heard the second wrapper being ripped open. Later comes a lot sooner when you're hungry.

CHAPTER 26

With a little time to kill before my stakeout, I went back to headquarters to do some spy work. Frank was still at the scene of the shootout, and Joy was holed up in her office no doubt breaking her arm by patting herself on the back for doing what she was told to do. The window was probably narrow, but it was enough time to get the job done.

My office chair squeaked in anger when I sat down. The act of spying was still foreign to me. In one way, it was the hardest thing I've done, what with the subterfuge and lying to anyone and everyone. Except Tommy. If it wasn't for him, I'd have lost my mind months ago. In another way, it was easy because I was trained not to be noticed as a spy and as a cop. Like the stakeout that approached. I needed to be as close to the conversation as possible while being invisible. Although the redness in the sky brought an eerie feeling, it was still dark enough to help. And hurt.

After keying in my security code, I went to the case file. Everything the CSU team and Dr. Washington told me was uploaded into the ICON case file. Seeing the information made the murder more important to me somehow. With the words in black and white, I felt the concreteness of the case. There was only one thing missing. The name of the killer. Everything inside me screamed to fill in the blank with the Antichrist, but I knew it would mean the guillotine for me and Frank, whether we confessed to being believers or not.

Once the case file completely downloaded to my computer, I put the thumb drive in and let it start invading the Beast. The Christian Resistance found ways around the walls set up by the Sovereign's specialists and former hackers, through plants like me. As a detective in the Peace Forces, I had higher clearance than most to use the Beast. Although I didn't have unlimited access, the flash drives were usually capable of invading the networks to help keep Christians safe from the Antichrist's regime in my region.

With the exception of checking my family's files, I did what I was told by Tommy, who mostly wanted times and places of raids and any military information I dug up. This time my curiosity got the better of me. The first name I looked up was Amelia. Her file was easy to find, and it was clean, with the exception of her not getting the Beastmark yet, but that was good for her and me. Everything she said about her past was correct, with enough exceptions to be believable. A perfect rendition would've ended our relationship. I thanked God for her.

Then I researched the new president. I never thought I had the clearance to get close to his file, but the software on the flash drive was able to get through the firewalls and other high tech safety measures. The new president's mug appeared on the monitor. As I perused through the file, I noticed a side note. It was a video file that was named, *The Goods*.

It was a video of the Oval Office. The placement of the camera was on the painting above the fireplace mantle. The new president walked in, but he was the vice president at the time. President Mason used the Resolute desk that was in the office in the video, but the new president moved it out and put in the Johnson desk. He walked behind the desk and sat down. It didn't bother me because I'd even sat in

Frank's chair once when I was in the academy. What the vice president did in the chair really bothered me.

He used the President's phone and made a call.

"I need to put an order in." He gave a code. "Yes, I'd like the Johnson desk taken out of storage and cleaned. Yes, it will be brought to the Oval Office in a couple of weeks. I'll let you know the exact date when I have it. Yes, she's aware. She asked if I would make the order. Thank you."

My mind started going into overdrive trying to figure out why this was important. It was plain enough that he was anticipating her death. Then it hit me. He said in a couple of weeks. Not days. This was planned out longer than I anticipated. It also proved that he was in on it. It made sense for the Antichrist to attach this to his file. If he started giving the Antichrist any problems, demanding more power, wanting more money, etc., he would become an instant Public Enemy No. 1 with this video. My case files on President Mason's murder would be brought to light and matching it to the video would be adding one plus one to the ignorant masses, who would eat it up and call for his impeachment, and the blade. It had to be Plan B, if this case fell through, because the new president was from New York. St. Louis wouldn't have made sense.

After copying the video, I typed in President Mason's name. I anticipated a file similar to the new president.

Her death certificate was already on file. I looked at the date it was entered and almost screamed. It was input two days after the announcement of her disappearance. The Antichrist didn't even wait until the conspiracy was completed. His arrogance knew no bounds.

Frustrated, I looked up the superintendent. Joy's grinning orange face gave me the creeps. Her eyes were dead, like a shark. Her pupils were dilated to the point of hiding each iris. I shivered and clicked on it hoping to add her to the conspiracy, if only as a minor accomplice.

Although the thought just crossed my mind, I knew the chances were slim to none. Her inexperience in the field made her an easy scratch from the suspect list. She just didn't have it in her. Plus, she was a cop, and I had a difficult time thinking a cop would be involved.

The meat of her file was opening when Joy entered the room staring at the screen of her phone without knocking.

"Can I help you, ma'am?" I wanted to say more but thought better of it.

She looked up as if she was lost. "Will, are you on your computer?" She went back to her screen.

I hit the escape and F1 buttons. Her file disappeared when the flash drive disconnected. The case file was the only thing on the screen. "Just looking at the case file. CSU and ME posted their results. I wanted to start putting everything together, hoping to close in on the identity of the victim."

She frowned harder. "No, that's not it. It says here that a HQ computer is being used to maneuver into ICON's global database." She tapped the screen.

"Not from this computer, ma'am. I don't have the clearance to go into that database without supervisor permission." I reached for the thumb drive from the CPU tower but pulled back my hand when she looked up.

"I know. It's weird. This app they installed tells me everything going on with all the computers in my headquarters. The problem is that the computer showing this hit isn't in our cadre, but it is resonating from this general vicinity." She looked over my monitor. "What's that thumb drive?"

"Downloading the case file, so I can look at it anytime I want. By the way, will I be getting a laptop? I forgot to ask for one the other day. But now that I have something to read, it'd be nice to have one." I gave an internal inhale hoping she didn't know about my K.C. laptop.

She pointed at the thumb drive. "Is that standard issue

from here? Have you had IT format it?" She wasn't buying it.

I thought quick. "It's one from K.C. HQ. Won't it work on these computers?" My heart rate went up a tick or three. Tommy trained me to kill in a situation like this and get out as fast as possible. I unsnapped my jacket acting like I was getting warm to have access to my SIG.

She frowned some more. "Detective Thomas, according to Peace Forces protocols, you cannot bring in outside tech from anywhere, up to, and including any other Peace Forces headquarters. Now give me that thumb drive." She struck her tiny hand out.

"If it's all the same, ma'am, can I take it to IT myself and have them format it? All I have on this is the case file. If I lose it during formatting, I can redownload it later. And my captain in K.C. will have my head if I lose another one." I went to pull it out when Frank walked in.

"Superintendent Everhart, we need to discuss your press release." His face was red, and his voice was demanding. He almost hit Joy with the door, but I couldn't tell if he meant to or not.

She gave a tiny squeal when she side stepped the door. "Watch where you're going you overgrown buffoon." She collected herself and pocketed her phone. "Captain Malone, you have no authority to demand anything of me. What I gave to the media was carefully considered and revised in a way that is both informative and professional."

"But you blamed the Christian rebels. According to Peace Forces intel, they weren't even in the city. This was clearly an ambush by the outliers on the Survivors Crew. We joined in to finish them both off." Frank's redness deepened.

"Captain Malone, there were some indications that the Christian rebels were among the outliers." It's a good thing she was a cop, otherwise Frank would've slapped cuffs on her because her lie couldn't have fooled a toddler.

"I went through all the evidence myself. There was nothing indicating the Christians were in this at all." Frank was insubordinate, but my fear was that he was looking like a Resistance spy.

"If I didn't know any better, Captain Malone, you sound like you're one of them." She put her hands on her hips. For once, she impressed me. She could hit a bull in the butt with a banjo. As my grandpa used to say.

Frank took a deep breath and blew it out slowly. "Joy, one of the reasons this city is enjoying a little peace, up until the ambush, is that we are not being constantly hounded by the rebels because we don't try to implicate them in anything that doesn't involve them. Do you want St. Louis to be the next Syracuse?"

The northeast Resistance had a large militia force in Buffalo. The Peace Forces had entered Syracuse in order to start pinning them in between the city and the falls. The Resistance got wind of it, through someone like me, and attacked from the south when the Peace Forces were expecting a head-on attack from the west. It was the largest Christian Resistance victory to date.

"We can easily handle anything those ignorant rebels can throw at us. And besides, Syracuse was a fluke. The ignorant military general has been dealt with. And follow decorum," she shouted.

Her loyalty was as high as her shrill voice.

"I just don't want to poke the bear, Superintendent Everhart. We have no idea how many rebels are in the area, let alone if they're armed or not." I was impressed by the way Frank improvised.

"The Peace Forces commander of the Missouri Marines knows, and he complimented me on the speech and press release."

She sounded like the class brown noser. Frank looked at her like he would like to smack her across the room. It was quite obvious how wide their differences were. My pity ran deeper with every confrontation they had in my short time in St. Louis.

Frank shook his head. "That man is a warmonger."

"I will tell him what you said. You'll be lucky if he doesn't slam the blade through your thick neck himself."

"Aw, come on. You know we hate it when Mom and Dad fight." I nervously giggled, hoping to de-escalate.

Boy was I wrong. They turned their heads at the same time, fast enough to do neck damage. I'd have rather them yell at me than the daggers that were flying from their sockets.

"Don't you have a case to investigate Detective Thomas?" Her scream was unwavering, which made me nervous. Had she started taking command of her shrillness? If so, I needed to be extra careful.

I nodded, feeling my eyes bulging.

"Then get to it. I'm not paying for your insolence." She stormed out of the room.

"She might be right." Frank rubbed his throat while he plopped down in the chair across the desk from me. "I wasn't made for this crap."

"Easy, sir. Don't let her get to you." I used my calmest tone.

He rubbed his face with both hands. "We need to talk. You up for a round of golf?"

I looked at my phone. "Sorry, Frank. I got a lead that requires a stakeout. I need to go if I'm going to get there early enough to set up my position."

"Who are you staking out?"

"I'm not sure. My informant told me two people have been meeting in the cemetery the last two days at fifteen hundred." I whispered, not sure if my office was bugged. "Since I don't really have any other leads, I thought it couldn't hurt. But I do need to talk to you about something. How about tomorrow morning?"

He nodded his head. "All right. Do you need backup for

this?"

"No, I doubt it's anything but a drug deal. I'll bust them and make you look good." I smiled.

He returned the smile. "I definitely need it." The redness left his face. "And by the way, if you refer to me in that way again, I'll show you the moves I didn't teach you at the academy."

I got up, saluted, and walked to the door. "Lock up when you're through."

He grinned. "Smart aleck."

CHAPTER 27

The cemetery was like a horror flick when added to the angry skyline and the red, dead air. Just stepping through the entrance gave me the willies. What didn't help was seeing the punctured gravesites of the believers who'd been raptured. I half expected some monster or zombie to jump out and start attacking. That just added to the dread I felt. Plus, the fact that there wasn't even a breeze blowing increased the creepiness factor higher than I'd ever experienced and gave my stomach fits.

Clay had told me to find the headstone that was tall and pointed to the sky in the middle of the cemetery. It was all he could remember, so I eased my way through the large graveyard, trying not to stumble on anybody mourning, grave holes, or any two people meeting for nefarious reasons.

Of all the landmarks I passed, none of them matched Clay's description. I checked my phone. Fourteen fifty-eight. I was afraid I might've missed it already.

After deciding to give it another twenty or so minutes, I spotted a grave marker that was in the shape of an obelisk that was close to the center of the cemetery pointing to the sky. I made my way around it to see if anyone was close. Sure enough, two people, one much taller than the other, were having a discussion near a tree close to the grave. Although sound doesn't carry very well without wind, I still lightened my footsteps to move around the scene and get as close to the two as I dared. The short one wore a dark gray hoodie and was similar in height to the senator. The tall one, about Tommy's height, wore an olive-green hooded coat. Both hoods covered their faces. With the light as bad as it was, I couldn't even make out if they were male or female.

When I got as close as I was comfortable with, about ten yards, I hid behind a thick trunked tree. The words were garbled to the point I couldn't even guess what was being said. Mourning the loss of sound carrying wind, I waited for a while. The decision to follow the one that came close to me when the meeting concluded was my only choice. I'd have to get the other one later. Maybe the first one would give him to us during questioning.

A couple of minutes later a bluebird called from the tree behind me, the tall one looked in my direction and bolted away from me without saying a word to his partner.

The shorter one looked around in confusion and began running in my direction.

He didn't come straight at me, so I waited until he got close enough. Then I darted at him.

When he saw me, he squealed. It was high pitched, like a woman, but I wasn't going to assume anything. I've met my fair share of squeaky male screams.

The chase was longer than I estimated. His short legs were humming as he navigated the headstones of varying size and height, trees, and bushes. I wasn't gaining much ground. I was faster in straightaways, but he took corners better.

He was going in the direction of Calvary Cemetery, just across Calvary Avenue from Bellefontaine. I was in good shape, but not great shape for this sprint. My hope was that he was the same. My heart was beating against my ribcage when we crossed Calvary Avenue. I tried to tell him I was a cop, but true to form, it seemed to make him go faster.

Wondering why the senator didn't recognize my voice, I began thinking he was part of the conspiracy to assassinate President Mason. The doe-eyed man in the dugout was an act. My anger rose in my gut as the foolishness rose in me.

He stumbled across the sidewalk, giving me enough time to close the distance then tackle him down near the main entrance. The high-pitched scream as we fell to the ground sounded familiar.

I wrestled him over and pulled the hood away from *her* face.

"Chief of Staff Brown, so good to run into you." I rolled off her onto the ground.

"Why are you chasing me, Detective Thomas?" She straightened her hoodie and sat up.

She was panting so hard it was difficult for her to speak.

"Why are you running from me, Kennedy?" I barely got out between large draughts of stale air.

"I didn't know who you were when we started. All I saw was this overgrown man chasing me."

She smoothed her jeans and took a final deep breath that transferred to a normal breathing pattern.

"I shouted 'police' twice," I said, still panting.

"Like I would believe anyone using that old word." She got up and crossed her arms. "Try Peace Forces, and I'll stop next time."

"Next time?" I stood.

"That's not what I meant." She huffed.

"Let's forget about the chase. Who were you talking to?"

"It's none of your business. Free country. It's my right." She sounded more like a high schooler than a college educated Chief of Staff of a federal politician.

"To dress up like spies and have clandestine meetings in the oldest cemetery in the state?" My heart had slowed to a more manageable speed while my breathing returned to normal. I made a quick mental note to get back to my cardio.

"If that's what we want to do, you have no say."

She shifted to one foot while tapping her other, still maintaining a childish disposition.

"When me we met earlier today, you took me to the senator. Now you're meeting this guy. Another cop investigating a case the senator is interested in?"

She looked around to see if anyone was listening, then motioned me to follow her with a sideways nod and started walking into the new cemetery. After we walked about a hundred yards, she stopped.

"So?" My patience was losing its grip on me. That's when I decided this must be what raising a teenager feels like, although I'd never experience it due to time constraints.

She looked down at her black and white running shoes. "He's involved in the assassination of former President Mason."

I took a double take. "What?"

She shifted from one foot to the other. "He's involved in the president's murder."

"Is he the assassin?" Two questions came to mind. Why was he still in the city? Why didn't he stage the crime scene himself?

"I can't confirm or deny the accusation."

Her facial markers lit up like a Christmas display. Although she sounded like a politician, she'd never make it through the primaries without working on her lying technique.

"And how are you involved in this?"

"You're a Peace Forces Detective. It's your duty to fight crime and keep the city safe. Right?"

The sound of conviction entered her voice. Second Thessalonians 2:11 came to life in front of me. She was definitely falling for the delusion. God was allowing her to believe the Sovereign's lies.

"Right." It bothered me that she told me my job. But I let her have the floor in order to get to the point.

"It's also my duty, as Senator Jon Staeger's Chief of Staff, to protect the country if I believe he's doing wrong."

She had my full attention. I nodded for her to go on.

"The senator is against the U.S. from getting soaked into the global government." She pulled the hood off her head and sighed. "He's old school. I get that, but look around. This country's going straight to hell."

She swung her open hand around for effect and exasperation while mussing her stringy brown hair.

She was right for all the wrong reasons.

"Okay, but what does he have to do with the assassination."

"Nothing. But he's about to be the pawn in the greatest overthrow of a government in history."

"Why?"

"Our new president will not be answering any of his questions anymore. In the last Foreign Relations committee meeting, which he weaseled his way into chairing, Jon demanded that the new president be subpoenaed to answer questions about signing the ratification of the Mid-East Accord as acting president."

"From what I understand, he had no authority, and President Mason refused to sign it."

"But she wasn't doing it for the betterment of the nation. She did it because she wanted to protect Israel, even though they were already protected under the Mid-East Accord. She put them ahead of us. And so is Senator Staeger, now that she's gone."

I took it all in. The question that was nagging at me started coming into focus.

"You're obviously not the mastermind, just a pawn. Where do your orders come from?" A line of conspiracy formed in my mind even while I asked the question.

She smirked like she was the only one who knew the answers to the test.

"Of course, you know I can't divulge..."

A loud pop like a large firecracker went off. Kennedy dropped to the ground as I turned. Reaching for my gun, I saw the taillights of a car speeding off. A new electric model that I could barely hear even without wind interference. I ran a few steps trying to get a shot off, a plate number, anything. But the car tires squealed as it took the corner and disappeared from sight.

I returned and looked at Kennedy's dead face. There was a small bullet hole above her right eye. Her eyes went from bright to dull brown the instant her blood flow stopped. Even though I knew it, I checked for a pulse as I phoned in the murder.

CHAPTER 28

It took a couple hours to finish up the paperwork, talk to Frank about what had happened, and collect my wits. The hard part was not giving the full account of the incident. There were only two witnesses to the shooting, and they were across the street in Bellefontaine, out of earshot. They could only describe the car, which was better than mine because they were closer in the dim light, but not the shooter claiming he had already slipped into the driver's seat. He was alone. Probably used the door as a gun rest.

Frank's workload increased significantly because Joy sent him a mountain of paperwork that wasn't his responsibility. The little orange insect gave him Evans' case files to digitize because Joy said that Evans was more effective in the field than behind the desk. It was an obvious retaliation for their argument in my office.

It was late, my nerves were shot, and my stomach filed its grievances in triplicate. Instead of finding a nice restaurant and treating myself to a proper meal, I chose to go to the riverside and food truck it out.

My bad luck held out as I entered the food truck patio, and the only choice was the chili dog truck. Before getting out of the beater, I popped an antacid and said a quick prayer of thanks for having something to eat—and for protection from the food. I dreaded the chili flavored mystery meat on something resembling a bun, but at least the onions were the reconstituted kind from before the Rapture.

"Sorry honey, we're fresh out of chili," the lady said.

After giving God a mental knuckle bump and spiritual thanks, I ordered two dogs with the works and a sweet tea.

While I waited for my food, I wondered what new scent had crept into my hotel room while I was gone. I didn't want to endure any more mystery scents that would add to my near future indigestion I was expecting from the chili dogs, so I chose to lean on the beater in the angry red darkness, staring at a reddening river I barely heard.

It was the first time since the shooting that I was able to process watching someone die from a GSW. The way her body went limp and collapsed. Her head slightly lurched back, but the small caliber bullet wasn't strong enough to make her fall that direction. She simply fell straight down and folded in on herself like a crumpled towel on the bathroom floor.

The hardest part of the memory was knowing where she was now. The weight of the Resistance felt heavier than ever. Watching her just before entering the gates of Hell, I wondered if there was a chance the northeast Resistance or a Jewish preacher had the opportunity to talk to her before taking the Beastmark.

"Your order's up, sweetie." The lady walked up to me and handed me the container. "I threw my last brownie in there. Hope you like it."

"Thanks," I said with no life in it, and a half-hearted smile. I walked over to a nearby table, sat down, and began forcing the food down my throat.

After a couple of bites, my brain began to focus on the case. The feel of conspiracy made me believe I was on the wrong track, like I was reading a movie script. But the reality of it was that the Bible told of a world leader willing to do anything to get and keep his power. Wishing I had Dad's journal, I tried to remember what he wrote concerning the Antichrist's power grab at the beginning of the Trib.

He was the White Horseman of the very first judgment. A world leader given a bow with no arrows. He used diplomacy to take over countries. His words were everything everyone wanted to believe. That humanity was on the cusp of greatness. That poverty and wars were near their end. That everyone belonged. And all they had to do was sign on the dotted line.

And they did.

Except President Mason.

Senator Staeger said she wasn't fooled by the Sovereign's promises after her dismissal from the Oval Office. He expected her to acquiesce like all the other world leaders. It wasn't just arrogance. The Antichrist believed it was his birthright. He even mentioned in a speech that it was his calling from the womb that the Possible Divine made him to heal the lands and peoples across the planet.

The scene around me made me chuckle. God was proving that the Antichrist had no say in the healing of the world. Not when God's fury was pouring out on a consistent basis and the Sovereign was powerless to stop them. But the Loyalists took the Beastmark willingly.

After taking another bite of the barely edible hot dog, which was better without the chili, I thought of the list of players I had so far, knowing that it wasn't a complete list. The victim was former President Mason. The assassin, yet to be identified, was still in the city. Senator Jon Staeger was also present but not accounted for because I didn't know his place in the assassination. Chief of Staff Kennedy Brown, deceased, was part of it by her own admission and taking orders from an unidentified source. Hector was told to stage the secondary crime scene, and used one of his people, the guy on the street cams, to do the work.

The line of conspiracy, as I thought it was, began with an unknown power broker ordering Kennedy to get the assassin to make the hit. She also set up the staging through Hector's community. The assassin killed the president, bladed and cleaned her, brought her to the city, handed her head off to Hector's man, who staged the scene. The power broker had Kennedy killed by the assassin to clean the network.

But where did the senator fit in all this?

Was he the power broker?

The more I thought about it, the less it made sense. Senator Staeger saw everything unfolding in the world. It would've been best to stay behind the scenes and let it all unfold.

I took the final bite of the second dog, and it hit me. That is exactly what he did. He was now trying to take the baton and finish what the president started. But to what end? Was he making a power grab for the Antichrist's position? Was he the real Antichrist who was letting someone else do the dirty work? He said he was running for president. It would be easy from that position to take out the Sovereign through the assassination and take over the world government while bringing the U.S. into the fold since he was the president.

I needed to talk to Frank as soon as I walked into HQ in the morning.

Good thing the antacid was fast acting and super strong because the food was trying to drill a hole to my spleen even without the chili. I wanted to get some rest. Tomorrow was promising to be the most challenging since I entered the city.

When I tossed my container and cup into a trash receptacle, the sound of conversation turned my attention back to the river. A couple in hazmat suits were walking the river using high powered spotlights to search the shore and water. The two stopped. One produced a telescopic pole with a hook that gleamed in the spotlight on one end and started fishing.

"What's the trouble folks?" I asked while I walked closer to them.

"Corpse Patrol. Just found one. You might want to get back," the one without the pole said when he flashed a badge attached to his suit.

I pulled out my badge. "Homicide." They stood straighter. "By all means keep up the good work." Everyone needed to be put to rest.

They slumped a little and finished dragging the dead body out of the river by a bra strap. It was a bloated mess.

"She's been in there a while." He groaned. "Don't want to puncture her."

The one with the hook was extra careful, and I hoped he was since I wanted to see the body in one piece. That and I didn't want my dinner coming out.

"Please don't," the other one said, "I've had more than my fair share of stink this week."

Nodding in agreement, I felt better about my apartment.

"Do you need me to check her out?" I walked closer.

One pulled out a scanner. "No need."

He scanned the usual locations, right hand and forehead. However, when it didn't ding, he began scanning the whole body.

"Why's he doing that? Did I miss the memo that people can take the Loyalist chip anywhere on their person?"

"No, it's still in the regulations. But a chip in a body that's as bloated as this one can move around. Had a Medical Examiner at the crematorium find one in a man's pinky toe once. He turned out to be a state senator from Iowa. Boy, did we have egg on our faces. Since then, we've been ordered to scan the whole body."

"Need me to make sure she wasn't murdered?" I didn't want to, but that was part of the job.

"Thanks, but you don't have to. The docs at the death center will call if they think anything's fishy."

He giggled at his own terrible joke.

His friend with the hook finished bringing her to the shore. The other one got on his radio and ordered a gurney and bag.

"Very well then. Have a good night." I turned and left.

They waved and returned to their work.

I walked towards the beater thinking of God's judgment. It hurt to think that people had sunk so low as to believe a night of fishing corpses out of the river was as normal as strolling with a beautiful woman. This world began working on me again.

CHAPTER 29

After trying to get the sight of the bloated corpse out of my mind, I returned to the beater, leaned on the hood, and tried to return to my conspiracy theory. I kept it that way in my mind to avoid tunnel vision in the case that makes even the most seasoned veterans chase rabbits down holes that led to cold case land. The sound of crunching gravel interrupted my train of thought.

"Detective Thomas. I thought you'd be here." Joy's voice grated inside my ears. "Helping Corpse Patrol now? You are a man of many talents."

It was her way of a compliment, but it fell flat.

"Superintendent Everhart. What brings you to the riverside? Slumming?" I had enough of being compliant. "I thought you'd be across town celebrating your press conference with your minions." I didn't come to attention. I just kept leaning and enduring the objectionable entity that entered my orbit. White knuckling it for Frank.

She tried to act like it didn't bother her, but she went a bright shade of red orange. It could've been the cheap light that hung over the distant picnic table area, but I doubted it.

"I will let that go without reprimand, but you do need to watch your tone in front of a superior."

She tried to sound magnanimous like she was doing me

a favor that would need to be repaid with the answer she was expecting.

My gut reaction, hot dogs notwithstanding, was to question her superiority. But something inside reminded me of Frank. His neck was as much on the line as mine. I took a long deep breath before I spoke.

"Sorry, ma'am. Getting shot at earlier and seeing a bloated corpse just now has made me a little on edge." It hurt to say, but I knew it was best. A typical lie. A kernel of truth wrapped in deception.

"That's a boy." Her beautiful smile needed to be shoved to the back of her throat. "You are correct. I am due to be at a dinner with the mayor. He is proud of how we accomplished the victory."

"Victory? The last I heard the body count was over a hundred." My anger became harder to harness.

"It could've been a lot worse." That was a load of crap, but I let her have it. "The casualties were minimal compared to what it could've been." She hopped up on the hood of the beater like she was mingling at a Saturday night party in the country. But there was no make out session happening at the food truck patio.

"Well, the numbers don't lie." But I knew numbers can, and were, manipulated to say whatever the manipulator wanted them to say. The Antichrist was a master.

"True. Can't get around that. It's nice when they actually work in our favor." She paused. "Well, that's enough shop talk. Let's get down to the matter at hand."

"What matter?" I mumbled out of resentment.

"Please, show some manners." She glared in a way that was almost cute. Maybe she wasn't a total loss.

"Sorry, again, Ma'am."

"Long hours were never what we anticipated when we signed up, huh?"

She was trying to relate, but I knew her route to where she was didn't include long hours of work, just kissing up and threatening her way there.

"True, but at least the pay stinks." I smiled at the old cop joke.

She laughed. It was actually quite lovely. Not a cackle, or hyena call, but a nice throaty chuckle. If it wasn't for that attitude, ambition, and bad spray tan, she would be pleasant company. Even datable. She turned to see if anyone was watching and then back to me.

"Senator Staeger is in town. I thought you should know because he wasn't scheduled to be here and is probably going to reach out to you about your investigation."

"Why would he be interested in my case? Does he know the victim?" I attempted to look surprised while trying to figure out where she got the information.

"Not to my knowledge, but it's not unheard of for a politician to be involved in a case or two. To show that he is connected to his constituents. I guess he's going to pick this one."

If she knew what I knew, Joy would've run to whoever she deemed high enough to make sure of her next promotion.

"I hope he doesn't." She looked surprised.

"If it were me, I would jump at the chance to have a senator on my side."

Trying not to show my real revulsion of her grandstanding, I said, "As slow as this is progressing, I don't want an antsy politician making decisions that might jeopardize my investigation. They have been known to do that on occasion."

"You do have a point, but they could also help if tough decisions need to be made."

She did have a valid point. Her wisdom finally came out. If it wasn't for the stupid things she did, she might've made a decent cop, but ambition has been known to cover a multitude of unrefined talent.

"True. You could be right." I sat up a little straighter. "I might take the senator's help. If he offers it."

The thought of trusting a man that I couldn't decide which side of the conspiracy he fit on didn't make me feel confident in what I said. Especially after his closest advisor, a woman who confessed to being a pawn in the assassination, died right in front of me.

The moment passed, and her expression changed.

"Will, you told me you would give me an answer today."

I sighed. It was time to choose the side I'd always been on. But I needed to know where she fit in the grand scheme of things as it pertained to my job.

"To be honest, I'm still confused. Why do you want me? I'll be going back to K.C. when this investigation's over. At best, my help would be minimal." I took a deep breath to avoid finishing off with an insult.

"Assignments can change, Detective Thomas. It wouldn't be difficult to have you reassigned to St. Louis. In fact, one call, and it's done."

She tapped her phone with a long, manicured fingernail.

Some acid came back up my esophagus and soured in my mouth and not just from my supper. Someone as egotistical and ambitious as Joy shouldn't have had that kind of power. I almost said yes to see if I was able to derail her plans, but I knew she wasn't my boss. God was. And He didn't give me the go ahead with an inner feeling. In fact, the red flags were full staff.

"Sorry, Superintendent. I've grown roots in K.C. I love it there. St. Louis is nice, but the Cards are gone, and I'm not ready to relocate just yet." I wiped my mouth from the feeling of ketchup hanging around its corner. "As for Captain Malone, I was never joining you against him. He's a good man and a great cop. He does have his temper, but that just shows his passion for duty. Sorry Joy, count me out."

The redness overcame the orange. "Fine detective, but

let's make this perfectly clear. There's coming a day when everything will change. Old cops, like Captain Frank Malone, will be eliminated. The Peace Forces have no room for his kind. If you place your loyalty to that dying breed, you will join them." She slid off the hood, then stepped away from the car. "I will make sure of that." With that, she stormed off. It was almost adorable, like a toddler getting mad that the ice cream truck didn't have her favorite treat.

I watched her get into her luxury electric car, paid for by the city no doubt. My gut was protesting the way I was treating it with the stress and food choice. I looked at the sky. The redness had increased and almost overtaken the black. The churning remained at full force. It felt like the judgment was close to breaking, unlike my case. Although there were a few answers, all they did was add to the list of questions.

The food truck had left, and the lights were off. I bowed my head and asked God for help. Either put off the judgment for a while or help me get this case solved before it begins.

CHAPTER 30

The next morning was as dark as the night before, except the sky was even more violent. Although I had the feeling of dread deep inside, I also felt like the case was almost over but no idea how it would end. Maybe my instincts were catching up to my training. After a quick shower and shave, I got a text from Frank to meet him at the golf course in twenty.

Frank was sitting at the table when I walked in. He looked demoralized.

"Hey, Frank. How's it going?" I sat on the bench across from him.

"The Survivors Crew and their offshoot are completely gone." With his elbows on the table, he wrung his hands as if he had arthritis. The pain didn't come from a remorseful cop, but from a Christian understanding that Hell had new occupants. I could relate.

"I figured as much. Hector seemed sure he was keeping the top spot in the city."

"His number two, a guy by the name of Tony the Fish, was reported to be telling some of his guys that the Spirits were all but brought into the fold." He looked up. "If that's the case, the only mob left is the second outlier group. And they won't last the week."

The thought of a single mob in the city was both troubling and interesting. The cops wouldn't have to try and figure out who to blame when any crimes came about, but the Free Agents' power would be almost unbreakable, considering their political backing.

"Not to change the subject on you, Frank, but the man who ordered the investigation is in town."

"Jon is in St. Louis?"

"You're on a first name basis with the good senator?"

"We go way back. When he was on city council here, I was a sergeant downtown. We met on a not-so-great night in his life." Frank grinned. "A patrolman brought him in on suspicion of a DUI. I grabbed him from the rookie, took Jon into the bullpen, and did a quick sobriety check."

"Did he fail?"

"He admitted to having a couple glasses of wine at a restaurant, but not enough to restrict his ability to drive. I let him off with a warning. It's what the rookie should've done." He paused and looked at me. "I was his go-to guy after that. But not for anything dirty. Just the odd parking or speeding ticket."

"Did he do anything for you?" I wasn't sure if I was repulsed or proud of my captain. Maybe I should've asked for more of the senator's help.

"He put in a good word for me to get the academy job."

"I won't tell Joy then." I laughed, and so did he. The tension was still there, but at least his spirit seemed to lift a little bit.

"So, what did Jon want?"

"To tell me that the Antichrist ordered the hit on President Mason and helped the vice president get sworn in."

"That figures. The new president is a pushover. He'll hand over this country without a second thought."

"With the loyalist chip in place, the Global Church putting their unholy temples everywhere, and the Peace

Forces in power, the only thing left is the paperwork." It hurt to say. Dad was wrong with his T.S. Eliot theory. America wasn't ending with a whimper. It was ending with a prostrate and a signature. A single signature from an overly ambitious hand that desired crumbs.

"I bet he wants to be king."

Frank gave me a confused look.

"Read your Bible. At the halfway point of the Trib, the Antichrist will assign ten kings. They won't have kingdoms, but they will have power."

Frank nodded.

"Yeah, I considered that after the inauguration."

A long, quiet moment passed between us as we contemplated the importance of the case. I felt helpless thinking President Mason's murder might go unnoticed. Then I remembered that you may not get everyone involved in a conspiracy, but you can get at least one of the participants. And who knows how the falling dominoes will place themselves afterwards? The rats will abandon the ship running over each other in the process.

"Since the Antichrist can't be stopped by us, I want to get the killer. The assassin."

"Do you think the assassin is still in town?"

A little life entered Frank's voice.

"I'm willing to wager a month's salary."

"Why's that?"

"The other thing I wanted to talk to you about."

"I forgot about that," Frank said, scratching his scruffy chin.

"You had your hands full with the shootout."

"Right." He moved his hand from his chin to rub the back of his head like he was trying to remove a bad memory.

"Senator Staeger's Chief of Staff, Kennedy Brown, was killed yesterday. She was at that meeting I staked out. I might've been the target, but I may be wrong."

Frank's eyes widened. He didn't know, so I filled him in. Except for the part that it was the same killer, I was still working on my theory of whether or not Senator Staeger and Frank should know all the details.

"If it wasn't you, then why her?"

"She was in Philly with the senator."

"She could be the organizer."

It seemed like Frank's brain went into overdrive with possible scenarios. It was impressive to watch my mentor at work.

"That's what I'm thinking. And so was Hector." I pointed at Frank.

"How was Hector involved?"

"Hector admitted to me that he was ordered to dump the head when it was delivered. So, he wasn't in charge of organizing the hit, but he organized the staging, maybe even the transport."

Frank sorted this new information while he listened to me.

"But he tried to lead me to believe that a politician ordered the hit."

"Do you believe him?"

"He is a liar. His chosen career demands it. So, I think it's a mislead."

"Who then?" Frank sighed.

"Senator Staeger?"

"Seriously? I know his ambitions are high…"

Frank wasn't buying it. Joy was right. Frank was old school. He'd blindly back Jon even though he'd never reciprocate.

"That makes him all the more dangerous. Think about it. If you are the Antichrist, who better to have this end of the hit done than a politician who is so blinded by ambition that he is willing to do absolutely anything to get in good with the top man? Plus, he has the authority to pull it off."

"No." Frank stood, shaking his head. He walked a circle

around the table. "Not Jon. I mean come on. He's been against the U.S. joining the global government from the beginning. And I've known the man for over two decades. He's as straight as they come." He sat back down still shaking his head.

I told him my conspiracy theory of Jon taking over the global government but left out the possibility that he's the real Antichrist. Frank could never handle that theory.

"You have a point, Will. But that's a lot to prove. With Kennedy dead, who can corroborate anything we accuse the senator of doing?"

"The assassin."

"But the assassination was somewhere else. Remember the CSU report. I'm guessing the Philadelphia area. The assassin probably dropped off the head and could be anywhere on the planet by now."

"The assassin's in town. Kennedy was shot under the eye with a small caliber bullet, just like the president. I couldn't see him because of the darkness, but I'm sure he's the assassin. We catch him, maybe we can cut him a deal and get whoever organized that side of the hit."

"Maybe so, but I think it's the Antichrist who ordered the hit. I gotta believe Jon is on the level."

Frank's body language cried despair, and I truly felt sorry for him.

I began believing Frank. Even though they had known each other a long time, it wasn't the type of relationship that was close enough to blind him.

"Let's say he ordered it. But he'd have someone in the U.S. doing the rest. I'm guessing a politician." My mind was spinning with the possibilities. "Maybe he had Kennedy organize it to keep himself with plausible deniability. But we need to find out where Jon was when it happened. And if he didn't do it, he should have a guess or two as to who did."

"He'll leave the city when he hears about Kennedy."

"We need to find him. He'll either need protection or be arrested."

"Jon is trying to expose the Antichrist and get rid of the new president."

Frank was desperately pleading. He was going against the cardinal rule of investigation. Check your biases at the door or you might miss the criminal. He all but beat that into his cadets at the academy. But when your world is literally and figuratively falling apart, anyone can become desperate and forget themselves.

"That's what he told me, but we can't take his word for it. As far as I'm concerned, he's still a suspect like the rest of the politicians." Even though I trusted Frank, I had to keep my wits about me.

"Until then, you have to keep this under your hat. If Hector is right, and it is a politician, we might be handing this case over to the military Peace Forces. And we can't do that, or it's guaranteed to be swept under the rug."

I ignored the hypocrisy because he had a point. I needed to keep calm. Cop training. Never allow your opinions or emotions guide your investigation. Pay attention to the evidence. That was one of Frank's big rules even if he was borderline breaking that rule.

Frank stood and stretched. "Let's get back to headquarters. I'm friendly with Joy's assistant. I might be able to sweet talk her into looking at Joy's phone records."

"Is she reliable?"

"She can't stand her boss. Joy treats her like a servant." Frank winked. "She'll talk."

There was more than sweet talk in his voice.

"Sounds like a plan, boss."

CHAPTER 31

We entered the building and were immediately met by Joy's assistant. A lady who adored desserts too much, with hair that was not its right color. I didn't even know the name of the color. She wasn't anything like Clara, Frank's first wife, but loneliness can be a driving force, plus she wasn't chipped that I could tell.

"Superintendent wants to see you in her office." She grimaced instead of smiled.

"I'll be there in a second, Marjorie." Frank winked.

"Both of you." She used two fingers to point at us when she winked back.

"Of course, my dear." He grinned.

She grinned and shimmied off.

"What's that all about?" I winked and gave him a knowing grin that riled him.

"I pay you to solve murders, not meddle in my private life." He punched my shoulder harder than I wanted, and not as much as he wanted by the look in his eyes.

"Great, what does she want now?" he asked as he walked to the elevators.

"Probably wants to rub her success in our faces." I doubted it. She saved that for the people she deemed important, and we both completely missed the mark.

The doors closed and the elevator took us to the top.

Since Marjorie hadn't made it to the office yet, Frank knocked on the door and Joy told us to enter.

Knowing this was an attempt to curry favor with her superiors, Joy had decorated the entire office in a European motif. It was stunning. Each piece of furniture was brought from select countries that accentuated each other. Mostly contemporary, the seats and sofa were brown leather that sat comfortably. And filing cabinets that opened at odd angles were black metal polished to a high shine. All of it was quite spartan except for the desk.

A woman I didn't know stood beside Joy's chair. Tall, maybe five-ten, not pretty but not ugly. Utilitarian. Dark, straight hair brought up in a sensible ponytail. She had a smugness about her I didn't care for.

Frank nodded to her, but she didn't reciprocate. Must've been someone from another department.

"Captain Malone, Detective Thomas. Have a seat."

Joy was reading something on her phone and eating an apple. The other woman stood in silence. Joy made us wait far too long. She didn't type anything into her phone, making me think she was doing another one of her petty power trip moves. What little respect I had for her disappeared. Anyone with those kinds of attributes didn't deserve to be put in charge of a preschool class let alone public servants putting their lives on the line every day.

"I was wondering where we are on the case." She put the phone down on the oversized mahogany desk that made her look like a child sitting at daddy's desk.

"We have a couple of leads to follow up on, but it's progressing," Frank said.

"From what I hear, you got less than squat." She took a bite and slowly chewed, then swallowed. "Maybe it's time to reevaluate and reinvest our time on other cases."

"What are you talking about? I was brought here to investigate this case. It's the only one I got." I sat up. "Are you sending me back to K.C.?"

"No," she said, with an immature giggle. "I was talking to Captain Malone. I have other plans for you. Now, why don't we put this case on the backburner while the shooting incident you were involved in earlier cools down? The media is having a field day with this."

"Why are they even interested in that? Will had nothing to do with her death. In fact, I believe he was the intended target."

Frank's temper was rising, and I wasn't far behind him.

"Well, I couldn't say that to the media. I would've sounded like a conspiracy nut bag. We all know the citizens of this fine city have no love for the Peace Forces. They are talking about Will killing the woman while he tried to get information out of her. He's lucky he's not suspended." She looked at me with disdain. "Or worse."

"We know the truth, Superintendent Everhart. Will was staking out a possible suspect, and things went sideways. It happens all the time."

Frank sounded like he was pleading. It put me in an inner rage. This little troglodyte was making a good man, and a good cop, feel like he was about to get on his knees and beg. It was all I could do to not put a bullet above her right eye. Maybe the killer felt the same way. The thought made me calm down. I was better than that.

"That's the problem, Captain Malone. It happens all the time." She said the last sentence slowly as she tossed the core in the trash by her desk.

The thought crossed my mind as to why Joy was spinning the story this way. It was almost as if she was trying to turn the case cold.

Frank rubbed the back of his neck in frustration. Although I knew he was weighing his possible responses, Joy smiled triumphantly at his silence. She actually believed she won the argument. He paused. Her immaturity in this conversation annoyed me to the point that I felt the need to respond.

"The investigation is only a couple of days old. Why are you wanting to put the kibosh on it so fast? Because it has nothing to do with the media." I held up my phone. "The only thing going is the shootout. There's nothing about the young woman's murder."

She stood and shouted, "I'm in charge here, and you will do as I bid."

She gathered herself like a true drama queen. Even the way she talked right now sounded like she was practicing for the big stage, trying to really impress her superior. I did a quick look around checking to see if there were cameras. Maybe she wasn't practicing after all. Maybe she was putting on a show for her superiors.

"Frank, get Will here to the riverboat casino. There's been a murder that needs to be investigated, and we need the help. I've already cleared it with your captain in KC. She says to keep you as long as I need you."

"What about Evans?" I asked. "Didn't you guys say that's her territory?"

The woman finally joined the conversation. "I will be lead, and you'll be my second."

So, she was Evans. And she had enough gall to not acknowledge her direct supervisor. Another Joy on the way up.

"She has plenty of work to do and could use a partner for now."

Joy completely reversed what she said earlier.

"She'll also do the evaluation on your abilities. Which I am questioning at the moment. And it's apparent that Frank is too biased to give an accurate one."

"But I'm entering her paperwork into ICON. What work does she have but to investigate?"

Frank tried not to shout, but his husky voice made it impossible. With Evans in the mix, I knew the answer. Joy was trying to bury my investigation. But why?

"And I am perfectly capable of doing an eval on Will. Are you questioning my ethics?"

Frank stood and turned away from Joy. He seemed to be trying to calm himself.

"I will *not* be questioned by subordinates," she raged. "You will do as you're told or risk suspension without pay. And with the economy the way it is, you'll starve in less than two days." She smiled that snarky smile and gave him the up and down look. "Maybe a little starving would help your waistline and your attitude, Captain Malone.

I sat up straight and was about to shoot back at her when Frank interrupted.

"Unbelievable," Frank whispered.

"Excuse me?" Joy shouted.

"Sorry. I just whispered to Will that it's unbelievable that there's been a murder at the old riverboat. Will and Kate are on it."

Frank knew when to quit and what needed to be said. His years on the force came out. While I wanted to take this argument to the mat, he knew when to walk away. The frown on his face wasn't from anger, but careful consideration I'd seen him give in other conversations with higher ups. I knew what he was about to say. Words he really did not want to say.

"My apologies superintendent. My temper got away from me. It won't happen again."

His voice was almost subservient. It hurt to see Frank in this position, especially to an inferior cop. She didn't deserve the apology. She was either trying to impress her superiors, or she was holding up the case, maybe permanently. I cringed at the thought that there were more like her in the expanded Peace Forces. I thanked God for people like Frank. The good ones trying to do the right thing.

"See that it doesn't. And please get your subordinate under control."

We stood to attention, saluted, and left.

Frank hit the first-floor button. I figured it was by accident. He caught my arm when I reached out to push the right floor. He shook his head without looking at me.

We had a lot to talk about.

Frank led me out of the building and to the beater.

"What about the cameras and mics?" I asked as I tried to keep up.

"The car is specially built to be soundproof. Compliments of the senator," he whispered.

I unlocked the beater and got in wondering what other surprises the old girl had for me. The thought that the senator had his own mics in the car came to mind. I let it go because I trusted Frank, and he trusted Senator Staeger.

"I can't believe she did that!" Frank sat hard on the passenger seat before slamming the door.

"I can. If she knew about the hit," I said aloud to myself.

"Now what are you talking about?" Frank sighed.

"The whole conversation seemed scripted. She just ended the investigation of a murdered President of the United States. That can't be her call." I said, running my fingers through my hair. "She has no authority to make that decision. She's just a city superintendent."

"You're right, but why bring her in?" Frank asked.

"If this goes up the ladder to Philly, you'd think the superintendent of the city, and known brown noser, would be in the loop." I whispered as my mind was reassessing the conspiracy. "We must be getting closer than expected. Now she's running blocker with Evans, her own person, being planted to make sure we don't go any farther by reassigning me. Evans is now a babysitter. Remember, she tried to get Evans as the lead investigator when I first got here."

"Right, but I talked her out of it." Frank's brow furrowed in thought.

"Sorry, but I believe she was told to allow it since a

rookie was put on it. Maybe whoever's in charge thought I wouldn't get far along this fast. Considering what's happened recently, I think we're closer than we realize."

"I can't imagine Joy being part of a conspiracy to assassinate a sitting president. Even though I can't stand her, she's still a cop." Frank's voice cracked a little. He was a cop to the bone marrow.

"Remember the times we're living in and what the Bible says. There's a line in the sand and there are only two options. Jesus or the Antichrist. As much as it hurts to say, cops have the same choice. Not all will make the same one."

Frank bowed his head and closed his eyes. It hurt to see my mentor and friend come to this powerful realization, but it was necessary. He needed to come all the way into the new world.

"Frank, all we can do is our job. God knows what He's doing." I shrugged. "Who knows. Maybe I'm wrong about everything and Joy is just trying to win a few brownie points with the mayor. It could be just a city problem, and not a global one."

"That remains to be seen." He smiled and raised his head. His eyes turned dark red. "The sky is getting scary."

It was the first time he mentioned it. Maybe he was coming around. We sat in silence for a few minutes to let the effects of the last hour or so to melt away.

"We need to do something about the president." Frank turned to me. "If America is about to die, we can't allow it to go out with unfinished business."

He always wore his patriotism on his sleeve. Always standing for the pledge of allegiance and the national anthem. His husky voice was heard over everyone. And this time, he was right. If we go as a nation, it will not be in this manner. My pride rose until reality hit.

"It's hard to do that when you're taken off the case," I whispered, not wanting to be the downer of the two of us.

"Not off the case. Just delayed." Frank had that deep, thoughtful look on his face.

"What are you thinking?"

"I think we should do as we are told. You go investigate the murder at the riverboat casino with Evans." He leaned forward and whispered, "And I'll go talk with Marjorie when Joy's on her lunchbreak."

CHAPTER 32

The riverboat casino didn't float. It was on land near Carondelet Park. In fact, it was penned between the river and I-55. The river had pushed the huge boat onto the land during the second quake. Originally in New Orleans, the riverboat was one of the last floating casinos that cruised the Mississippi River to Vicksburg and back. The Spirits salvaged it when New Orleans was overtaken by the Gulf of Mexico.

It looked like a giant silver turtle that got stuck upside down in the mud, although the reflection of the red and black sky made it look like roadkill. I had to park on the interstate to get close enough to board. There were two marked Peace Forces SUV cruisers in front of the gang plank that served as the main entrance. The patrol officers were on the roadside.

"Are the others on the boat?" Evans asked.

"No, ma'am. It's just us." His deer-in-the-headlights look wasn't promising.

"Why aren't you protecting the crime scene?" She was acting like she wanted to investigate.

"They won't let us aboard." He pointed to the edge of the gangplank where three shadows lurked.

"We'll see about that." Evans took out her phone and

punched the screen.

"Who are you calling?" I asked.

"Superintendent Everhart." She rolled her eyes as if I should've already known.

"Why not Frank?" My rage went immediately to boil. "He's our direct supervisor."

"Captain Malone is not to be in on this investigation." She looked like the favored child of poor parents. I waited for her to stick her tongue out at me, which nearly made me smile. "Superintendent's orders."

"Unbelievable." I pulled out my SIG and headed for the gang plank. "A real pair of brave souls you two are." I glared at the two patrolmen.

"They got guns."

"We have guns." I waved my SIG.

"Ours are bigger." A voice from the boat laughed.

The man standing under a deck light pointed to an MP5 his guard was toting.

"Mine will get the job done." I walked on the gangplank.

"We didn't say you could come across."

The man was drug-addict lean with too many teeth missing. His weathered face looked grim in the mixture of the weak deck light and red reflections from the sky and river. But I knew his kind. The type that buckled under pressure. And a little violence.

"Detective Thomas, I'm the lead on this case, and you will stand down until I report the situation," Evans yelled, holding the phone to her ear.

"You need to listen to your superior," the scrawny junkie hollered. "I didn't say you could cross."

"I didn't ask. There was a murder reported here. We're here to investigate." I held out my Peace Forces badge.

The man pulled out a handgun of his own. "I said you can't come over."

"And I said I'm a cop," I screamed while stepping from

the gangplank to the deck.

After closing the distance quickly, I did a front kick to his gut, sending him flying across the deck. He landed flush against the wall behind him and slid down to a sitting position, eyes closed, with a slow, pain-filled inhale.

"Detective Thomas, I am putting you on report for striking a civilian in the course of your duty." Evans swiped her phone's screen and pocketed it while she darted across the gangplank.

"He was obstructing justice. I'm within my rights." I pointed my gun at Leo's forehead.

"Leo, what are you doing?"

The calm voice coming from the top deck sounded put out, but I couldn't see his face to confirm it.

"I didn't say he could come aboard." His guttural response was just loud enough.

"Didn't I tell you to let me know when Detective Thomas arrived?"

I raised my gun from Leo's head and holstered it. The voice knew my name, but it didn't sound familiar. I was getting tired of people knowing me before we met.

"Yes, sir. But I didn't know it was him." Leo stood, massaging his gut, and looked to the upward deck.

"Be a good man, stand-down, and escort the detective to the casino to start the investigation. I will join him in a little while."

"Yes, sir." Leo turned, glared, and waved me to follow him.

"He knew you were coming, but not me."

Evans sounded quite hurt, but I was paranoid.

We followed Leo into the enormous casino. It covered the width of the boat and over half the length. Leo told us it was once the largest riverboat in the world. I wasn't sure if he was telling me the truth, but I let him prattle about its history. At least I kept him from thinking about shooting me. Most of the gaming tables were either overturned or broken. The Spirits apparently weren't into gambling yet. Smart considering of the current state of the American economy. The room was sparsely lit by a grand chandelier with too many bulbs burnt out.

The victim was underneath a roulette table. The poor lighting did little to help me see much. I pulled out my flashlight from my Cards jacket, turned it on with a quick click, and inspected the body. A bloody entry wound lay above his right eye. Same bullet in the same place as the president's and Kennedy's wound. Joy's luck ran out. I was back on the case. Which made me reconsider her involvement in the conspiracy. She should've known the whereabouts of the assassin.

"Thank you for coming, Detective Thomas." The voice now had a man attached to it. He was late-thirties, early-forties. Tall with a limp. His pointed nose rested above a mouth that had a smirk that needed knocked off. He ignored Evans.

"Do we know each other?" I asked.

"No, but I have heard of you." He stopped by the dead body.

"I have a reputation before I even get here." I grinned at Evans, who wasn't smiling, and shook my head.

"Maybe, but you do make a lasting impression. My partner gave me the heads up on you and your investigation." He offered his hand. "James Franks."

"Will Thomas." I shook his hand. "Detective, Peace Forces."

"And I'm Detective Katherine Evans, lead investigator on this case."

Evans forced the handshake like she was a politician trying to win a voter.

James was polite but kept his focus on me.

"Detective, who called this death in?" He slightly shrugged. "I didn't. And I know none of my associates did."

Evans wasn't about to be pushed to the side. She stood between James and me.

"I'm not sure. I'm just doing what I was told to do by my superior, Superintendent Joy Everhart. She told me there was a murder and gave me the case." She tried to bulldoze him with her words but missed the mark.

He quietly listened to Kate as he leaned to look at me.

I mimicked his shrug.

His mouth twitched as he looked back at Kate.

"I'm not sure that it wasn't suicide. Probably open and closed."

"The wound suggests the bullet came from a distance longer than his arm." I looked around. The windows of the casino were almost all blown out from the hard landing during the quake. "I'm guessing the shooter was over there." I pointed to a blown-out window that faced the river.

"But we'll have the CSU team do a complete analysis of the scene to be sure."

Kate shot me a frown. I wasn't falling in line like I was expected to. That'll go on my eval. It was obvious she didn't like babysitting the newbie. But you can't make points with the boss without doing the occasional annoying task. It's part of the job description. Take care of the boss's dirty laundry.

"Why there?" Franks ignored Kate and looked at the spot I pointed to.

"Angle and trajectory points to it. Unless the body was moved." I raised my eyebrows, turning the statement into a question.

"He wasn't, sir."

Leo's face had a certain genuflect to it. He was telling the truth out of fear of a terrible punishment. He was a broken man in front of James Franks.

"You seem to know who did this unspeakable act."

James' look of sorrow fooled no one, especially me.

"This is the work of the same assassin who killed a young woman I was talking to last night at the cemetery. Same bullet wound, same location on the face." I pointed to the wound, then looked him in the eye to see his reaction, half expecting a Hector reaction. His face lost its blood. Like his dead associate.

"But we can't be sure until the CSU analyzes the area."

Kate lost control of her emotions along with the conversation. "And we're not even sure if these crime scenes are connected. I'm sure Superintendent Everhart…"

"Has no intention of letting this go any farther than needed." Now I lost my cool.

"Detective, I will have the two men who were here when this one died give you their accounts of the incident." James limped out of the casino in a hurry.

I looked over at Leo. "Seems like your boss had some unexpected business to take care of."

"He's a busy man." Leo sat and lit a cigarette.

"Those are hard to come by." I nodded at the cigarette when I stooped to look at the body.

"They are if you don't know somebody."

He took a long, deep drag and blew it at me. Unfortunately for him, the smoke lingered in front of him before floating to the ceiling.

"Superintendent Everhart will walk you to the guillotine herself. And I'll ask to pull the handle," Evans shouted as she left the scene, her phone over her ear.

Doing my walk around, as Leo smoked another cigarette, revealed nothing of importance. And there was nothing else the body was going to tell me, other than it was the same guy toting a .22 mag rifle. The close proximity made the shot, about ten to twelve yards, much easier.

"No one was in here when he got it?"

"Nope. He was here alone." Leo took a deep drag.

"Doing what?"

"Collecting."

"Collecting what?"

"His thoughts." Leo grinned.

If it wasn't for the fact he was a lowlife, I'd probably be friends with Leo based on his impolite sense of humor.

"Can you at least tell me his name?"

"Tony the Fish."

The name hit me right between the eyes. Hector's number two. Confusion swept across me and the whole case. Who would dare go against the number one mob boss in the city? Maybe even the river. I looked up and saw two men enter the casino. They crossed the casino and stood next to Leo.

Leo stood. "Tell him what you saw."

"I heard a pop, but I was on the other side of the boat. Al, here, was the one who saw more of it."

"I saw a tall man. Thin with a hooded coat. It was about all I could see. Seems like the storm front is sticking around. The darkness made it hard to see anything. Didn't even see the man climb aboard. But he did jump overboard. Then I heard a boat fire up and light out, quiet like."

"But you didn't hear it before the shot?"

"Come to think of it, no."

"Must've drifted from upriver."

"Must've," Leo mimicked.

He lowered his arrogance when I frowned at him.

"I guess that's about it. You can go now, detective. We'll take care of Tony." Leo coughed.

"I'm staying until the CSU gets here."

"Nobody comes aboard." He almost shouted.

"You said that before." I spread out my hands. "And you see how well that worked."

Leo went out the same door James exited.

I turned back to the two men. "Did you happen to across gun?"

"Rifle's all I know. It had a scope. But the rifle was

short."

"Like a squirrel gun?"

"Yeah, that's it." He sounded like it had just come to him.

".22 mag," I whispered to myself. "Just like the one that got her." Then I saw Leo come in scowling.

"Like I said, I'll stay until the CSU team gets here. You make sure they get aboard safe and off the same way."

About thirty minutes later, Jenny and Ruth walked into the casino. I had the main witness take Jenny out to the place where he saw the shooter jump from the boat. I figure Bobby would drone the place soon enough.

Ruth stayed inside to process the body and the crime scene. Her trepidation caught my attention as she nervously looked at Leo and his associates who leered at her. I walked to the door where I entered and hollered for the two officers to get on board.

"You make sure all the CSU team members are safe from beginning to end. Got it?" I shoved my finger in the lead partner's chest.

"Yes, sir." He flinched and rubbed his chest. "But we're off in less than an hour."

"You have just been approved for overtime. Your superintendent will see to it."

Their frowns needed a lot of work.

Leo was mad when I ordered everyone but him, and the other witness, out of the casino to avoid any further contamination of the crime scene. I guess James told him to give us full cooperation because he didn't fight the order.

While they were working the scene, I went out to see if Kate was still on the phone begging for my head on a platter. Her cruiser was gone. It stunk not being able to hear when a vehicle drove away.

I checked the time, calculated when I would receive the call from Joy for my sentencing, and decided to go and see if Clay had anything to report. But first, I needed to get some food for my informant.

CHAPTER 33

The door to Ballpark Village was blocked by a chunk of debris. I had to crawl through a hole in the wall that I barely fit through to get in. I opted to use the flashlight on my phone to see if there was any imminent danger inside. Outside of the debris, it all looked peaceful and void, which made me uneasy. I couldn't shake the feeling of impending doom as I walked across the place that housed sports fans and other various revelers throughout its time of operations. Something was wrong.

When I reached our usual meeting place, Clay was lying in his little cubby hole, facing away from me. He used his coat as a pillow and covered himself with a sheet that I guessed he stole from one of the empty hotels. But was it really stealing when it was abandoned?

"Clay, you okay?" I sat on my chunk of ceiling. He didn't move. "Clay, wake up." My heart rate increased. He still didn't move.

I stood and gave him a light kick to see if he was a heavy sleeper.

He lay there silent as a corpse.

Dread filled my gut when I reached down to turn him.

"Don't kill me," Clay whispered.

My heart jumped out of my chest. "It's me, Will." I sat

back down and collected my wits.

"Will?" He turned over and grimaced. "I thought you was the killer." His voice cracked in fear.

"Why would you think that?" I asked, then took a deep breath in relief that he wasn't dead.

"Because he's killin' everybody. That woman, the senator's girl, and Tony the Fish."

Clay's face was as ghostly white as mine felt. But facing your own death would have that effect. He was terrified. I wondered if he got caught spying by Hector.

"I'm afraid what he'll do if they find out what I'm doing," Clay said. A tear landed on his new sheet when he turned and sat up.

"They don't know anything about you, Clay," I assured him. "Have you heard anything new?"

He rubbed his face with both hands and began rocking. "Just that Hector ordered the hit on Tony."

"Who said that?" This case was getting more confusing by the minute. Maybe my gut needed more practice, or less hot dogs.

"Hector, of course." Clay started rocking.

"What did Hector say exactly?"

"That Tony was tired of being told what to do by a bunch of Europeans. But Hector made a deal with the head European to keep the river."

"Where did you hear this?"

Clay stopped rocking, looked down, and smiled. "I got in."

"In? In where?"

"They were looking for a gardener. One of the capos came out and said that Hector needed another gardener. Said one keeled over. Probably from stealing veggies. He picked me because I told him I did gardening when I had a home."

"Is that true?" It dawned on me that I knew very little about my C.I.

He looked at me, wounded. "I had a job, a house, a wife, and two kids."

"Sorry, I didn't mean anything by it."

His new tears were for the past. "They died at the beginning. But I didn't kill them like that piece of Eurotrash said. The kids went first, then my wife poisoned herself the next day."

I watched him shake and vehemently wipe his wet cheeks. He'd been through a lot. Not wanting to upset him more about the past, I let the silent moment pass.

"I've been doin' it ever since. Slowly."

He stared at the track marks on his arm. He was more than an addict, he was suicidal. I gave him another minute to collect himself, and silently prayed for God to intervene in this man's life. It was hard not to tell him about Jesus. But that was part of the job. Then Tommy entered my mind. But first, I needed the information.

"Tell me everything you heard, and I'll introduce you to my friend. He helps people needing help. Like you." I patted him on the shoulder for reassurance.

"I might take you up on that. It gets lonely out here."

He wiped his nose with his shoulder. After a minute or two, he took a deep breath and seemed ready to continue.

"I made sure to stay as close to Hector as I could, without him noticing me."

He sniffled while I handed him a bag of food from a burger joint on the west side. "Here, eat this. It'll help."

He smiled, blew his nose with a napkin and dug into the fries. It's amazing what some food can do for a drug addled body with a depressed mind. His demeanor lightened.

"Anyway, Tony came out and talked with Hector. He wasn't happy that you came to talk to Hector, and that Hector talked to you. Said the cops were causing a lot of problems for their plans. Especially with the shootout."

It felt good to know there were some on the force who didn't help.

"My conversation was a little one sided. I let him talk, but he didn't say much." I stretched the truth, feeling a little foolish at how Hector led me through the conversation.

"Oh, by the way, Hector was the one who ordered the cops in on the shootout," Clay said before taking a sip of water. "Said he wanted them in case the Survivors Crew were better than he thought. And that Tony had no say in strategic plans like those. Hector reminded Tony that he was there because of his connections with the girls."

He wiggled his eyebrows and grinned at me.

"What did Tony say?"

"Tony didn't want any more help from the cops, so he wanted to call off the attack on the other outlier mob. Said the heat needed to cool."

"And Hector didn't agree?" I pulled out a handful of energy and protein bars.

Clay quickly put the bars in a scrubby backpack, and said, "No, in fact, he ordered the plan to start earlier. Tonight. Of course, your people won't be involved. Hector said he had assurances that there'd be no more cop influence in it," he said, pulling out the burger.

"Influence in what?"

"The takeover." He shook his head while he wiped fry crumbs off his mustache. "You don't have it figured out?"

"That Hector's taking over the city? Yeah, we figured that…"

"No, the whole river. His mob covers almost all the river, north to south. Incoming and outgoing. That's why the people in Europe are supporting him."

Clay acted like he couldn't believe I hadn't pieced it together. And he was right. It was all there. Frank had told me that Hector had other associates outside of the city. I thought they were just political informants. Another thought hit me. "Why did he say he had assurances of the cops not getting involved?"

"He didn't say, but I'm guessing it's that woman at the

top."

"Superintendent Everhart?"

He pointed at me. "That's the one. Short, bad tan?"

"Yeah, but why her?"

"She comes to the gardens all the time. One of the other gardeners told me. He gives her meat and fresh fruits and vegetables, and she does what she's told." He tore into the burger.

Although I believed she may have had a part in this, I didn't want to believe she was corrupt. Just overly ambitious. I guess Frank rubbed off on me that way. My stomach turned at the thought. "Seems like a small payoff to take orders from a man she's supposed to be fighting."

"Oh, not from Hector. She's just a messenger. She tells him what's going on, and he feeds her. My new gardener friend told me that she likes bossing him around a little too much. Hector talks behind her back that he will eventually kill her when the time's right."

The idea of her death wasn't fully repugnant, but I wondered out loud. "Who's her boss?"

"That European guy. You know, the one who got the Jews and Muslims to stop killin' each other."

"The Sovereign?"

"That's the one." He quickly pointed a French fry at me. "How do you know that?"

"The gardener has heard her say that the Sovereign said this and said that. And that Hector better get on board or be left behind." He belched loudly and smiled. "Tank's full."

"Left behind?" I asked.

Clay slashed across his throat with his finger.

"I thought the Free Agents were just that. Free."

"There's no freedom in this world, Will. Just a lot of ants playin' king of the mountain."

He put the trash in the bag, wadded it up, and handed it to me.

"Toss this outside. I don't want it stinking up my place."

"King of the mountain. I played that when I was a kid."
I smiled as I stood, tucking the trash under my arm.

"You better remember the rules or you'll be at the bottom catching the noggins." Clay fluffed his pillow and yawned. "When will this bloody night end?"

"Don't worry, buddy. The storm will be over soon enough."

Praying inwardly for Clay, I crawled out of the hole in Ballpark Village.

I stood over the crime scene to put on a show for the cameras. The thought of Joy being on the Sovereign's speed dial didn't make sense. She might be important here, but on a global stage she was still a tiny, little orange guppy. Maybe she was under Kennedy. I had a hard time believing Joy ever took orders from her, but it was possible. If Clay was right, I needed to find whoever she was setting up, or I'd be investigating another staged noggin. Maybe even get a small caliber bullet to the brain for my troubles.

There was some movement in my peripherals. I turned to see Tommy hiding behind some stadium rubble. His hat turned while he was recording me, or at least he acted like it.

I rubbed the back of my left ear to let him know I couldn't meet. He disappeared into the rubble, clearly put off.

CHAPTER 34

Even though it was early, it felt late. I was hungry and went to the food truck patio.

The line to Hector's truck was short. Too late for lunch, too early for dinner. I made a mental note for future reference since it looked like I might be sticking around longer than I originally anticipated.

"Hey there, stranger." Amelia's voice didn't have its usual life.

I looked at my phone. "Late lunch?"

"Yeah. The weather is really doing a number on my internal clock. I usually am good about knowing when it's lunchtime without looking at my phone. The constantly dark sky makes it feel like quitting time, not lunchtime."

She stood by me at the end of the short line and laced her arm through mine. She made sticking around worth a long consideration.

"Me too. It feels like an exaggerated daylight savings time."

"I know, right?" Her widened eyes accentuated her words.

It was difficult to try and decide between the Cobb salad and the Greek salad because I was glad to see her. Especially considering the events of the day.

"If it stays dark too long, it'll be like an Alaskan winter," she said, then stepped forward to give her order.

"I hope that's not right." I walked up to the counter and ordered the Greek salad. "I like the rays."

"You and me both. England can be so dreary at times. My dad used to say the sun avoids England, so it doesn't have to bow to the king."

She giggled at the memory, then ordered the Greek salad, same as me. We went over and sat at the same picnic table we'd sat at on our date. While we ate, I noticed that she itched her wrist. Fear coursed through me. Did she get the Beastmark?

"How's the case coming? Do I need to warm up my lips?" She wiggled her eyebrows, making me forget my fear.

Feeling like a lovesick teenager, my mood improved. "Sorry, I'll have to take a raincheck. Just got taken off it today."

Her eyebrows raised. "Are you serious? What did you do?"

I raised my eyebrows in protest. On one hand, it was nice to see she still wanted the kiss. On the other hand, I took exception to the idea that she thought it was my fault. That I did something to merit getting kicked off the case, even though she may have been right.

"I didn't mean it like that." She searched for the right words. "I mean, why did they take you off the case? It just got started."

I watched her take a bite of her salad. It was nice to enjoy her company, unlike the other women in my life at that time. She was beautiful, graceful, and great company. I knew my parents would've approved. She caught me staring. I quickly looked down and acted like I wasn't.

"I guess the superintendent decided the trail was cold enough to call me off and put me on another," I said, hoping she wouldn't call me out on staring, although anyone would've agreed that it'd be difficult not to stare at the British beauty.

"There's been another murder? It's not even on the news yet." She took another bite and waited till she swallowed to smile. "So that's what it feels like to have the scoop. Now I wish I was a news reporter."

"I'm glad you're not." I took a sip of my water and noticed her giving me a surprised look. "Then we wouldn't get along, and I couldn't get that kiss. Conflict of interest."

She grinned and wiped her mouth. "Who was murdered?"

"Sorry, ma'am. That's all I can comment on." I tried a western accent that really stunk.

"What if I bribed you?" she asked, smiling wryly.

"Depends on the payoff." I returned the smile. These kinds of negotiations were fun. Unlike those with Hector.

"Well, since the first deal died. Pardon the pun. I guess a new deal is necessary."

I almost giggled. Which would've sounded like a goofy teenager. Which would've turned her off. Which would've caused me to commit self-harm. So, I kept it in.

"What deal do you have in mind?" I asked.

"Same deal, different corpse." She stared at me and took another bite of her lunch.

"Deal." I grabbed her hand and kissed the knuckles on her right hand. The smoothness of her skin made me shiver inside. That, and there was no chip. Two birds, one stone.

"Ooh, a gentleman." She blushed, checked her phone, and got up. "Sorry, I need to be at a meeting in ten minutes. Can I see you tomorrow?" She took my phone and entered her number.

"Sure, where and when?" I said it too fast. Such a rookie in so many ways.

"Dinner, but not here." She handed my phone back and collected her trash. "My number in case you get busy with the case."

"Dinner?" I felt my face heat up.

"Yes." She deposited her trash in the receptacle and left.

I suddenly felt very alone. The high tide allowed the river to ease close by the patio, and I decided to stay for a while to contemplate the situation. She wanted dinner which meant a sit-down restaurant. Since she was calling the shots, I knew I needed some nicer clothes than I brought. I'd ask Frank for his tailor's number.

After finishing the salad, I got in the beater and watched the river. The arch had turned a color I hadn't noticed before, metallic red. It almost shimmered. It was also troubling, looking like the tentacle off one of the robot monsters from the old movies. Although it troubled my spirit, I took comfort in knowing the coming storm wouldn't hit me. I bowed my head and gave thanks for God's blessings during the Trib.

Returning back to the problem at hand of not understanding the conspiracy trail, and also not wanting to believe cops were involved, I started with the people who appeared to be involved. Joy came to mind first. She got her orders from Europe. Although I doubted the Antichrist knew her name, but one of his minions did. Next was Hector, who took orders from Europe, as well. Joy's just the messenger. It was efficient.

They didn't order the hit, but Hector planted the president's head for the world to see. I'm guessing Joy was behind the scenes to make sure Hector did his job. But to what end? President Mason was in the Antichrist's way of taking over the country. He had her assassinated and put his man in the presidency to keep the Americans happy until the time was right to sign the treaty.

Why kill Kennedy? Who was she in the grand scheme of things?

It was difficult to keep the ties between the assassination and the St. Louis mob issues separate. Hector had many irons in the fires, but he seemed more like an iron in this particular fire. For him it was about control of the river as much as it was of his life. The river wasn't that important to the Antichrist, or he would've taken it over long ago.

I started the beater, then I heard popping coming from the west. I guessed the last of the outliers was being eliminated by the Free Agents. Clay was off on his timing. Or maybe it was the darkness playing with everyone's clocks. Although I knew what was happening, it was futile to call it in. Joy would just block it. That, and Evans was tattling at that moment. I'd talk to Joy soon enough. The helpless feeling raised my anger. It's hard to know things and not be able to act on them. That's not what cops are supposed to do. Especially when your own boss is blocking for the killer.

Hector once said that the Free Agents were a community. He was also known to have said the Free Agents were tired of having their destiny decided for them. Yet, they did as they were told. Strike that. He did what he was told. Thus, the problem that led to Tony the Fish's demise.

The people eating began staring at me too much, like they were tired of the noise and air pollution. I drove around for a while. Unfortunately, driving didn't help my thought processes anymore because I spent too much time navigating the obstacle course that was the city streets. So, I went to my hotel and tried to guess the new smell that invaded my room.

Cleaning products?

My room was spotless, and the odors were pleasant. After shutting the door and doing a mental victory dance, I pulled out my K.C. Peace Forces laptop, plugged it into an outlet, and started it. I needed to put the information of Tony the Fish's murder in the case file while it was still fresh in my memory.

To my surprise, the autopsy was already done. In fact, the autopsy on Kennedy was finished as well. What didn't

BLOOD STORM RETRIBUTION

surprise me was that the cause of death for both was a gunshot wound to the head. And that the bullet was from the same .22 mag rifle. The rifling matched perfectly.

That was brazen, especially for an assassin. This guy didn't care who knew. It was as if he wanted us to know it was him. That made me wonder what else had he done?

After considering it, I went into the case file of the shootout, and my guess was right. He was involved in that, too. Although there was only a half dozen bodies completed, three of them, all Survivors Crew, had the same bullets. Even though they weren't in the same place, the bullets still hit vital organs. This guy was good. Real good. I relegated the placement to the movement of the battle. It's hard to get a perfect hit every time when people are in constant motion. So, the mob war and President Mason's murder were connected. I sat back in the hard hotel chair and stretched. Even though it was only fifteen hundred, my body thought it was well past midnight.

The evidence and autopsy files came out quicker than the president's. Why the expediency? Ruth was overwhelmed with work, but she was obviously told to do these ahead of the other bodies. It clearly implicated the assassin with the mob war. Was he on loan to Joy? Or did he go rogue? No, then he wouldn't have been used to kill Tony the Fish.

The wheels in my head spun but didn't land on anything. What was the connection between the two cases, besides the same assassin? Did the Antichrist help Hector obtain St. Louis as part of the deal to get the river from one crime boss, instead of many like Clay suggested? Why was the river so important to kill the president and help a mobster gain control over it? And why plant the head for all to see? That part confused me the most. And just the head. Why not the whole body? Was Senator Staeger leading this to take over the world? Or was he the one being set up, and not Hector?

Although things were starting to line up in one way, another thread appeared and tore the line completely apart. The multidirectional conspiracy annoyed me. I thought for another hour trying to play connect the dots, but all I got was more confusion.

My phone dinged that I had a text. It was Joy.

COME TO MY OFFICE IMMEDIATELY!!!

She seemed overly stressed, so I ignored it.

It was time to talk to Hector to see if he had any insight into his partner's murder.

CHAPTER 35

Hector sat at the same bench. His goons let me in without a word. They already knew my face. That could be good or bad. While I walked toward Hector, I noticed the construction workers raising what appeared to be the final section of a transparent roof over the gardens and some of the trees. It looked like a giant greenhouse like the Climatron.

"Detective Thomas, so good to see you at this inauspicious time. Did you come to give your regards?" He nodded for me to sit beside him.

"I'm sorry for your loss. As you probably already know, I've been assigned to Tony's case."

"And Detective Evans?" He grinned as he tsked. "That was bad form the way you dismissed her. She was, after all, the lead detective." He shook his head like a disapproving father. "And she is to evaluate you. I must say, your youthful energies may lead to your dismissal. And I was starting to enjoy your presence in our fair city."

His disappointed demeanor and scolding tone shouldn't have thrown me off. Why would he care? After all, the Spirits were all but soaked into his mob, and the city was, for all intents and purposes, his. My temper had been tested since I arrived in St. Louis, and letting it fly would be counterproductive, even deadly for me. So, instead of flying off the handle, I decided to act the part of the rebuffed student. I lowered my head and shrugged.

"My apologies. I didn't mean to admonish." He crossed his legs as if ready for the conversational topic shift.

"I have some questions. Standard stuff." I was about to fire them off.

"Yes, he was my partner over the community. No, I didn't send him to the Spirits' boat. No, I don't know why he went there. And yes, we weren't in complete agreement as to how the community should be run, but we were working things out like gentlemen." His voice was calm and collected, but it didn't sound rehearsed, just very factual and very hard to read. I hated when he did that.

"You've done this before." I threw it in hoping to stall while I pulled out my notebook and pen and furiously took notes.

"No, but I know how cops think. Sorry, but it's best to know these things when the community is always under the Peace Force's scrutiny."

I gave a quick point at the roof, then started writing again. It was a ploy for me to catch up. "What's with the structure?" I kept scribbling, hoping I could read it later.

"Just preparing for the very near future." He smiled. "You didn't say anything about it when you were here last time."

"I just thought it was a wall to protect your garden from thieves."

He laughed. "What a detective you are! The dome was under construction while we talked."

Feeling my face redden, I looked down at my notes. What a detective indeed.

Hector slapped me on the thigh. "I am sorry my friend. I jest at your expense. The workers were on a break then. The dome should be finished by day's end. I have them working round the clock. They work efficiently because I promised a big bonus if they finish on time and the structure is properly built."

"Don't the plants need rain?"

"I had an irrigation system installed six weeks ago. It's now time for the covering. The transparent roof will allow the sunlight through for photosynthesis, but it will protect my crops from the potential dangers of the times we live in."

"Are they bulletproof?" I was half serious and half kidding.

"As a matter of fact, they are. But that's not the foremost reasoning behind their installation. You see, I believe there is a storm coming unlike any humanity has seen since the days of ancient Egypt." He looked at the sky.

My gut tingled. Was he a believer? Did he know the next judgment was coming and what it entailed? "Are you into meteorology, Hector?" I asked.

"Of a sort." He pulled out an old, tattered Bible and opened it to the back pages. "The first angel sounded, and there followed hail and fire mingled with blood, and they were cast upon the earth; and the third part of the trees were burnt up, and all green grass was burnt up, Revelation 8:7." He closed the book and set it back beside him.

"Are you a Christian?" I used my cop voice to hide my hope.

"No, but I am a pragmatist concerning recent events." He grinned and turned to look me in the eye. "My dear mother was a devout believer. She used this very book to try to win me over to God. Unfortunately, my father was a repellent man, who only lived for the pleasure of women and booze. So, as you can tell, I was caught between two worlds. When I left home, she gave me her Bible and begged me to read it. I promised her I would keep it.

"Soon after, I began living my father's life, but it didn't satisfy my desire for greatness. I knew I was put on this planet for greater things. That's when I entered the community business. It was rough at the beginning, but I fought my way to the top. Although I never knew what happened to my father since he left me and my mother when I was fifteen, my mother always answered the phone for her degenerate son. She was seventy-six when she disappeared a little over a year ago." He shifted his crossed legs.

"Was she murdered?" I was baiting him.

"Absolutely not. She was taken from this world by her God."

A slight emotion came from his voice. Even a lawbreaker has to love someone. Why not his mother?

"Do you believe in God, or the Divine Possible?" I needed to know.

"I believe in me." He tapped his chest. "It doesn't matter if you call the deity God or the Divine Possible. What matters is that this book is accurate." He patted the Bible. "Thus, my pragmatism."

"I don't understand. You believe the Bible, but not what it preaches?" I scratched under my hat with my pen.

"Of course, I believe what it says. I just reject the idea that I must give my destiny to an unseen God."

He waved the idea away with his hand. He seemed more like a believer than he wanted to admit. The blade must've kept him leery of strangers, and he obviously wasn't in the resistance by the way he ran his mob. However, his mom appeared to have more of an influence than he wanted to fully disclose.

"However, the Bible is getting it right concerning recent happenings," he said in a tone that sounded disconnected from the source mentioned. No emotion or zeal.

"Let me get this straight. You reject God's requirement for belief in order to keep your freedom, but you're following the Bible because it luckily predicted a couple of disasters? Nostradamus did that, but I'm not going to call him a god." It was hard to act like a nonbeliever. Especially since I was a new believer.

"You are correct. Nostradamus was no god." He held up the book with one hand and laid his other hand on the top as if he was taking an oath. "But there is a God, and this book contains His game plan for the future. I'm just using it to increase my place in this world."

"By knowing what comes next, you think you'll come out on top when it's all said and done?" I'd never thought of that. It was wrong, but brilliant. I considered taking out stock on the chip market to make some extra money when the Beastmark became mandatory.

"So far so good." He winked. "I've had to pretend to be more compliant than I'm comfortable with, but all's fair in love and prophecy."

It was a good thing I was a believer, or I might've been won over by his ideology. His appearance of success would appear otherworldly to someone looking for an alternative to Christ and the Antichrist. It was like he was looking into a crystal ball and getting it right every time. Then I remembered my dad talking about antichrists predicted by Jesus. Was Hector one of them and not a believer? I prodded to find out.

"If the prophecy you read is true, then you're going to make more money from this garden than any other enterprise the community can dream up."

He sat back. His smile turned into a grimace. "Not exactly. This is for survival." He stared at his garden like a starving man would at an all-you-can buffet.

"Because almost all the plant life will burn?"

"I'm afraid so."

He looked around and leaned closer to me like a man about to let me in on a major secret that only he was privy to. One that needed to be maintained at all costs.

"I've been hoarding grain and hay, from the farmers in the surrounding states, to store it, and my livestock, in underground facilities I had prepared based on the Bible's predictions. If everything goes to plan, and my resources are unaffected, people will be coming to me by the thousands. My community will be the most powerful in the country."

"But will the Sovereign be persuaded to play ball with you? He's not the type to share anything, especially power, from what I hear."

"He will have to." Hector shrugged and leaned back. "Unless he is reading the same book I am."

"There's rumors flying around that that book is about to be banned." I wanted to know what he knew. In fact, I was shocked that it hadn't already happened.

"Possibly, but I doubt the Sovereign cares if a man so far from his reach has one. Especially since I know some of your people."

He was goading me into telling him if I had inside information. I did, but I didn't. Playing dumb was my best, and only choice.

"I'm the newbie around here. Just came in the other day. I don't know much about the goings on in the St. Louis Peace Forces." I shrugged.

He looked at me with admiration. "Well played, newbie."

"There is one thing I'm confused about." I knew I was playing with fire, but the fire that was coming from God gave me reason to push harder than I wanted. "If you reject God because you don't want to put your destiny in His hands, then why are you compliant with the Sovereign? You told me yourself that you planted the president's head as you were told."

Hector went stoic. I couldn't tell if he was angry or just searching for the right response. Then he grinned and said, "He is the most powerful man on the face of the Earth, so I must make my dealings with him." Hector then sighed. "If you are wondering, yes, I knew it was former President Mason's head the whole time."

"I guessed that, after the fact. But getting back to the Sovereign. If he can get the president killed without repercussions to him, aren't you afraid you'll be the fall guy?" I started taking notes again, looking down at the pad to avoid him reading me. I needed to know if Hector was the one to take the fall. If anyone, he would know.

"That was something that weighed heavily on my mind, but then I was reassured by his people that this will not land in my lap. After all, his empire is just beginning. And if history shows us anything, it is that every empire also has an ending." He pointed to the Bible. "And I know that this empire will end in less than six years."

"Is that what the book says?" I played ignorant for my own good.

"You can bet on it." He smiled.

"What's the next empire? Does the Bible predict that?" Staying with the ignorant cop routine was working. Why not keep it up?

"God will send His son, Jesus, to defeat the Sovereign and his army, then take the throne of this world for himself."

His surety was that of a devout believer. It was hard to think that he wasn't. It didn't make sense to me. So, I pressed some more. "Then what about you and your community?"

"Then I make a deal with Jesus to let me keep my community when He takes control."

His matter-of-fact tone was one of the most arrogant I had ever witnessed firsthand. But I let him think this could happen. It was obvious he didn't read the rest of the Bible concerning the post-Trib world. When Jesus takes the throne of the world, people like Hector will find no place. Jesus will rule with a rod of iron. There will be no deals. I wanted to argue with Hector to get him to understand the folly of his plan, but I had let him swim in his delusions and let Jesus take care of him in His own time. The desire to pray for Hector's soul overwhelmed me. He would be a great brother-in-arms for the Resistance and a strong addition to God's kingdom. I prayed internally for him.

"Is there anything more you can tell me about Tony's murder?" I stood knowing the answer.

"Just that the killer is the same one who killed the woman you met with."

"We knew that already. We did a bullet comparison."

His eyes narrowed for the first time since I met him, as if he didn't believe me. "That was fast," he whispered.

"Excuse me? I didn't catch that." I raised my eyebrows and leaned towards him.

"It was nothing." Hector stood and looked at the structure. "If you have nothing else, I must make sure my project is finished on time. And please be careful. When that judgment comes to pass, I wouldn't be caught in the open if I were you." He smiled and reached out to shake hands. "Unless you are fireproof."

After shaking hands, I started for the way out. Smiling, because I was fireproof.

"I forgot, Detective Thomas," Hector called. "Please give my condolences to Senator Staeger for the loss of his Chief of Staff."

My smile left my face before I turned. "I'll do that the next time I see him."

On my way back to the hotel, I remembered I needed to talk to Frank first thing the next morning.

CHAPTER 36

The next morning, I went to the mini golf course on a hunch Frank was there avoiding Joy. I parked on the other side of Union Station to avoid the cameras, then walked into a familiar area.

Strolling past the shops of St. Louis' Union Station, I thought back to the only time I saw Kat after the beginning of the Tribulation. I had just transferred to Kansas City and was on my way to meet Tommy for the first time. The world was as alive as it was before the disappearances. We were to meet at the Kansas City Union Station to get to know each other and plan our first infiltration of the police department. Even then, things were changing, and the Antichrist didn't even seem like he was in control to the American public.

Kat was sitting in the Grand Hall, near a restaurant that had closed. My first instinct was to run to her and hug her. But when she saw me, she rolled her eyes and laughed out loud. She stood and walked to me with a vicious sneer. She made fun of me for being a hypocrite with Mom and Dad. She said they would've been ashamed of me if there was an afterlife. I didn't get a word in edgewise. She basked in her virtue of staying true to her convictions. Then she grew quiet, frowned, slapped me and walked away. I stood there with a stupid expression on my face. At first, I thought God had just given me my sister back as a way to make it through the Trib. Now I realized it was His way of letting me know she was still the same.

I said a quick prayer for her, then went to the mini golf course.

I walked to the door and saw Tommy beside a Ferris wheel cabin. He turned his hat. I gave the sign we'd meet. He was still frowning when I turned the corner. We needed to straighten things out. But not now.

Frank was putting on the final hole when I walked in.

"How's it going with yesterday's shootout? Are Free Agents planning a parade in front of headquarters while Joy waves from the Santa Claus float?" I sat on the table.

Frank pulled the blue ball from the cup, threw it at the downed Ferris wheel, and screamed. He stomped away from me. His face was as red as the river. I'd never seen him this angry and decided to stow the humor or face his wrath that was clearly meant for Joy and her people. De-escalation was needed, so I sat at our table and waited.

After an awkward minute, he looked at me. "How did you know about all that?"

"I'm a detective. I went out and detected." I was doing my best to calm him, but my effort was failing miserably.

"Boy, don't play with me. How did you know?" He walked towards me, pointing the putter at me.

I raised my hands. "Easy Frank. James Franks from the Spirits told me when I looked into Tony the Fish's murder."

He stopped. "Tony the Fish is dead?"

"That's who was murdered on the casino boat I investigated."

"What was he doing on the riverboat?" He said it to himself as he sat across the table from me.

"Getting killed. It was a hit."

"Hit? Tony got hit? He is one of the most careful people

in the business. He's completely paranoid."

He half stuttered his words. It was plain to see the shock in his face. Even I knew that mobsters that high in the food chain were rarely killed like that. Tony had to have been set up by Hector, or James Franks. I wondered if this had anything to do with the dead president, or was it business as usual in St. Louis?

"I'm guessing Hector had someone Tony trusted to send him. Maybe on the request to negotiate the transfer of power."

"Any idea who killed him?" Frank acted like he already knew the answer.

"Same guy who hit the president, Kennedy Brown, and at least three of the Survivors Crew during the first shootout."

Frank shifted his weight on the bench while he shook his head in disbelief. "All those people by the same guy?"

"The bullets all came from the same rifle. I saw him when I was with Kennedy, and the Spirits' guard on the riverboat described the same guy. I will wager my pension that someone from the shootout, if any survived, would describe a similar man who participated. This guy is everywhere. Killing a lot of people." I looked Frank in the eyes. "And I'm willing to wager there are more to come if we don't catch him."

"But why did he get involved in a mob war after he killed the president? He should be on a private island sipping the good stuff."

"If he could find a stable island. You remember that everything shifted from mountains on land to islands in the water. I heard of an airline pilot who got lost trying to find Hawaii. The plane was in the air during the first quake, and the islands disappeared. They were nowhere to be found. The plane ran out of fuel taxiing from the runway they landed on, when he finally found one of the islands. A reporter said the islands were spread in a way that a person could argue they weren't part of the same chain anymore." I hoped the change in topic would help Frank return to his normal, analytical self.

"It still doesn't answer the question."

It didn't. Frank was always like a dog with a meaty bone.

"I've been thinking about this." I looked up through the glass ceiling. The sky was enraged. The black and red colors were at war, violently churning to gain the advantage.

"We need to get this figured out today. The next judgment's about to start any minute."

Frank didn't need to look up to figure that out.

"We need to find the killer, but I don't have any description other than he's tall and wears a hooded coat," I said in a frustrated tone. Frank's mood was starting to rub off on me.

"We need to find someone who knows what he looks like."

"How about Hector?" I asked.

"Is he in on it?"

"Yeah, my CI told me that Hector was ordered to plant the president's body. Possibly a fee for helping the Free Agents gain control of the city."

"And you believe this guy?"

"Yes, but I corroborated his story."

"How?"

"Hector told me."

"He told you?"

"Yeah. Yesterday he told me he was ordered to drop the head in a public place."

"By whom?"

"Joy Everhart." I drug it out properly.

Frank's entire face bulged with rage. "I don't like the woman, but you better be joking about a fellow officer, or so help me, boy, I'll drop you here and now." His clenched fists worried me.

"Easy, sir. I don't like saying it myself. Do you think I would accuse her if I couldn't prove it? My C.I. told me she comes to Hector's for groceries and to give orders. The way I see it, she gets the orders over the phone in her office, then personally goes to Hector to avoid any internet implications."

Frank dropped his head into his hands. "That's what Marjorie was hinting at."

"What did she say?" I leaned in closer.

"She said that Joy was getting calls from a European number."

"One of the Antichrist's people giving her orders."

"So, this is all connected?"

"That's my gut feeling. What cements it for me is that the assassin was used to help take out the Survivors Crew." I hesitated. "And so were the cops and military."

Frank almost turned the table over in his fury. "Don't go thinking that good cops were in on this. I won't stand for it." His red face matched the red in the sky.

"Then sit down. I believe Joy sent the cops and soldiers on orders from the Antichrist as payment for Hector planting the body. The cops and soldiers probably weren't in on it."

Frank nodded while he listened, and I saw a tear fall on the picnic table.

"I never thought I'd see the day that cops would be pawns for a megalomaniac. We're just grunts to implement his plan." He wiped the tear streak from his cheek. "You read the Bible and know it's coming, but when it happens there's no preparing for it."

"Amen, brother."

A moment passed in the inactive air. It was necessary. Frank and I were too worked up to formulate any sort of plan. I tried to empty my mind when I heard Frank clear his throat.

"I'm not going to make it to the end," Frank whispered.

"End of what?"

"The Tribulation."

"That's crazy talk. We can get through this together."

He shook his head and pointed at me. "Not we. You."

"Me?" I got scared thinking Frank was becoming suicidal. Tommy warned me that being undercover as deep as I was would make me think about a date with a bullet meal. The look on his face made him look hungry.

"Yes, you. Will, God has a big plan for you. Not me." He smoothed his tie. "I'm not cut out for this spy stuff. I'm an old beat cop who's in over his head, in a police force that I don't understand and won't work for." His smile was weak. "Maybe I'll go to the dessert and play some real golf for a few years."

"Over my dead body." I felt my blood raging like the sky. Frank was all I had left from my pre-Trib life, and I wasn't about to let him go.

"I'm tired of this world already, and it's barely started. Corruption is rampant all around. I feel trapped. Like I'm standing on one leg while someone's taking a pot shot at my other leg." He rubbed his bowed head with both hands. "And I can't keep up this charade of not being a Christian. You know me. It's hard to keep quiet when someone slams a Christian, or brags when one is beheaded. I'll slip. They'll catch me quick enough. They'll find me out, torture me, and then off with my head!" He whistled while he slashed across his throat with his thumb.

"I'll break you out." Now my eyes were watery with rage.

"No, you won't."

He put his beefy hand on my forearm to calm me.

"Your people need you. I'm just a soldier in God's army. I'll do my part." More tears hit the table and formed a small puddle. "And so will you."

I didn't have a response to the truth that I didn't want to

be true.

"Who knows? Maybe I'll make it to the halfway point. See the souped-up Antichrist." Frank grinned.

According to the Bible, the Antichrist will be assassinated, and his body possessed by Satan, newly exiled from Heaven. Then all hell will break loose. Truth be told, I was dreading that the most. So, I changed the subject.

"Let's not talk about death like this. I'm a homicide detective. I deal with this all day. Let's get back to headquarters and find an assassin." I stood. "And get that superintendent arrested."

"Maybe I can help."

Senator Staeger stood inside the entrance of the indoor minigolf course, staring at us and looking haggard. Like he had ran a mile at full speed. I was quite surprised to see the senator here, but not completely shocked. He had the ability to sneak around without being noticed. Although the thought that he could've been caught on camera crossed my mind, my gut said that he knew where the cameras were to avoid detection.

"Jon, are you okay?" Frank jogged to his old friend and shook his hand.

"I'm better than I look. I had to power walk all the way from the stadium to here."

He took a deep breath, but it didn't help much. Frank led the tired senator to a chair and helped him sit. He looked his age with sweat beads coming off his bald head, trickling down his neck and cheeks. Frank pulled out a handkerchief from his pocket and handed it to Jon.

"How did you find us? And were you followed?" I cautiously asked. My paranoia kept waving the red flags that had kept me alive to fight another day.

"Kennedy saw you two the other day and found out this place is unseen by the cameras." He dabbed his forehead, while catching his breath. "I made sure no one followed me. I doubled back twice and kept an eye behind me at all times. Something I learned from an old Secret Service friend."

"I'm sorry for your loss." Frank patted his friend's knee.

Senator Staeger nodded at me.

"I understand you were with Kennedy when she died," he said as tears welled up in the corners of his eyes.

"I was, but I hate to tell you this." I uncomfortably shifted my weight in the chair. "Kennedy was about to turn you in to the Peace Forces. She didn't believe in your agenda for keeping America out of the global government." This was one of the hard parts of being a cop. To tell someone that a close friend was not their friend, but an enemy. This news was difficult to reveal with the tact it deserved.

"I was aware." He looked down at his patent leather shoes as if nothing surprised him anymore. "She was my Chief of Staff, but I learned one thing early in my political career. Trust no one."

That hit me between the eyes. To see them at the stadium, I would've sworn he looked at her like she was his daughter. The rookie in me needed to learn the lesson of never trusting politicians, even one acting as an ally. They were all misleading.

"What do you need from us, Jon?"

Frank sat on the chair beside me, across from the senator. The determination in my mentor's eyes was clear. I'd been around Frank long enough to know when his patience was gone, but he kept it cordial for the senator. A man Frank clearly respected, no matter Jon's profession.

"I need you to catch a killer." The look in Jon's eyes were that of a man on the run. "And implicate the superintendent and the Sovereign. If you don't, I'm afraid that I will lose my head. Pardon the pun."

"That's what we've been discussing. But the trail is cold." I shrugged and Frank nodded.

"But I know where he is." The senator gave a grim grin.
Frank and I looked at each other in disbelief.

"Do you think I would come here asking for help if I didn't have anything to help you with?" Jon asked.

I wondered if this feeling of inadequacy would ever stop.

"So, where is he?" Frank asked impatiently. He opened his hands, as if begging for a handout.

My phone vibrated. Another text from Joy.

IF YOU ARE NOT HERE IN THE NEXT TEN MINUTES, I WILL PERSONALLY BLADE YOU MYSELF!!!

"A push boat stuck in the river, south of the Spirit's base of operations." He straightened his tie. "But do be careful. He is a trained assassin after all."

"How do you know this?" The red flags were waving fast. Was he setting us up to get rid of the rest of his unknowing conspiracy team?

"I have been a politician longer than you've been alive. My contacts run deep in Missouri, especially my city." He spread his hands like a proud father. "Even in this time of darkness, both in the physical world and the political, my sources are more than reliable."

"That's good enough for me." Frank stood.

Frank looked at me with his old fierceness rekindled.

"Come on," he commanded.

"Just the two of us?" I had to ask. It was a risk I didn't think was necessary, but I'd follow Frank almost anywhere.

"No, I'll call for backup." He made for the exit.

"Okay." I tried to keep up.

The red flags were beating me over the head. This got way too easy, way too fast.

"You stay here." Frank turned and pointed to the senator. "I'll come and get you when it's over."

"That will be fine." Jon settled into the chair. "And happy hunting."

235

Before we exited, I said, "By the way, I might be fired and guillotined by the end of the day." I used my matter-of-fact voice.

Frank stopped and looked at me. "What are you talking about."

I told him about what happened at the Spirits base of operations with Kate and showed him the texts.

"I'd tell you to go and straighten this out, but I need you." He pulled out his phone. "I'll square it with Joy for now, but you need to get to her office when we nail this guy. She won't hold out for long."

We got in our vehicles and made for the tow boat.

CHAPTER 37

Although the red had taken control of the skies, it was still dark enough to make it hard to find the boat until what appeared to be a flashlight in the pilot house was switched on. We would've missed the river as well if it wasn't for the redness in the sky reflecting off the water. The redness of the horizon where the river met the sky gave the appearance the judgment had already started, and the land was burning. I said a quick prayer of protection while I followed Frank's SUV cruiser.

Frank killed his headlights before parking out of sight from the push boat, so I did the same. I pulled in behind him, parked, then got out. The flashlight beam from the pilot house made its way across the port side of the main deck like a small spotlight searching for escaping prisoners.

We quickly formed a plan to catch him by surprise by walking along a row of trees near the boat, then swimming to it using the current to help us save energy for a potential fight. I told Frank I wanted him to implicate Joy, so he needed to be captured alive. Frank figured he had military training and wouldn't come quietly. He ordered me to take no chances. We'd get her with or without him. Our safety was of the utmost importance to make sure the senator was kept safe from the blade, and to make sure we didn't lose the killer one way or the other.

The boat faced the river, so we worked our way to the stern from the tree line. The closer we got to the back of the push boat, the harder the already saturated ground was to navigate. Frank started sinking to the point he had to retreat a few steps and try new ground. I did alright, but I had to navigate the last twenty yards like Frank. Then we entered the river and used the current to wade the last few yards.

The hull was firmly planted into the riverbed. Frank led the way to the starboard side, and we raised ourselves onto the main deck. After quietly shaking the water from our clothes, we went to the port side.

We looked for the one carrying the flashlight. We didn't see anyone, so we made our way along the side. The narrow aisle to the front was just wide enough for Frank, so we went single file, hoping to fool the killer into thinking there were more of us. He might give up, thinking he was outnumbered.

We did the best we could to stay quiet, but it was hard because we were soaked and were still dripping all over the deck. Fortunately, our shoes didn't squeak. But that was the only thing going for us. Just when I noticed a camera mounted to the ceiling at the end of the deck, an arm with an MP5 at the end came out of the front cabin and recklessly sprayed bullets at us.

"Frank?" I looked for guidance once I hit the deck.

"No planning for this. Hope you're ready for a fight." He charged towards the open door just in front of us and disappeared into the darkness behind it.

Another spray of bullets went aimlessly into the river when I got up to follow my captain's lead.

"This is the Peace Forces. Put down your weapons and lay flat on your stomach on the floor." I shouted, hoping the killer would at least stop firing.

"You people aren't supposed to be here. Now go back

home to mama." The gunman screamed before firing another spray.

"Will, we need to get this guy now. If he makes it to his narco boat, we'll never see him again." Frank peered out the door.

"Remember, we need him alive." I checked my SIG to make sure it was in working order.

"I know that, but the situation may not be in our favor. We need to get him before he gets away." Frank did another quick peek out the door.

Before I could respond, Frank bolted to the gunman's door. It was impressive to watch a man of his size and age fly down the narrow walkway. It wasn't a reckless abandon maneuver, but a controlled flight.

After hesitating, I followed and heard more firing, then a scream. It sounded like Frank. My mind went numb as I entered the room. My fear was that my hesitation just cost Frank his life. Thank God that wasn't the case. One man was on the ground with a bullet hole center mass, his dead eyes staring at the ceiling. And another one was on top of Frank strangling him with a rope, reaching for the MP5 with his bare foot.

Frank's thumbs, struggling between the rope and his throat, were the only thing keeping him alive. However, his bulging eyes and protruding tongue indicated he was in dire straits.

I leveled my gun quickly and fired two rounds into the man's head. It was a risky shot, but it was either that, or maneuver to a safer angle. Frank may not have made it that long.

Frank gave a long inhale and a raspy exhale. "Not bad, boy. Must've had a great teacher."

"He was a great teacher, if a little immodest." I stood.

"Wise guy." He coughed for a moment, then stood as well.

"Neither of these guys are him." I pointed at the one

Frank shot, then the other.

"How do you know?" Frank checked them for a pulse.

"Too short. The guy I saw with Kennedy was taller than me. These two are shorter than you."

Frank stood to his full five-foot eleven height. "You callin' me short, boy?" He rasped, then cleared his throat some more.

"No, just stumpy."

A muffled thud came from the front of the boat. The still air wasn't helping the sound travel.

Frank retrieved his sidearm, then quick stepped toward the door. "Did you hear that?"

I nodded to Frank. With all the commotion that had gone on, the killer had the opportunity to board the go-fast narco boat attached to the bitts between the two tow knees of the push boat. If speed was needed, that boat had plenty to spare. Three oversized outboard motors mounted side-by-side gave the look of a jet boat on steroids. If the assassin got a short start, we'd never see him again.

We rounded the corner to see him fire up the outboards. He was about to cast the mooring line when Frank and I holstered our guns. While the killer was stowing the lines, we jumped onto the narco boat.

"Sorry bub, your cruise has been canceled."

Frank went to the man's left, and I went to his right. He held up his hands. He was as tall as Tommy, who was six-foot-six and two eighty, but the killer was about a hundred pounds leaner. I didn't take that for weakness, though. I had plenty of scraps with wiry guys who nearly bested me. I wasn't about to take any chances.

"You might as well let me go." His cocky grin needed removing. "You got nothing on me." He bent slightly at the knees and lifted his fists in a martial arts fighter's stance.

"Funny, but the senator told us where you were. Seems he wants you in cuffs as bad as we do." Frank grabbed the man's duffle.

His smile lost its flare. "He did, huh."

"And this should've been in the river long before you boarded this vessel." Frank pulled out a short rifle with a scope.

"You're pretty good with this," I said.

"Pretty good? I killed the president with one shot from almost a hundred and fifty yards."

"So could I without wind interference." I mocked his cockiness.

"Come in and tell your side of the story, and I'll see what can be done about leniency. Maybe take the blade off the table." Frank's smile was genuine. He had plenty of experience talking guns out of hands, but this guy was a pro.

"No can-do, boys." He grunted as he sucker-punched Frank in the cheek so hard it sounded like the rifle had been fired. It was so fast, I barely saw it.

I grabbed the killer by the shoulders and tried to wrestle him down. Like I said, he wasn't going easily. He used his height to his advantage and swung me into Frank, who was shaking the bats from his belfry. I let go, trying not to land too hard on Frank.

Frank shoved me to the side and tried a grapple move to take the killer down to the deck of the boat. The killer anticipated his move and side stepped just enough to shoulder tackle him, which sent Frank straight into the console of the vessel.

God was watching over us then. Frank hit the throttle hard enough to make the boat lurch. The killer lost his balance. Already on the bench, I was able to jump up, grab the killer by the waist, and kick down at his right knee. He grunted in pain but didn't go down.

We wrestled for a bit until the man gained full control of me for an arm bar. He then screamed in pain. Frank grabbed him by his hurt leg and cranked down on the knee. He was about to roll over and kick Frank, but I put him in a rear choke hold and held tight until he calmed a bit.

Frank cuffed him while I used the assassin's phone to call and find out what happened to our backup. Joy said they'd be there momentarily. I noticed when she was vague, she was either lying or hiding the truth.

CHAPTER 38

It took a while, but we got the assassin to Frank's SUV and put him in the back seat. We left the door open to question him while we waited for backup.

"It's still pointless to bring me in."

I shook my head. His arrogance was weak. Like a wounded animal about to give up after the last energetic attack failed.

"Why's that?" Frank leaned on the edge of the door.

"Who do you think sent me here?"

"I'm guessing someone from Europe," I said, standing guard beside Frank.

He gave an inquisitive look. "You know about him?"

"We know a lot of things. So why don't you start from the beginning and fill in any holes we might have," Frank said.

"I was in the Marines. Sniper scout. Then the murders occurred, then the earthquake. I was in Iraq, stationed in Babylon, when this all happened. Instead of discharging me before the aftershock, like they should have when my time was up, they made me an offer. Kill someone for my discharge."

"The president?" Frank asked.

"No, a Saudi Arabian royal who was against the Mid-

243

East Accord. So, I did. When I was discharged, a woman approached me and asked if I was willing to work as an assassin." He gave a low chuckle. "She actually said assassin. To get me to say yes, she sweetened the offer with a bank book that showed a balance of ten million with my name on the account. She told me that was for the royal job, and that there was plenty more where that came from."

"Nice origins story, but can we skip to the part where you assassinated President Mason?" I was growing tired of his arrogance.

He looked up at the raging sky as if in deep contemplation. "She was the last one on the list."

Frank stood upright. "What list?"

"The woman gave me the list…"

"You have a handler?" I asked.

"I have no handler, just someone who gave me the list of people to kill who also checked in to make sure I was on schedule. That was it. She never helped me with the jobs."

"What's her name?" I prayed to hear Joy's name come out of his mouth.

"No name. She's just tall, medium build. I doubt the rest of her was real." He grinned. "Including that horrible French accent."

"When did you kill the president?" Frank asked impatiently.

"A couple of weeks back. The list ended with her. But there were some differences with the orders on the list for her."

"What differences?" He had my full attention. I glanced at Frank and could see his face clench. He was trying to hide his anger. A shared anger that I was trying to learn to hide on the spot. My respect for Frank as a cop grew,

"I had to get her body in a refrigerator and make sure it was delivered to Hector in St. Louis the next week."

"Was decapitation part of that list?"

He blushed. "A mistake on my part. You see, the

president isn't the easiest target. The only way to get to her was at her vacation home in Virginia. I was told she would be there and that the Secret Service would be taken care of. I snuck onto the property and got the lay of the land. She spent a lot of time in the hot tub on the back deck.

"It was perfect. Her two Secret Service agents had moved away from her to another part of the house. That was the opportune moment I needed, and I shot her. The problem was that she slid underwater the second the bullet hit her. Although dead, she still inhaled some water. My orders were to make sure the evidence didn't lead back to anyone in on the hit. So, I took her to a private Global Church guillotine, sent the rest of the body to the nearest crematorium, put the head on ice in a beer cooler, then made my way to St. Louis."

"Why scrub the head and get rid of the hair and teeth?" Frank scratched his cheek.

"I was told to do it because the hit was early. They wanted to stall the investigation until the right time."

"Then what?" I gritted my teeth.

"Then I had to stay here and wait for orders from the top cop and my payoff."

That was exactly what I was waiting for. Joy was officially implicated in the assassination of President Mason.

"You mean Superintendent Everhart?" Frank asked.

"That's the one. She usually gets her orders from Philadelphia. Some Chief of Staff of a senator, but the European told me that she'd contact the superintendent directly to make sure everything was done properly, and that the Philly girl wasn't in the loop anymore."

"Kennedy Brown?" I asked.

"Yeah. Then the order came in to kill her." He grinned "Top cop wanted to kill her personally, but the European told her to have me handle it. To make sure it was done right."

Frank shifted from one leg to the other. "Why did Joy want Kennedy dead?"

"Said she wanted her job." He caught his gaffe. "I mean as the one who got the orders directly from the European. She's ambitious."

"That she is." I tried to piece more of this together in my mind.

"You know. I'm wondering why you boys haven't asked about why the president was on the list." He scratched his cheek.

"She was against the United States losing its freedom. The Sovereign wants us to get soaked into the whole global government." I was still trying to connect Hector to this in my mind.

"Close." He giggled.

Frank's brow furrowed. "What?"

"It's not just that," he said, waving his hand in circles as if I was right but not completely. Then he sighed impatiently. "She was about to make a speech to the people of this country."

"What speech? I didn't hear anything about it." I was referring to my Christian Resistance contact, Tommy.

"And you won't." He turned to Frank. "She was about to claim the Sovereign is the Antichrist. Can you believe it? She was going to call him that." He laughed.

"The Christians have been calling him that for over a year," Frank said. "So why is she different from them?"

"Their time is coming." The killer lost his mischievous attitude. "I have killed almost twenty people since the murders. Over half of them were Christian Resistance leadership. The rest were non-Christian leaders who were trying to do the same."

"What agenda are they trying to stop?" I tried to sound naïve.

"You idiot." He gave a surprised look. "World domination."

"Now who sounds crazy." Frank giggled, but I knew it was fake.

"Listen, I don't care who's in charge of this planet so long as I get paid." He sat back and sighed.

"What about the megalomaniacs who tried it before? They were killing everyone in their path, including their own people."

Frank was reaching, but I admired his tenacity.

"That's why I'm staying out of his path. He stays on one side of the planet, and I'll stay on the other." He tapped his temple.

"But he's not alone. He has an army no one knows about who knows about you." I lied trying to follow Frank's lead in a combined effort to try and scare this guy.

"Keeping one step ahead isn't my plan, boys." His grin widened to a smile. "I plan on staying off the path entirely." Again, with the temple tap.

The pause in the conversation was maddening with the clouds rolling in the background, but they seemed to be slowing. So, I decided to change gears. "There's one thing I was wondering." I rubbed my chin. "How do you fit in this whole mob war? We have some of your bullets in a few participants of the first shootout, and one in the Free Agents' number two man."

"I wondered that myself. I think I figured it out." He pointed at the river. "It's easier to gain control of the river when there's only one mob to get it from. Superintendent said Hector needed his second in command gone, so he would stay compliant longer."

Clay was wrong for the first time. Hector didn't order the hit. I was impressed with my C.I. He was better than I gave him credit for.

Frank looked at the sky. "Is Hector on the list?"

"Nope. But I guess his time will come. The Sovereign doesn't share power. He only takes it."

A question started bothering me. "Now that the list is

completed. What happens to you? Time isn't on your side anymore."

The killer's arrogance was completely gone, as if he realized something. "Everyone's time comes. Doesn't it?"

Frank caught on. "Sounds like yours might be sooner than you think."

"Maybe," he whispered.

"Why not let us take care of you. We can keep Joy at bay for a while." I was hoping to use him to implicate her, and who knows, maybe slow down the Antichrist.

"Can't." His shoulders dropped a little. "Part of the job."

"You don't have to end it this way." Frank was almost pleading.

"You're protecting someone." I saw it in the change of his demeanor.

"People." He grumbled. "I have some friends in Saudi Arabia trying to get out of the country. They're not what you'd call friends with the Muslims or the Europeans."

"Go on."

Frank's prodding showed he smelled a way in, and I waited for my queue to follow along.

"They're not Christians, if that's what you're thinking." He looked up at Frank. "They're free agents of a sort."

"Like the mob?" I didn't know where he was going with this.

"No, like we don't want to be on either side. We're fighting to be independent. We want to find our own country and be allies with the new world government while still maintaining certain freedoms not given by the Sovereign."

"Hector sees himself that way, too," I said.

"But he doesn't want to be the leader of a country, just a mob," the killer said. "We want autonomy."

"And you'd give your life for this?" Frank asked with mock disbelief.

"Wouldn't you? I mean that's what this country was

built on. But now, America is hemorrhaging. It's in its final throes. I mean look at it." He waved his cuffed hands at the sky. "This is the end of America. Europe and the Middle East aren't taking this as hard. In fact, the people over there are saying this country was overdue for some humbling."

He missed the mark. We were in the throes of the end of the world. The Middle East and Europe had their turn coming. And soon. But I needed him to focus on the assassination.

"You said the president was the last one on the list. Is there another list?" Frank asked.

"No, the woman said as soon as I finished, I'd get paid, and my people would be freed. The last ones were part of the deal with Hector. They were side jobs. And I got extra pay."

"Why is keeping the river so important?"

He shook his head. "Boy, you guys are really thick. The river is important because America is divided."

"Divided? You mean philosophically, politically?" I had no idea what he was saying.

"Geographically."

He was in complete awe of our ignorance, and at the moment, so was I. The feeling of incompetence coursed through my mind. A feeling that appeared too many times in the past five days.

"I thought everyone knew. The first earthquake widened the Mississippi River and took out a lot of cities and land. The aftershock joined the river with the Lawrence River in Canada through the former Great Lakes. The entire eastern half of the U.S. is an island."

The words hit me hard. The idea of the U.S. being divided this way was not in Dad's journal.

"Why doesn't anyone know about it besides you?" Frank acted like he didn't believe him.

"I thought everyone did."

He raised his hands like he was surrendering all over

again. When Frank nodded, he reached into his coat pocket and produced some folded papers that were shriveled like they had been in water. He handed them to Frank. I watched Frank's mouth slowly open when he unfolded it. It took him a minute to collect himself.

"This right?" Frank asked the killer while handing the papers to me.

The top page was a printout of what appeared to be a satellite photo of the U.S. The entire eastern half was cut off from the rest of the continent. The Lawrence and Mississippi Rivers connected to separate it from the rest of the continent from the Atlantic above Maine to the Gulf of Mexico. The single river would be permanently salt water.

I wondered if Amelia was lying or being lied to.

"It was on the patio deck. The president was looking at them when she was in the hot tub." He nervously scratched his cheek. "Kennedy confirmed it. Said the government was hiding it so people wouldn't panic. They might join the Christians, or people like me, and the Free Agents. The rest of the papers were the speech she was working on, calling the Sovereign the Antichrist."

I looked at the pages to confirm. "If America is as bad off as you claim, why all this? Why doesn't he just let it die naturally?"

"Sovereign isn't a patient man. Plus, Kennedy said he has plans for this land." He pointed at the island on the map. "But I'm not sure what. He just needs America to be compliant as soon as possible."

It was hard for me to believe. "But the media would…"

"They can't do anything that will hurt the ones in power. First Amendment's dead, gentlemen." He sat back and sighed.

I remembered what Frank told me.

"So, what's the play?" Frank asked.

"There's one more thing I have to do. But I can't tell you. And I won't. My people's lives are at stake, and I won't fail them."

"You told me where they are, but who are your people?" I asked.

The red and blue flashing lights of Joy's so-called backup were piercing the still night air.

"I'll call Joy to try and stop her from taking him," Frank said, pulling his phone from his pocket.

"Wouldn't have told ya anyhow." He looked at me for a second. "You're Will Thomas, right?"

"Yeah, so?"

"So, your boss is not a fan." He shook his head.

"What do you mean?" I asked, afraid of what he was about to say.

"Superintendent Everhart told me the European didn't care if you died or not. That if I could line you up with Kennedy, I could end you too." He didn't smile.

"My boss wants me dead?"

He rubbed his hurt knee like a kid who didn't want to get involved in his parents' argument. "She acted like it was hard to give the order. She said it wasn't right to kill a cop who was doing his job. If I had to guess, I'd say she was under strict orders on that."

"Why didn't you follow through?" I asked, using my calmest voice. Although I wanted to shoot him myself.

"Kennedy was facing my direction. I thought she saw me." He shrugged. "Plus, I didn't have the right gun for the job. Bullet wouldn't have gone through both skulls. Lucky you that Kennedy was the primary target." With that, he said nothing else.

Before I could respond in an unprofessional way, Frank's voice raised to a level I hadn't heard since the academy. He balled up his fist while he listened to Joy give orders over the phone. He argued a little, but finally relented to the authority of her position. The assassin was put in the other cruiser and shipped to headquarters.

Frank was about to get in his SUV to follow them when

I pulled him to the side.

"Frank, I need to meet my handler," I whispered.

"Don't waste a lot of time. I might need you at headquarters, and you need to straighten things out with Joy and Kate." Frank took a long draught of stale air. "By the way, I wanted to give you your..." He looked in his cruiser.

"I'll get it at HQ. Go get our killer back or Joy will bury him."

I got in the beater and left.

CHAPTER 39

The alcove wasn't far from the sunken push boat, but the road was almost nonexistent. In fact, it felt like off-roading from my pre-Trib days.

I couldn't see in to know if Tommy was there until he lit his phone screen for me. I hurried inside to make peace with him before returning to HQ to help Frank.

"I can't stay long. We just caught the assassin. Joy took him away from us, and Frank is going to HQ to try and wrestle the guy away from her."

Tommy's scowl told me enough.

"Listen, Tommy. I'm sorry for questioning your manhood and dedication to the Resistance. I was just trying to help you..."

He raised his hand.

I stopped.

"They arrested Senator Staeger."

"Where?"

"Just outside the stadium."

"I told him to stay put."

"You talked with him?"

"He told us where to find the assassin. What does his arrest matter to the Resistance?"

"According to my contacts with the northeast

Resistance, he was a major ally to the cause."

"So, he's not a believer?"

"I don't know. All they know is that President Mason was recruiting him. They thought she might've had him by the way he stood up with her against the Mid-East Accord."

He pointed to my chunk of rubble, then turned his attention to the sky as we sat.

"When the clouds stop rolling. It's on."

I had to shake myself out of my conspiratorial thoughts at the topic change. "What's on?"

"The next judgment."

"How do you know?"

"One of the Jewish witnesses told us."

The hundred and forty-four thousand Jewish witnesses had dispersed throughout the world preaching the Gospel to anyone and everyone the year before. Though the Antichrist tried his best to slow them down or kill them, they could not be touched. Another Bible prophecy coming true. The Resistance tried their best to let them do their work while we did ours. However, they knew our work and helped us when God wanted them to give advice. This included warning us from other dangers that moles, like me, couldn't find out, and, most importantly, giving us the heads up when a judgment was about to commence.

"Did he happen to give a specific time? We've almost wrapped this up."

"No, just that when the clouds stop rolling it'll start." He didn't keep his eyes off the skies.

So, the senator was the target. His friendship with the president was used against him. That and the fact the Sovereign anticipated his moves perfectly. He knew Jon would come to his city and try to implicate the Antichrist. And I was willing to wager that the killer was right. Hector would be taken care of when the river was his.

Deciding to get back on topic, I asked, "Am I supposed to get Staeger out?"

"No, it's too late for him, he's already on his way to Missouri State Pen."

"The new due process is a joke." I was disgusted by the new laws.

"Tell me about it. Now that all capital court cases are handled by a Peace Forces military tribunal, you can lose your head in a matter of a couple of hours."

"What about interrogation and torture?" I remembered what Frank said when we found out about each other's faith.

"A paid informant said that Staeger's blade is being sharpened as we speak. Rumor has it the Sovereign will broadcast throughout the nation about the killer of the president just before the blade drops tonight. He's creating outrage to encourage American citizens to demand that the treaty be signed, so he can be their new leader."

"We wanted efficiency."

"And we got it." Tommy stiffened. "The clouds are getting slower. We need to get to shelter. Give me the flash drive and let's get out of here." His giant hand opened.

"You go on. I need to find out if the killer is going to be bladed with the senator. He knows things that the Sovereign is keeping from the world. And I need to make sure Frank is going to make it to a shelter. I won't be far behind." I reached into my pocket.

"What sort of things does the killer know?" Tommy turned his focus to me.

"Here." I handed him the map and speech. "This is a major game changer."

Tommy turned on his phone's flashlight. His face went grave. "I need to get this out to all Resistance groups."

"Right. The killer mentioned the Sovereign has plans for the island, but he wasn't sure what. Right now, everything centers around the treaty." I looked at the slowing clouds, still searching my pockets. "I've got to go. Frank needs help at the precinct."

"You be careful. That place is a snake pit."

Panic set in when I remembered that I never took the flash drive out of my computer when Joy came into my office.

"What's the matter?"

"I don't have it."

"Those drives are to never leave your person. That's rule one."

He almost shouted at me.

"Sorry, Joy burst in my office looking for spies." Even in the light of his phone's flashlight, I could see the questions in his expression. "I mean she has an app on her phone that allows her to keep up with every computer in her HQ connected to the Beast. She knew that someone was on it but didn't know who or how."

"I'll pass it along to the techs. But you need to get that drive before we all hear the blade dropping over us."

His voice was loaded with disappointment, which made me feel worse than I already did. There was also a disconnect that startled me. Like he was about to cut ties with me because I had broken a cardinal spy rule. Leave no discernable trail or evidence that could indict you.

"There is one thing on that drive we need to expose the new president. He was in on the assassination. Maybe it can be used to get him out of office and slow the treaty being signed."

"This goes a long way up."

"All the way to the Antichrist."

He returned his gaze to the sky, and the fear in his eyes made me uncomfortable.

"You need to get out of here now. I'll get the drive and bring it back with me. I'll give it to you in our meeting place in K.C.," I said as if I were his son looking for some sort of hope that he wasn't cutting me out of his life.

"Fine, but you know the rule."

My heart sank. He was giving me only one chance to

make it right.

"I know. If I can't get it. Don't come back."

He stood and walked away, putting his phone to his ear.

I walked out of the alcove. The redness of the slowing clouds heightened the uneasiness in my gut. I said a prayer that I would get the flash drive back without any repercussions that included Christians meeting the guillotine. Up close, and personal.

CHAPTER 40

On my way back to headquarters, I had to take a wide detour because the media had filled downtown from the stadium to HQ. Between the press vehicle lines and the unpassable streets, I had to park farther away. Near an empty stall, I noticed a familiar sports car in front of a government building. Although Frank needed help, I decided to stop by and give Amelia the heads up about the judgment without calling it that.

When I got out of the beater, a familiar figure came around the corner of the building. It was hard to see because of the weather and a few broken streetlights. I pulled out my mini-mag light and shouted for her.

She smiled.

"Hello, stranger. Unusual weather we're having."

She was dressed in black yoga pants and black turtleneck that accentuated all her curves. I almost forgot what I was supposed to be doing.

"What are you doing here? It's not safe. The weather could get dangerous."

"First, I had to go back to my office for some plans and then do some yoga by the river before our date." She pointed to a rolled-up yoga mat in her backseat. "Second, the weather is fine. Not a breath of wind. If anything, we'll get a much-needed downpour."

If only she knew the kind of downpour that was coming.

"Fine, but you need to go home and do your yoga. The mobs are kidnapping women alone in the dark and putting them to work in a not so nice job."

She looked a little concerned. "Hadn't thought about that. But it's been dark for days. Am I supposed to just sit around in fear until the sun comes out and rescues me?"

I thought about the Son who could rescue her forever.

"After all that's happened in the last two days with the mob war, don't you think it wise to be more cautious?" I caressed her hand with the tips of my fingers.

"You're probably right." She smiled. "I'll go home and get ready for our date."

Her whole face lit up. I felt the gooseflesh come up on her forearm. I felt excited thinking about the date, but there wasn't any time for us to be together. It was hard to tell her about the coming storm without sounding like one of those fake psychics who go around predicting vague omens. Although the coming storm wasn't vague. God's fury was about to be felt by the unbelieving world. So, I focused on the case.

"I can't make it tonight. We just closed the cases." I moved closer to her. "There's also the matter of collecting a debt."

Leaning in, I gave her a kiss. The passion I felt from her outweighed mine by quite a bit. And that was saying something.

"You caught the killer." She wasn't asking.

"Actually, I should get two kisses, since it was the same killer in both cases."

Before I could think, she dove in for the second payoff. Her lips were soft and full. She tasted like fresh vegetables and salad dressing from Hector's food truck. As I drew her in, not wanting the moment to end, a sudden clap of thunder came from overhead as if God was telling me to wake up and help Frank.

I pulled away and looked at her in the small light from my mini-mag. Her beauty was unmatched. Another clap of thunder brought me around.

"Whoa. I guess I wasn't meant to do my yoga outside. Since we can't go out tonight, how about you coming over and doing some yoga with me?" Her smile said there'd be more than just yoga.

A flash of lightning across the sky reminded me that speed was of the utmost importance.

"Sorry ma'am. I have to get back to headquarters. The case isn't closed until we question the killer and get all the paperwork done." I kissed her lightly on the cheek. "Raincheck?"

She nodded with a satisfied smile on her face. It made me feel good to see that smile. It meant she liked the kiss as much as I did. It meant there were more of them to come.

"How about tomorrow night after the storm?" she said, caressing my cheek that sent a flash of adrenaline through my body. "At the food truck patio?"

"Lord willin' and the crick don't rise." I smiled at her but cringed inside. I sounded like a bumpkin trying to woo a girl at the county fair.

She gave me an odd look that confirmed my fear.

"Sorry, it's an old saying my family used for decades. It means that I'll meet you if everything works out. And in this case, there's a mighty big crick near the patio." I thumbed towards the river.

"Too true."

She gave me another kiss. It was clear she wanted me to stay. And I truly wanted to, but duty called. And this time it was of the utmost importance. Otherwise, I might have been persuaded. I eased back, immediately feeling the lost moment. "I really have to go."

"Okay, flatfoot. Call me after everything ends, and we'll set up our next date. But this time, no contract kisses."

She gave me another deep kiss, then we walked to our cars.

I opened her car door for her and helped her in her vehicle. Then I stood by the beater and watched her drive away, I asked God to send someone who'd help her find Him. It would be difficult to date a woman who I wouldn't see after the world ended.

CHAPTER 41

Headquarters was subdued when I exited the elevator. Uniformed Peace Forces officers either gave me sideways looks or just stared at me as I walked to Frank's office.

"Detective Thomas, so good of you to finally show up." Joy was sitting in Frank's chair. "Have a seat. We have a lot to cover in a short time."

Kate was in a chair in the corner trying to glare a hole through me. She really needed to work on it.

My rage was near impossible to keep under wraps. "Where's Frank?" I grumbled.

"Where's Frank?" She stretched it out as if coaxing me to finish the sentence.

"Ma'am." It was all I could do to not snatch her from that chair and end her.

"Not quite there, but close enough." She sat back and pointed to the chair across the desk from her and raised her shrill voice. "Have a seat, detective. We have some things to discuss. And I have a helicopter waiting to take me to Jefferson City."

Again, the thought of throttling her and watching those beautiful blue eyes dim to gray coursed through my mind. But I stopped myself for Frank's sake.

"What's there to discuss ma'am?" I refused to give in.

"Well, first things first. We need to talk about your insubordination at the river boat." She nodded at Kate who sat up straight like a spoiled child about to get her way.

I raised my hands. "I did my job." I leaned in with my hand's edge on my cheek and whispered too loud. "Did you know she doesn't pee without calling for your advice?"

Kate flew out of the chair in a rage and shouted, "You were completely out of line the entire time we were together."

"That will be enough for now, Detective Evans. I'll handle this." It was the first time Joy went against Kate in front of me.

"At the rate she was going, we'd still be on the road by the boat waiting for permission." Then I looked at Kate. "She should know the new law enforcement regulations well enough that when a crime has been called in, we are allowed to get to it any way we see fit. She was calling you on the phone to see what to do next. It was ridiculous." I turned back to Joy. "And don't blame me. James Franks refused to acknowledge her presence and talk to me. I didn't encourage it."

"But you didn't discourage it either."

Joy acted like she had the upper hand.

"He was telling us about the crime. Why stop him when he's willing to talk just to make him look at the right person?"

Joy looked at Kate and shrugged. "He does have a point." She looked at her phone. "I don't have time to play referee. Detective Evans, is what Detective Thomas saying true?"

Kate sat back hard against the seat back and folded her arms in a huff. But she nodded. I wanted to smile, but again held back. The satisfaction was enough without rubbing it in.

"I guess there is nothing else to be said. And I do expect that your evaluation won't include this incident that wasn't really an incident at all," Joy said, smiling at me as if I owed her one. "Now to the second order of business."

"I'm not following." Confusion coursed through me like a charging bull.

"Detective Thomas, it is with great pleasure that I commend you on a job well done." She stuck her hand out.

"I'm not following, ma'am." I looked at her hand.

"As you know, the suspect you apprehended earlier was the assassin of former President Mason. He broke under interrogation and gave us everything we needed to send him and his co-conspirators straight to the guillotine." She pulled back her hand and glared at me.

"Co-conspirators?" I knew she meant Senator Staeger. But the plural threw me. I sat to think.

"Of course. All mercenaries are given their orders and their payments from their employers."

She looked like she was about to give a spoiler to the audience before the scene ended.

I sat back against the chair. Her happiness was a little over the top, even for her, especially considering what the assassin had told me and Frank about her involvement in the conspiracy. Something was wrong.

"Senator Staeger and Kennedy Brown?" I asked without asking, afraid my meeting with the senator would implicate me. He must've talked during interrogation.

"How did you know?" Her smile faded.

"He mentioned the senator when we questioned him." I slowly sat up straight, trying not to show my nerves.

"What else did he say?" She leaned forward.

"Not much, only that a woman with a bad French accent gave him the orders and transferred money to an offshore account in his name to kill the president." I wasn't about to give her everything. Especially not knowing what she knew.

She fingered her phone while she thought.

"French accent?"

"Yeah. He said it was real bad."

"He never mentioned that during his interrogation." She looked at Kate who confirmed with a head shake.

"Ask the captain. He was the one questioning the suspect." I got up, walked to the door, and looked down both ends of the hallway. "By the way, where's Captain Malone?"

"Since you mentioned him. How long have you known Captain Malone?" She acted as if she didn't want to broach the subject.

"Since I was a kid. He went to the church where my dad preached. He was also my academy instructor." I frowned as I came back and sat. "What's that got to do with the assassin?"

"That's quite a while to know someone. Wouldn't you say?"

She was worse at this than me.

"Not really. We never talked at church because of our age difference." Which was true. "And we didn't consort all that often at the academy. It's what you would call a professional relationship." Which wasn't. "Where's the captain?"

"Interesting." She fingered her phone some more.

"Again, what does this have to do with the case?" I raised my voice.

"Listen, Detective Thomas, don't give me that insubordinate tone when I'm patting you on the back. In fact, I'm also letting you know that you will receive a full commendation for a job well done." She acted as if she didn't want to give any accolades, just receive them.

It took a second to sink in what was really happening. Then I realized she had no idea about where I'd been and who I talked to the last forty-eight hours. Then Frank's absence began making sense. My gut wrenched in anger.

"Where's Frank, Joy?" My voice was calm, but my emotions were about to cross lines.

"That's Superintendent Everhart to you, detective." She raised her voice as stood.

I towered over her when I stood. "Where's Frank, Joy." My voice was still calm, but they had murderous undertones.

She melted under my fury. "On his way to the Missouri State Penitentiary." Her voice cracked enough to know she understood my point.

My fear left me. I quickly calculated what it would take to kill her and Kate, then making a quick escape out the side entrance before anyone knew what happened. It was a long shot, but one that seemed worth taking.

Her hand shook as she pulled out a flash drive from her shirt pocket. "Look familiar?"

"Yeah, it's a flash drive." I kept my tone.

My heart dove down, with my stomach, to the floor. It was my drive. She must've taken it after I left. The plan, and my anger, died along with any hope of getting Tommy the info I had promised. She wouldn't have shown it to me without making a copy.

I was out of the Resistance. And worse, brothers and sisters in Christ would pay the price for my incompetence with their lives. I nearly puked on Joy.

"Not just any flash drive." She pushed them forward. "It's your flash drive."

"Yes ma'am. I must've left it in my computer after our talk." I tried sounding as if it wasn't a big deal.

But the smirk on her face showed that she had the upper hand.

"Interesting." She sat and fiddled with it between her fingers. "Because we found it on Frank's person when the assassin implicated him and Senator Staeger in the presidential assassination." She didn't even try to hide her glee.

And I couldn't hide my anger. "And you believe him? Did you check out his story before acting on it?"

She shouted, although it was more like a shrill squeal, "That is enough, detective. I'm not sure how things are done in Kansas City, but I assure you we are beyond thorough when proceeding with charges this severe. Frank told us he took it from your computer when he saw it yesterday during his insubordinate conversation with me in your office. He admitted he used it to get intelligence from ICON to help the Christian rebels. In fact, he said he was on his way to give it to his handler when he was called in by you to help with the assassin's arrest."

I had nothing to say. My mind was in overdrive wondering why Frank took the blame for my mistake. He knew the blade would land on whoever was found in possession of that flash drive. Then I remembered what he said about not fitting in the new world and my importance to the Resistance. The failure felt like a mountain wrapped around my neck as I sank.

"And I'm sure what will be found on this drive will drop the blade on that treasonous lowlife." She sat down and held it up, looking at it like a trophy she'd just won.

I fought the urge to run and find Frank and help him escape, like I said. Then I remembered. Frank was about to give it to me when I went to see Tommy, but Frank admitted to it all. If I had just taken a second of my time, Frank would be where that little insect was sitting. Doing her vocal victory dance.

"I promise I will make sure this investigation will be under the full scrutiny of Internal Affairs. And if you get one thing out of line, I will watch you lose that power you're clinging to." I pointed at her, stood, and started for the door.

"And just where do you think you're going, detective?" She gained a little more malice in her voice.

"To talk to Frank." I turned and shouted.

"He's already given his statement and signed it. Frank Malone…"

"That's Captain Malone to you." I shouted, ready to jump the desk to kill that little fame whore.

"He's no longer a member of the Peace Forces." She grinned. "He's been fired and, like I said, is on his way to the state penitentiary for processing and tribunal." She giggled. "He's with the killer and their accomplice, former Senator Staeger."

"You're insane. He's the best cop you have. And the straightest." My voice strained under the force of my shouting.

"What are you implying, detective? And do be careful. You're close to a meeting with the disciplinary committee for insubordination."

She tried to grow three feet as she stood but failed miserably.

"I am already going to have you suspended for threatening a superior officer." She tsked and looked out of the side of her eye. "Isn't that right, Detective Evans?"

Kate sat up and nodded vigorously. "I witnessed the whole thing, Superintendent Everhart."

"Don't join your friend at the blade ceremony." She mocked while she turned her attention back to me.

"Only in rank are either of you my superior. You'll always be worthless cops." Before I started for the door again, I looked at Joy. "And dirty. Hector's little whore." With that, I stormed out of the office before I pulled my SIG and guaranteed my place beside Frank. The only thing on my mind was getting Frank out of the mess I put him in.

I went into my office, slammed the door, and clicked to open ICON. Flopping into my chair, guilt washed me into despair. Frank was going to the guillotine because of my incompetence.

The senator was the target. The last one in Philly to go against the Antichrist. Two birds, one stone. Frank and Kennedy must've been part of Joy's payoff. The Sovereign had no intention of burying the president's death. He was making it part of the narrative that would bring the U.S. into the global fold. When the president was identified, it should've made perfect sense. The Antichrist was eliminating the competition, exactly as Kennedy told me. This was the opening act of the great coup that would eliminate the U.S. from the world stage. Why didn't I see it?

Praying was useless. I didn't even know where to begin. My thoughts were everywhere. Anything I wanted to say and ask God seemed amiss. I rubbed my face with both hands.

The network came to life. I entered my ID and password, then entered Frank's name into the tribunal network. His name came up. The charge was conspiracy in the assassination of the president of the United States. It's funny how a group of Europeans was considered qualified to oversee the trial of an American involved in the murder of the president. Especially, when the evidence hasn't even been collected yet.

I tried to see if the senator had the same charges, but the screen showed that I was locked out.

Joy.

The mouse shattered against the monitor, which turned into a spider web. I decided to go see if I could help Frank out.

Or break him out like I promised.

CHAPTER 42

Speed was needed, unfortunately I-70 couldn't accommodate. It was probably the best highway in the state because the governor put almost all the infrastructure resources into clearing it and repaving it to reconnect the two major cities, but there was still a lot of work to be done. And Highway 54 left a lot to be desired. Even though it connected Jefferson City to I-70, the money ran out when the bridge over the Missouri River was completed. A two-hour drive turned into three and a half.

While I drove, I listened to the media droning on about the swift justice provided by the Sovereign's new world government and how their due process overshadowed ours. It's funny how President Mason's disappearance, and announced murder at the hands of the Resistance, barely garnered a blurb, but now that the trap was set, outrage filled the airwaves and internet of her death at the hands of a senator and his accomplice. It showed that Jon was the target all along. Another point I missed.

They kept going on about how the evidence was overwhelming, and when faced with it, the three conspirators threw themselves on the mercy of the tribunal. All I could do was scream at the radio that there wasn't any evidence, and the true conspirators weren't on trial, with the exception of the trigger man.

Then she was introduced.

"We have a special guest joining us from a helicopter on her way to Jefferson City as we speak. Superintendent of the St. Louis Peace Forces, Joy Everhart." The host seemed to gush. "Welcome to the program, Superintendent Everhart."

"Please call me Joy." Her voice was as phony as her tan, but I listened intently. "It's a pleasure to be on your show in these dire times."

"I know you're about to land soon. Please give us the rundown of this heinous conspiracy to turn America on its ear." His tone was also fake. This guy was known for preaching that America needed to get into the global fold. He even said we needed to change our name to show our progression in the new world order.

"Former Senator Jon Staeger was frustrated with the lack of support from President Mason in his bid to become the next president. With him being the frontrunner for the party nomination, he needed the president's endorsement to seal the deal over our new president. According to his chief of staff, Kennedy Brown, the president balked, and he became irate to the point of murder. And that's just what he did."

"Sad, just sad. The need for power overwhelms even those chosen to protect us." His tone of disappointment made me want to puke. "Please, keep going. You're doing great."

"Thank you." She gushed over the attention. "Staeger then called in a few favors and hired Jason Ewing, a former Marine sniper and known assassin, to kill the president and Staeger's chief of staff when Staeger found out she was working with the Peace Forces. Poor Kennedy didn't have a chance. Our own Detective William Thomas was there when she died. In fact, I believe he was also being targeted because he was lead on the investigation. But his Peace

Forces training kicked in and he narrowly avoided death."
She was playing the drama card hard. I couldn't believe she
used my name after suspending me.

"Why was the president's head found in St. Louis?"

"Kennedy said that Staeger lured President Mason to St.
Louis under the guise of a private meeting to discuss her
supporting him. Then Ewing shot her."

"Shocking." The host didn't sound shocked at all. "I
hear your own Captain Frank Malone is implicated in this
conspiracy."

"Yes, he is." Her voice cracked. Anyone listening
would've thought she was emotional from the betrayal of a
fellow Peace Forces officer, but I knew she was holding
back laughter. "In fact, he was caught with a flash drive
that contained highly classified information he'd stolen to
give to his contacts in the Christian Rebellion."

I nearly drove off the road knowing that was my flash
drive.

"He's a member of the Christian rebels?" the host asked
incredulously.

"We believe he's the only member in the Peace Forces.
He was a long-time police officer before the murders and
an active member of a Christian church. Internal Affairs
should've done a better job vetting him and his kind."

"I'm one of his kind, and you have no idea." I screamed
at the radio. "You moron!" It was as pointless to shout at
the radio as it was to her face, but it was hard for me to
hold back the rage I had for her. And for me.

"I'm sure the Peace Forces will do a better job." The
host sounded magnanimous. "Please go on."

"Thank you. Detective Thomas and his team did a great
job of figuring out the conspiracy quickly. And I did my
part as leader in apprehending the assassin, who has given a
complete confession, implicating the former senator and
former captain."

"And I'm assuming the decapitation was their way of

making a statement against the Sovereign, the greatest human in the world's history if you ask me, and our new president's efforts of progress towards the next step of human evolution, and complete globalization." This time he was emotional.

"Yes, the Tribunal has concluded that very idea in a press release from the Tribunal's media relations team a minute ago," she said.

"Are the other two conspirators linked to the Christian Rebellion?"

"Yes and no. The assassin is part of an independent group wanting freedom from the new government. They want to be autonomous." Her mocking voice followed by that cute laugh echoed in my ears. "And according to Kennedy Brown, the senator was working with the Rebellion to further their agenda to take over the United States, but as far as we know he wasn't a member."

"Will he and Malone be questioned to get information concerning the rebellion?" the host asked.

"No, they will be executed with Ewing tonight. The Tribunal believes they're nothing but informants, simple cogs at best, and have no knowledge of the inner workings of the rebellion at large."

"What about this flash drive?"

"The drive erased itself when the Peace Forces techs began opening it. But they saw enough to know what was on it, which wasn't much. Proving that Malone wasn't deep enough in the rebellion to be trusted. They booby trapped it because they knew he would eventually get caught. I guess you can't teach an old dog new tricks." That beautiful laugh resonated in my rage.

After a short chuckle, the host said, "It sounds like the Tribunal has everything well in hand."

"That's why we need to plug ourselves fully into the Sovereign's amazing global network." A muffled voice came over the radio. "I'm sorry, but the pilot just announced that we're about to land. Thank you for the time. Love your show."

I slapped the knob to turn off the radio and cursed. Frank was going to die because of my carelessness. I let my focus shift to petty office politics and a beautiful woman. The flash drive would never have been found if it wasn't for my ineptness.

As I drove, I thought the case through. The real conspiracy came from Europe. The Antichrist, wanting the U.S. to enter the new global government, and the eastern U.S., that's now an island, couldn't wait for the election the next year when he found out about the president's speech.

He had his minion, the woman with the bad French accent, organize the assassination. She hired Jason Ewing, who shot the president, had her bladed for his mistake, and transported her personally to Hector's man to stage. Not wanting a trail to the Sovereign, Kennedy Brown became expendable when Staeger, being lured there by Kennedy, showed up in St. Louis.

Once the investigation started, Ewing was told to help Hector gain control of the city for the river. The rumor that the Sovereign wanted Hector in control of the entire river seemed to be accurate, especially considering the geographical information Ewing gave us.

As for Joy's part in the conspiracy, Frank was implicated because she hated him. She also requested Kennedy's death to take her place as an American organizer for the Sovereign.

As for Tommy, he never told me the flash drive was rigged to self-destruct. He told me to get it or don't come back. It seems that maybe Joy, thinking she was talking about Frank, was right about me. Being a novice spy was too much for the Resistance to trust. Maybe they were right. It felt like Tommy gave me the heave ho.

And it hurt.

CHAPTER 43

By the time I reached the state pen, a massive crowd had congregated on the soccer fields beside the penitentiary. After parking the beater in the Peace Forces lot, I called the warden who told me the governor gave direct orders to not let anyone see the prisoners. He also let me know that Frank was in good condition, meaning that he hadn't been beaten.

After giving up my SIG, a couple of pat downs, and showing my credentials more times than I needed, I started my trek across three soccer fields to the front of the crowd.

People are horrible creatures. Give them the opportunity to witness death, and they'll come running. Unless they know the person dying, then it's a whole other matter. In this instance, the people were also misguided through patriotism. Only one participant was guilty.

The guillotines were on an elevated stage for the crowd to see, and those who couldn't were treated to a giant video board that rivaled old football stadiums. It was a festive scene. People celebrated the capture of the killers, even though they didn't even know the president was assassinated until a few hours before. There were even tailgaters in the parking lot. I couldn't fathom how a crowd this large could be put together on such short notice. There were thousands in attendance.

Then I realized this was probably in the works for at least a month. That and guillotine parties were known to break out after raids of Christian Resistance hiding places. Without any sports to enjoy and Hollywood underwater, public executions were the new entertainment.

There were people guzzling beer and other alcoholic beverages, along with various drugs, which were about to be legalized through the generosity of the Antichrist, who wanted all global citizens to be thoroughly compliant as he dragged them to Hell with him and his kind.

And the people were thankful.

I had given up on the idea of breaking Frank out even before I left St. Louis. Rule two of the Resistance, even though I wasn't a member anymore, don't go beyond your abilities. And they didn't include jailbreaking. I was a cop.

It would've been harder if I didn't know where Frank was going in an hour, according to the video board countdown timer. The problem I had was that Joy was winning. That ignorant, orange face, two-bit cop wannabe was winning. And it was my fault. She hated him, and I gave her the evidence to kill Frank.

Tears were hard to hold back as I navigated the mass of humanity. Guilt driven tears hitting the soccer field. I had to be there for my friend, my brother. I prayed that God would let me apologize to Frank for getting him killed when I reached Heaven. Trying to remember the good times was difficult when my sins against my friend weighed heavy on my mind. He called me in to help him in a tight spot, and all I did was throw him to that tiny wolf and her kind. I swore to never forget my mission again, if they gave me a second chance.

There was an eight-foot-tall chain link fence that wrapped around the guillotine stage. I stood at the fence looking at the place where I'd see my friend for the last time until I made it to Heaven. Three guillotines, side-by-side in a row, had blades that glistened in the stadium lights that surrounded the facility. No doubt they were sharpened to a razor's edge considering a few horrific outcomes in the first few decapitations of the Head of Religion's reign. People who held a grudge against the condemned paid the blade-man, as they came to be known, to dull the edge to make it painful. The outcome was so horrific that even the Antichrist joined in the outcry. I guess that even the devil's minion has his limitations, but I didn't believe it. A new church rule was put into effect that all blades were to be inspected by at least two impartial observers. Since then, the cuts were clean and precise.

Listening to the conversations and arguments made me glad I didn't have my SIG. The debates ranged from blade, to rifle, to rope. Then some went historical. Drawn and quartered, burning at the stake, and other sundry ways to bring pain during the death process. Then there were those arguing over the condemned trio. Of course, all agreed that the one who did the shooting needed to die. Then the debate over the senator and Frank being subject to public decapitation lasted only a few minutes when the countdown from ten began. The crowd pushed forward to get a closer look. Prison guards on the opposite side of the fence shouted orders for the crowd to not push the fencing or they would shoot on sight.

The clouds were almost at a standstill. Then I thought of something. Without bowing my head or closing my eyes, I prayed. I asked God to free my friend using the judgment. I didn't know about the senator's spiritual standing and the killer made it perfectly clear about his. So, I prayed for them all to be busted out as the hail, blood, and fire caused havoc among the crowd. I pictured Joy's smug little smile evaporating watching Frank and the other two escape. I wanted God to show a little mercy in this time of judgment.

When the timer hit zero, the crowd's cheer was almost deafening at the first signs of people coming to the stage.

The first was always the warden, a man who was short, fat, and ugly. Next was the Governor of Missouri, a formidable woman with over forty years of political service to her beloved state. Then, there was the mayor of St. Louis, looking tragic in the face of his disgraced captain. Then, there was Joy. My gut tightened. What was she doing up there? She had on her dress blues. But she didn't look tragic, not even ashamed. She looked giddy, like it was Christmas, and she knew the pony was for her.

My mind raced to the historical death sentence methods argued earlier. Burning that little witch at the stake sounded good.

The Decreed Holy Person was the real joke. He wore a dark robe filled with every kind of religious quotation, runes, and symbols from all the religions of the world, except Christianity. The tattoo surrounding his Beastmark on his forehead shimmered gold and silver. In a pluralistic religion set forth by the new Head of Global Religion, every Decreed Holy Person was to consecrate the justice proceedings, as they called them, with a prayer to the Divine Possible, in order to include all people's faith in anything, everything, and nothing. They weren't allowed to minister to those being executed because it would allow a potential lighter sentence in the possible afterlife, where they should live in eternal punishment as well.

Then, surrounded by eight guards, the three men were last. Shackled hands to feet and to each other, the assassin, Senator Staeger, and Captain Frank Malone appeared. The path from the holding cells to the stage was eighteen feet wide with an eight-foot-high chain link fence on each side and a chain link ceiling so no one could jump it and try to kill the soon to be deceased.

The crowd booed, jeered, and screamed awful things at the three men as they marched to the stage. It was all I could do to hold back a rage that wasn't enough to do anything more than make the spectacle more entertaining for the spectators.

They were unhooked from one another at the bottom of the steps that led to the stage. As they climbed, the assassin began shaking uncontrollably, then he lurched over the handrail and dry heaved. No last meal. But they were only there for about four hours. Jon and Frank were rocks. They didn't act scared, didn't shake. They walked up the stairs with their heads held high. The look of the innocent.

CHAPTER 44

Putting my hands on the fence, I looked up to see if any help was coming. I believed if God wanted them free, nothing would stop Him. And I prayed. I prayed hard. God heard me, that much I believed. But did He listen to my request? Or did He have another plan in mind? I didn't care, just so long as Frank, at least, lived.

The governor walked to a microphone stand and tapped the mic to make sure it was on. The taps quieted the crowd. These people had experience. My gut churned.

"In this unfortunate time, we are reminded that there are those who believe they are not just above the law, but beyond it. And in this mindset are willing to commit the most heinous crimes against their fellow humans. But we will not despair for we are now under the auspices of one who can bring true justice, not only to our country, but to our planet. It is my honor to introduce to you a leader whose name brings peace and safety to everyone, the Sovereign." She motioned to the giant screen.

The giant screen lit up as the Sovereign and the Head of Global Religion sat on what appeared to be thrones and the new president sitting in an office chair. With media cameras placed by the stage, it was evident this was being broadcasted throughout the world.

"Thank you for the kind words, governor." The Sovereign was a striking figure on the screen. It was difficult to tell his age, but he had the bearing of a man with many years of experience. His blue eyes felt as if they looked into everyone's soul at one time. His rugged facial features gave the impression of a strong individual who answered to no one.

"It is during the darkest of times that humanity must make those who hold us back from our true calling of greatness accountable for actions that are both abhorrent and divisive. But it is the blade that will divide the lawless from the lawful." He paused for effect as the crowd cheered. "The United States of America has been one of the leading countries for the progression of humanity over the last decades. But the past two years have witnessed this greatness falter through the actions of men such as these three who are about to meet justice. Their weakness will be outshined by our collective strength."

The crowd cheered once again.

"It is with great pride that I make the announcement that the president of the United States of America, and its congress who voted unanimously in both chambers, is prepared to sign the Declaration of Unity. This is a memorable day in human history because this great country is the last to come into the global fold and officially make Earth one society."

The crowd cheered as the president, with a small table rolled in front of him, signed the document ending the country's holdout. My stomach churned as the moment when one of my father's predictions of why America was not included in Biblical prophecy came true. We would give our country to the Antichrist of our own free will.

With that, the Antichrist began. "For the sole count of political assassination, Jason Ewing, you are sentenced to death."

The crowd cheered as two guards removed the

assassin's shackles. They had to carry him to the bascule and secure him.

Then came the senator. The best way to describe him was stony. Everything about him suggested he was ready to die. Glad I never played poker against him. "For the sole count of conspiracy to murder the president of the United States of America and slowing the progression of human evolution (he held the treaty up both to mock Staeger and for the world to see), Jon Staeger, you are sentenced to death." After his two guards removed the shackles, Jon finally showed his hand. A tear landed on the bascule as he leaned over to lie down on his stomach. I doubted that anyone else caught it because the morons were cheering so hard. He was secured to the bascule.

Then it was Frank's turn. The whole time he waited for the other two to get positioned, I saw his lips moving. At first, I thought they were quivering in fear. But when the senator's turn came, it looked like he was praying. His lips weren't quivering from fear, he was talking.

The crowd died down when it was his turn. He wasn't a big enough name to be harassing. "For the sole count of conspiracy to murder the president of the United States of America, Frank Malone, you are sentenced to death."

The crowd gave a mild cheer, then quieted.

That's when I heard it. He was singing. His deep baritone voice started echoing through the loudspeaker, even though his was the farthest guillotine from the microphone stand. Joy reached to turn it off, her frown prominent in the strong stadium lighting. But the governor took her wrist and whispered something in her ear. Acting like a spoiled child, she pouted as she leaned back into her original stance.

He was singing the old hymn, "The Old Rugged Cross." The song echoed throughout the soccer fields. What surprised me was that no one reacted. It was as if God shut their mouths, including the Antichrist and the Unholy

Prophet, if only for a moment. Frank was in the middle of the chorus when the shackles were taken off. He then, with no help, walked to the bascule and sat on the end. He stopped singing long enough to bow his head for just a moment, then reclined onto the board.

Of the three, Frank was the only one facing skyward, and the only one not secured. My gut tingled. Maybe someone paid off the two guards. Frank was about to escape. He needed backup. My mind began reeling with ideas of knocking guards out, ripping chain-link fencing from its ties, and other activities assigned to a prison break.

Then my hopes died. The bascules were slid toward the montant. All three heads stuck out of the lunettes as guards secured the bascules, then the lunettes. My fingers ached as I gripped the fencing. A couple of the links bent against the pressure.

Frank began singing again. Same song.

The Sovereign, with a severe look, said, "For these crimes you three have been found guilty, I hereby give the order to complete the sentencing."

The Unholy Prophet spoke. "In circumstances like these, it is my duty and honor to announce to those here in this reality that I banish these men and make my request to the Divine Possible that they be condemned in the possible afterlife." He paused for a moment. "May you never find relief."

The crowd stayed silent. It was an unwritten rule to be quiet, so they could hear the mouton singing down the montant, sending the blade to its resting place on the other side of the neck.

Frank's voice was still strong. It never wavered. "*I will cling to the old rugged cross.*"

The executioners positioned themselves near the trigger, in front of the casket that was placed next to the prisoner so their headless corpse would be transferred unceremoniously into the casket by a hinged and spring-loaded bascule. They turned to the screen for the signal, hands on the death levers.

"*And exchange it* today *for a crown.*"

The Sovereign nodded.

Three levers were pushed.

I wanted to scream with all my might that it was my fault Frank was there. I wanted to beg Frank for forgiveness for putting him there. I wanted to be there in his place. But I was behind the fence. Safe.

Three blades fell.

I kept my eyes open as wide as they could go. Even if they popped out. I needed to see the injustice that was served.

Three heads landed behind three paravents.

Three corpses were flung into three caskets.

Although the world seemed to halt, the crowd went crazy. They got even louder as the executioners retrieved the heads and hoisted them as high as they could in front of their own for all to see.

Rage flew through me as the executioners tossed the heads into their respective caskets.

The Antichrist's feed was cut.

Then I saw her.

Joy Everhart was jumping up and down, waving her fist, and shouting like a cheerleader at a ballgame. The others around her smiled at her like proud parents.

As the group on the stage started for the steps, she strutted to Frank's coffin, grinned at him, and spat into the casket.

The crowd cheered again.

She waved and sauntered to the steps.

I turned from the fence as the crowd noise diminished.

"She'll pay for that!" I shouted, following it with a litany of curse words.

While making my way through the crowd with the horrible scenes permeating my mind, I felt a drop on my forehead. I wiped it and looked. Water mixed with a hint of blood. I heard a woman scream, then another.

The bloody rain went from a sprinkle to a light shower, mixed with pea size hail that was fully red. Then the crowd started stampeding towards the gate leading to the parking lots as the drops turned fully to blood. I managed to get to the side and wait it out, remembering Joy's actions on the stage. By the time I exited the field, the hail increased to quarter size.

After getting my gun back at the guard station and considering finding her right then to finish her off, the rain and hail started to catch fire on the ground and a few nearby trees. The parking lot became a demolition derby of people trying to get to shelter. Cars and trucks ricocheted off one another as the drivers swore and flipped the bird to any and all comers. Fortunately, the Peace Forces parking lot was nearly empty.

Adjusting my focus to my friend, Frank, I jogged to the beater covering my head with my Cardinals jacket knowing only one thing. It should've been me.

Getting behind the wheel, the scene outside the car was from Dante. As soon as some of the rain hit the ground, sparks of flame erupted, consuming the soccer fields where Frank went to see Jesus and Clara. My tears landed on my lap. But they weren't tears that wished my friend back. He was in Heaven, perfection.

This was the precursor to Hell. And my mind was filled with fiery vengeance. Joy's future had been decided by me. I was the judge, jury, and future executioner. And I didn't need the Antichrist's permission.

Rubbing my face with my hands, I noticed the blood on my clothes.

And wondered whose it was.

EPILOGUE

It took over four hours to get to my shelter, an apocalypse prepper had built it before the Rapture. The drive over might've been quite scary for anyone not a fan of the slasher film genre. The white beater turned blood red as the crimson hail splattered on the windshield, looking like a hellish ice storm. The wipers left a wake of gore-filled slush with each swish. Beyond the car, all the grasses and most of the trees were ablaze, just like John the Revelator prophesied. But I was in such an irate mood that I barely noticed. Thoughts of Joy cheering, jumping, and spitting terrorized me all the way to the hayfield a couple miles east of Smithville Lake. My mind filled with rage and the desire to see her corpse floating on a sea of blood with fire shooting out of each ripple consumed me.

There was a tree by the entrance to the hayfield that apparently God had decided to spare. The field itself was completely burnt. The embers from the fescue looked like a hoard of reddish lightning bugs snacking on the uncut hay. When I parked behind the tree and got out, I noticed the beater had seen better days. Not only had it changed color, but the heat from the fires I passed, produced by the fiery hail, turned anything plastic on the body to dripping blobs. The tread on all four tides had smoothed. I was surprised they made it all the way to the shelter. God had my back. Although I wasn't affected by the downpour or the fire consuming the hayfield, I ran to the shelter entrance, a steel door covered with faux hay that fit in with its surroundings, in fear that the light from the fire might show my position. The steep steps leading to the living space of the shelter was dark, but I had used them enough to let muscle memory guide me to the light switch at the bottom.

Anger switched to confusion when I flipped the switch. The lights did not come to life. I pulled out my mini flashlight and sat hard on the bottom step as I stared into the barren space. At first, I thought the Peace Forces had found it and emptied it, per regulations. But it didn't make sense. They were supposed to blow the place to ensure no one else would inhabit it. I put my head in my hands when I realized that Tommy was calling his people to empty the shelter as he walked away from our last meeting. He had no faith that I would get the flash drive. To him, I was already a burnt asset.

A flash of hunger pushed from my stomach to my attention. The galley had been fully stocked with MREs and dried foods, with five-gallon buckets filled with food stock in a storage room behind the living quarters. The small chest freezer, which ran on a small underground generator to cover its heat signature, was stocked with frozen meat that Tommy gave to me after a successful deer hunting expedition a month before I went to St. Louis. There was also a full underground tank of water that would easily last me several months or more. There was also the ability to pump water from an underground source as needed.

Although hungry, I had no appetite. Then exhaustion set in. The bed that had stood along the south wall wasn't memory foam, but it slept well enough. Gone. I already knew the answer, but I did a sweep of the entire shelter anyway, hoping at least my personal belongings had been spared. Nothing was left. Dad's prophecy journal and Mom's Bible were gone, too. Rage entered my body. Tommy and the Resistance had no right taking them. My other personal belongings meant nothing to me. But those two items were all I had left of my pre-Trib life.

I decided that me and Tommy would have a long talk about this. And it would end with him bloody on the ground. My heartrate dangerously increased.

Screaming at the top of my lungs, I threw the flashlight across the vacant living space. It was sturdily made, bouncing off the wall and spinning on the floor where it landed without a crack. It was a short walk to the light, but it felt like a mile. Tommy abandoned me, and Frank was killed for my stupidity. The loneliness overpowered me. There was nothing left for me to hold on to.

Leaving the flashlight where it landed, I sat on the steps again. The SIG felt like the only friend I had when I unholstered it. All the bullets that I put in the chamber and magazine before driving to St. Louis, were still in the pistol. There was a dull reflection of the flashlight on the barrel that made me think. Maybe Frank was right. This world wasn't for cops like us. Maybe he knew the blade was waiting for him, and he decided to go and meet it. Maybe he wasn't thinking of protecting me. Maybe he just wanted to leave this unfamiliar world. This repugnant world.

Maybe I wanted the same.

Feeling the weight of my gun, my cell phone dinged. An email was waiting to be read. Putting the SIG beside me on the step, I pulled out my phone. It was from Joy.

Detective Thomas,

Although you did a good job in finding and apprehending the assassin, and you will still receive your commendation, I was troubled by your lack of respect to me, your superior. I spoke with the mayor and your commanding officer in Kansas City, and we decided that this attitude must not be tolerated. Although firing you would be the obvious choice, we agreed that your skills as a detective cannot be put to the wayside, considering the workforce shortages we are incurring.

We have decided that it is best to help you learn to control your insubordinate temper. With that, you have been transferred to the Peace Forces Military Corps. You will report to Colonel Curtis Longstreet at Ft. Leonard Wood tomorrow to begin an abbreviated boot camp based on your time served. We believe he is just the man to straighten out your lack of respect to superior officers.

I wish it didn't have to be this way, Will. You brought this on yourself. I do hope the time you spend in the military will be both beneficial for you and our global society. Who knows, maybe in time, you will return to the Peace Forces Police. You are a gifted investigator, and I'd hate to see that gift wasted.

Sincerely,
Superintendent Joy Everhart

The only thing that ran through my mind was that Joy needed justice enforced on her. She murdered Frank. She needed to pay her debt to society.

I put the SIG back in its holster, thinking how foolish I had been in believing that I didn't have a place in this world. But I did. To get justice for Frank. So, I decided to go into the military to appease her until the time was right to get that justice.

Trying to get away from my anger, I found a place in the corner of the shelter to get some sleep. Tomorrow was not going to be fun. I took off my Cards jacket, folding it into a pillow, and lying down. A calming technique that worked for me was thinking back to my father's sermons. Remembering his voice and his mannerisms behind the pulpit brought comfort in the most difficult times. The only thing that came to mind was a sermon he did from Isaiah.

Not sure of the topic of his sermon, I remembered that it was Isaiah 59:6-9, I could hear his husky voice reading it when I closed my eyes.

"Their works are works of iniquity,
And the act of violence is in their hands.
⁷ Their feet run to evil,
And they make haste to shed innocent blood;
Their thoughts are thoughts of iniquity;
Wasting and destruction are in their paths.
⁸ The way of peace they have not known,
And there is no justice in their ways;
They have made themselves crooked paths;
Whoever takes that way shall not know peace.
⁹ Therefore justice is far from us,
Nor does righteousness overtake us;
We look for light, but there is darkness!
For brightness, but we walk in blackness!"

Although this passage was referring to Isaiah's

confession of Israel's sins and judgment God put on them for their wickedness, I wasn't in the mindset to think it over. I just reacted. To me, it was showing that Joy had no ability to understand justice. She had only one desire. Power. The kind that brought darkness to her heart and mind.

I had only one desire.

Justice.

Or was it vengeance?

It didn't matter which, so long as she stopped breathing and I was the one to make that happen.

I turned off the flashlight, remembering Frank's song and realizing that he had already received his white robe and asked for vengeance, that's from Revelation 6:10.

It should've comforted me as I tried to get to sleep, but it left me quickly. In its place, the thought of vengeance and justice overwhelmed me. But it was cloudy. What's the difference? Both require punishment. Both demand payment. But who is the bringer of either?

With no answer that suited me, I pushed it aside and tried to find something in my memory to focus on. Amelia entered my mind. But trying to remember the way she looked the first time we met, or the way her luscious lips tasted was hard to hold in place. Before my mind completely left her, I sent a text message asking for a raincheck on our date. Another injustice at the hands of Joy.

Exhaustion overtook my hunger, and I unwillingly drifted to sleep. After violently waking up a couple of hours later and shouting for Frank to forgive me as he floated away into the light, I wiped the cold sweat from my forehead. The pain of losing Frank along with the knowledge that his death was my fault overtook my attention the rest of the night. A new feeling grew inside me that night. Injustice. And it needed to be dealt with.

She needed to be dealt with.

ABOUT THE AUTHOR

Ken Gardner graduated with his MFA in creative writing from the University of Southern Maine in 2018. He recovered from COVID-19 in November 2020 while deciding it was time to get serious about publishing. Since then, Ken is an award-winning writer of short stories.

Ken lives in southwest Missouri with his wife, Shelly, son, Hunter, and German Shepherd, Tank. He is a Christian, with an inherent interest in Bible prophecy, and an active member in two writing groups. Sports are a point of great distraction, especially, the St. Louis Cardinals, college football, and the NFL draft.

www.ingramcontent.com/pod-product-compliance
Lightning Source LLC
Chambersburg PA
CBHW071849220626
47052CB00002B/42